Don't get Blood in my House
Independently published
First edition. August, 2025
Paperback ISBN: 979-8-9998229-0-1
Edited by Brandi King
Cover art and illustrations Copyright © 2025 Matthew King

Don't get Blood in my House

A Novel by Matthew King
Edited by Brandi King

PREFACE

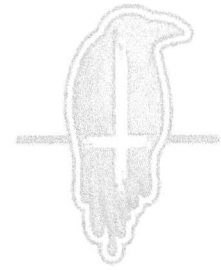

This book isn't perfect. I know this because it's my first piece of serious writing, but it's done. I poured myself into it and I'm happy with the result. And in an age where we barely have enough time for ourselves, I was given a chance to do something creative through the support of my family and without that help this writing wouldn't exist.

Having now, gone through the process of completing a book, I've realized that seeing your work through to the end is far more important than ensuring it's flawless. I hope you enjoy your time with this story and forgive any minor mistakes you may find in exchange for an exciting time with memorable characters. If you get the chance to write a book yourself, take that chance.

This book is dedicated to everyone who has helped me.

I hope you find your Sky Twinkles.

CHAPTER ONE

Natural Selection

"You're invited to dinner with three other killers."

A black letter stamped with a bird's foot, white, "Arrive at Black Manor on New Year's night."

A late twenties witch named Custard "The White Witch" steps her bite-sized self onto the moon-beveled, early 2000s road outside a backwoods Kansas diner. Custard smashes her lacey-white witch hat into the stale backseat of Cotton Bend's only taxi. She wipes straight black hair from bright blue eyes and a dying chef's blood off her new chef's knife. A faded sticker reads, "Your driver's Dusty". A thirty-something dad-looking guy with a taxi driving side gig, yellow trucker hat matching his junkyard cab. His sun-bleached hair slicks to his neck and his scruff smells like sunburn. He looks like a nice guy, weighted with the exhaustion of an older one. He drank a little too much at the New Year's party. A

1

hard worker trying to drown his responsibilities away for the night, but he couldn't remember who gave him his hat. It reads, "Blackout with your rack out." Appropriate party apparel.

Of all the passengers hiding something, Custard was Dusty's worst, missing her knife as he rearview-peeks her white button-up in the fingerprinted mirror. Custard slides the knife's cold blade between the holy seat and her unholy ass cheek of waist-high business pants. Dusty's a little intoxicated, even more now by Custard's black lipstick, extending in four directions across her face like an upside-down cross. Custard's uninter- ested face meets Dusty's confused reflection as she adjusts her small necktie from choking her anymore tonight. Dusty's never seen a woman like her in Kansas. He's never seen a woman like her period, greeting her with New Year's beers-breath, "Little late for Halloween, must have a hell of a party tonight, huh?"

Dusty takes his jacket off, revealing work-built arms, squeezing out a white shirt. Custard manages to cross her legs nice-like, owning the cramped backseat, "I already partied tonight, now I have business."

Dusty jokes, "Costume contest?"

Custard sucks her lips, "You've poked fun at me twice now, is it all out of your system?"

Dusty already forgot, "Wait, when was the first one?"

Custard holds her breath, "Your joke about Halloween clothes. Please stop bullying me."

Her far-off stare snaps to statue-esque judgment into his rearview eyes. The glare halts Dusty's fun as he side-glances the rain, rubbing his eyes already over her shit. He agitates in place, hand-combing his prickled blonde jaw, "Gonna be one of those nights, huh? Alright, miss, where to?"

Custard checks the invitation, "141, Black Bird Ave."

She listens for his reaction as he shifts a sticky shifter stuck in park, "Never been."

The National Weather Service interrupts the low playing typical New Year's jams, "Scattered storms across Kansas tonight, we don't want to rain on your parade, but keep an eye out as conditions for a tornado watch are in effect. We may very well see the first day of the New Year starting out with a massive storm. We'll keep you updated as information becomes available, so stay tuned."

Dusty's 'tuned' into the storm of a woman brewing in his backseat as he pulls onto the wet road, no blinker, "So, why you headin' to 'Black Bird Ave'?"

She checks her white fingernails for precision, "It would scare you."

Dusty flicks on the wiper blades, the passenger's works, the driver's vibrates, "Listen, my job's, take you where ya' gotta go, judgment free."

Custard laughs a small gust out her painted nose, "You've already judged me."

Dusty smiles in shame, "Okay, no more judgment."

Custard rolls her eyes at his attempt to charm her, "A town called Cotton Bend full of Corn. I'd say someone fucked up, Dusty."

He smiles the best he can over his shoulder, "So ya' do got a sense o' humor."

The taxi drifts as Custard's smile follows, "Keep your eyes on the road, Dusty. Normally, I wouldn't put my life into a man's hands, but it's raining, you have a car, and I'm paying you, so do your job."

She demands shifting her stare from his reflection to the back of his head. Dusty revs the engine sucking rain, "Boy, you sure like bossin' people 'round, got that little business outfit to go along with that mouth too, you some kinda manager?"

Custard dusts lint off her thigh, "I dress this way because it empowers me with nonverbal dominance. It's simple, Dusty, if I dress better than you, your brain intuitively positions me as the superior. This is thanks to your Ventrolateral Prefrontal Cortex. It's the part of your brain that responds to status cues. These chemical reactions coupled with my undying will to 'Take no shit from men', puts me in the driver's seat. Don't get confused, Dusty, you're still driving, just with a newfound respect."

Dusty lifts an eyebrow, "Any woman got a damn upside down cross on 'er face ain't gettin' no respect from me. You lookin' like a big city witch lost in the wrong town an' that big city money's the only thing makin' this ride worth the torture."

Custard puffs her tiny chest, "It's curious, Dusty, on occasion, men have paid me to torture them, but it's an interesting situation, me paying to torture you. Don't get me wrong, it's not out of the realm of possibility. Maybe if I had as many drinks as you tonight, luckily, Dusty, I don't drink. To be honest, you're

4

the only person to ever consider being in a tight space with me as 'torture'. Do you not enjoy tight spaces?"

Dusty laughs at grown-ass words from a woman ten years younger and at least a foot shorter, "Ya' know, you gotta be the weirdest chick to ever plant an ass in my cab. You city folks into some wild shit. So, you meetin' a customer at this 'Black Bird Ave'?"

Custard deflects his digging, "Just others who share the same passion as me."

Dusty digs, "'Same passion'? Lady, you talikin' 'bout torturin' men for money, meetin' others that share the same passion as you, so what you in for, a man torturin' orgy or somethin'?"

Dusty's thoughts drift to Custard getting nailed as the car drifts nailing a pothole, she warns, "Drive like it's not your first time, Dusty. If I was going to an Orgy, It wouldn't be in the backwoods of some corn town, I'm not an animal. However, a romp in a cornfield does sound exciting, pull over."

Dusty laughs, "'Pull over?' Ain't nothin' here. You wanna be dropped at an empty field? You get lost out here, that's on you an' if the sheriff comes askin' questions, I ain't gonna have shit to say."

He pulls off beside a sopping cornfield as Custard straightens her hat, "You're a small-town hillbilly type of guy so, I'm assuming you like to hunt?"

The broken wiper blade vibrates with the idle engine's growl as Dusty's in disbelief at her seriousness, "Yeah."

Dusty turns to the back, "But I ain't goin' huntin' with some witch-lookin' chick in a rainy cornfield past midnight. I ain't too smart, but I ain't that dumb either, girl."

Custard perks up at the word "witch." "Do you have a rifle?"

She waits, deadpan, fixated on his answer, blinking once in the last minute as Dusty scoffs, "Ya' know, I forgot it. Usually got it 'case some crazy dominatrix wants a huntin' lesson to start off the New Year."

She sucks her lips, a disguised hyena, "So, you pick up strangers hoping you won't need protection?"

Dusty explains, "I got a revolver in the glove, but we ain't huntin' with no handgun. We ain't huntin' period. Look, my kids are home sleepin', I'm just tryin' to make a quick buck, so, this your stop or what?"

Custard's a white wolf, seducing a brain-dead buck, "This isn't a stop, Dusty, it's a detour."

She moves her clean, white, long-sleeved arm to the beer-stained thigh of his jeans. The wind picks up, pelting the cab with the smell of rain. The vibration of the busted wiper blade rumbles, synchronizing with his nerves. Her clean nails gouge holes in the unclean fabric. Dusty's morals gouged with unclean thoughts.

Custard reaches from behind, covering his throat as he watches her hand in guilt, "Lady, I got a girlfriend."

He manages out through sheer will as Custard has an unseen stare of control, "I'm sure she's lovely. Introduce us sometime."

She whispers hot breath in his ear, sliding her hand to his knee. He feels the alcohol doing what it does best, still, he finds self-control, "Look, if this is where ya' wanna go, pay up an' get out. Else, let me get ya' where you need, alright? No hard feelins'."

Custard drips low words from a salivating tongue, "I can sense you already have 'hard feelings', Dusty. Don't worry, I'll get what I want."

The cold cab's window's steam up as the vibrating wiper blade throws Dusty on edge, "I ain't messin' around, lady, in 'er out."

He turns as their noses smash, witch's breath on his lips, her words entering his mouth, "Out."

Custard leans forward, pulling Dusty's keys from the ignition. The taxi's lights and engine die as Custard moves out of reach, Dusty cursing, "Hey, stop fuckin' around lady, gimmie' them keys and get the fuck out!"

Dusty struggles to grab her as she snickers, "I don't usually follow men's orders, but I'll choose one. Let's see. 'Give you the keys.', 'Get the fuck out.'."

She holds up a finger on both hands for each option, inspecting them both. Custard grabs her knife and steps out into the storm as Dusty loses it, "This bitch for real right now?"

Custard steps out the back, walking to the passenger side door, her shirt already soaked. She presses her button up against the trickling glass, putting the keys between her small chest and the window, "Will you give me a riiiiide, Dusty?"

Custard mocks with a storm-dripping neck as she glides back and forth, smearing rain into her shirt, Dusty's face smeared with loss of control, "Funny shit, now gimmie' my fuckin' keys!"

Dusty punches the car horn, as his knuckles swell purple, "God, mother fucker!"

He grits his teeth, looking over to find Custard leaned over outside the window, an amused devil embarrassed for him. She opens the door, peeking her head in, dangling the keys between their eyes, "You said you like to hunt, hunt me."

Custard bites down on the key ring, swinging them from smiling teeth. She wiggles back and forth like a hellhound, challenging him with playful growling. Her face has a fucked up smile like she's buzzed off his fear. Finally blinking, her smile drops to a serious face as she stares like a drooling statue. Dusty hesitates, afraid to move as the keys drip with saliva. Custard gives a beast-like smile, darting from the car, knife scraping the glass. Her white hat disappears into black corn, keys smacking her rain-covered cheeks, a cute and concerning scene. Her knife slashes corn stalks as she growl-laughs with a metal-flavored bite. The sound of jingling keys fades into the thickness, leaving muddy footprints and Dusty behind as he panics, "You gotta be fuckin' kiddin' me. God dammit!"

Dusty stretches for the glove compartment, fumbling for his revolver as the rain pours into the now rancid, sponge of a passenger seat, "'Get a taxi' they said, 'it'll be easy money', yea, kiss my ass!"

He grabs the gun and manages his brown leather on while stepping into the storm. He's already drenched, slipping around the car, stopping outside the hole she made in the corn, overwhelmed, "Fuck me."

He shields his face from the storm above a soggy hat, staring at a rain-covered screen, "Shit phone! Course I ain't got no service in these damn sticks. The fuck I do now?"

Dusty wipes his forehead, staring into an empty field, the kind of dark even adults fear, "Shit!"

He feels his blood turn to anxiety, gripping his revolver, taking the plunge into the corn. His pulse throbs and his ears are hot with paranoia, every plant feeling like insects. Things he can't see touch his face as he follows Custard's faint path into endless vegetation and stress. His wet hair touching his neck fills him with anxiety as Dusty curses every branch that trips him, slimy and itchy with scratches, "You better hope to hell I don't find you bitch cause, ain't no way I'mma' let someone else find you after this shit! Got me out here on a god damned witch hunt! Ow, fuckin corn, shit. You gonna pay a whole lot more than ya' owe by the time I'm done! Psycho chick got me out here lookin' crazy, you gonna pay my therapy bills after this shit, ya hear me!?"

He looks back at the taxi as he shivers, turning his back on Custard even for a second, "Why city folks always ruinin' shit? Why crazy fucks always end up terrorizin' small-town folk? Out here in these fields growin' yur' food so you can shank us in it!"

Dusty's eyes adjust to the dark, pushing through the stalks, "I hope that knife deflects bullets, else, you better keep runnin'! Freaky ass talkin' 'bout torturin' people, oh you gonna get some torture tonight ya' goblin, don't worry!"

He stomps weeds, sliding across mud as his face grinds corn. He loses his nerve at the slightest noises, feeling helpless, far from the road in deep, suffocating husks. Dusty fires his gun in the air. BLAM! "You hear that? Gonna be the last thing you hear, ya' don't come on up out this shit with my keys! Damn, succubus think this shit's a game."

The road's no longer visible, but the rain stops, "Guess, somethin' had to let up, god dang."

Dusty's boots drown in mud, "I know ya' hear me comin'. Better come out, hands up, keys in hand, knife on the ground, lady."

Suddenly, he sees his taxi, "Wait, what the fuck?"

Dusty turns around to see the path he was just walking now behind him, "Did I turn around?"

He turns back to the taxi, Custard in the back seat, her arm reaching around the driver's seat to his throat, "That's me! But, how am I there and- What!?"

He panics towards himself, Custard mouthing words from behind the other him, "Fuckin' she-devil, don't touch me!"

Dusty trudges towards the Taxi, the other Dusty closing his eyes again at her touch, "Dusty, don't let that demon get me!"

Dusty screams, but the other him can't hear himself over the rain that hasn't let up yet, "How's it stormin' again? Fuckin'

10

nightmare, wake up!"

He reaches the outside of the car, sliding on gravel as Custard steps out again with the keys. She slams the knife into Dusty's gut, blood exploding into the rain as red chunks splatter on The White Witch's face, "Gaaaaaahhhhhhh!"

Dusty wails hard enough to eject his own stomach, the moon shining off the tip of her blade, sticking out his back, the other Dusty watching him lifelessly. The knife's jammed so deep, Custard's arm's lost, tangled in warm guts. Dusty slouches down at her arm now halfway in his stomach, a blood-flooded shirt up to red, speckled witch, "I told you I'd get what I want."

Custard smiles as Dusty slumps backward off her knife, slamming into a blood-mixed puddle of bubbling death. His nose fills with muddy, bloody liquid as he drowns, fading into blackness, no longer feeling the rain.

He's dead on the road.

Custard steps on his hat, a small empowered witch, "Blackout with your guts out, Dusty."

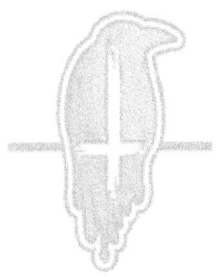

Dusty wakes up in the backseat, finding his feet and hands tied by rope from his trunk. He has one boot on, gagged with his sock-stuffed mouth duct taped shut as Custard drives the taxi. There's no hole in his stomach, he's not bleeding, he's not in pain. He wishes that needing money hadn't taken him away from his bed tonight. He tries yelling through the taste of wet sock as Custard pulls up the driveway of an abandoned mansion, Black Manor, 141 Black Bird Ave.

The National Weather Service tunes in, "The Storm Prediction Center has placed Cotton Bend in a Tornado WARNING status. Many power outages across Kansas are in effect as the state braces for what looks to be a significant threat. We encourage everyone in the area to take shelter in a basement or interior room on the lowest floor of a sturdy building. If you're outdoors, in a mobile home, or in a vehicle, move to the closest substantial shelter and protect yourself from flying debris. Stay tuned as we track the storm for updates and please stay safe."

The news chimes out, Custard chimes in, "I got that rope and duct tape from your trunk, Dusty. Of course, you know that means I know something about you now. Looks like we both have secrets. Also, Carol Lin messaged. I texted her back since you're a little tongue-tied. Get it? Figured she might be worried, you being out so late on New Year's without her."

She holds his cell phone up, swiping through the photos. They're of Dusty, passed out with Custard's face against his cheek, her licking his sleeping face and him lying on the hood while Custard straddled him, riding Dusty like a piece of dead driftwood. All these pictures sent to Carol Lin.

Dusty violently moves his body, screaming muffled sock-flavored spit towards a psycho-ass chick. He flails the best someone tied like a sausage can manage, as Custard explains,

"Dusty, you pick someone up like me and wonder why these things happen to you. Nature calls this natural selection, we'll just call it poor judgment. Oh look, Carol Lin messaged back. Well, I'm not gonna lie, Dusty, Carol isn't thrilled. She's cute, but needs to work on that temper. She's saying rude things. "Bye, bitch."

BLOOP. She pockets his phone, stepping out into the wind-blasted driveway. Black Manor still drips from the storm, decrepit and worn wealth of the past. Custard starts fangirling, "Dusty, you like haunted houses, right?"

She knocks on the car window, pointing like a tourist at Draculas, "Hey, Dusty, don't go anywhere, okay?"

Her face goes from an emotionless stare to a wide smile. She mumbles a spell as she walks up the driveway, the car locking itself, Dusty unable to see the now invisible demons holding the doors shut. Custard adjusts her bra from the bottom, holding her hat at the top, all while fighting against howling gusts, marching towards the mansion like a grown-ass trick-or-treater. Black Manor lives up to the name as its massive presence in the middle of dark farmland is ominous. The mansion has burnt parts, broken parts and parts unseen, buried alive under dead parts. Custard walks past a moldy fountain surrounded by cobblestone in the center of the courtyard. Splintered steps of the mansion lead up to a large black door littered with crickets, dancing around the porch. The windows are violent shards of glass and the rain effortlessly floods in from every inch of warped wood. The sound of drips can be heard echoing from inside a large entranceway. Custard peeks her neck past splintered glass, a tattered curtain ghosting out, the inside of the mansion abandoned and dead empty.

She turns from the porch to the courtyard, the Cab now far as wind in the corn carries sounds of animals beyond the manor, eating prey that howl past the fields to the smell of leaves. She grabs the car keys and presses the alarm button as the horn wails on repeat from a distance. Dusty jumps in terror, hitting his eyebrow on the back window as the cab's lights strobe the courtyard to the blaring horn. He yells unheard curses through the sock at a witch too far away to care. She cares enough to see him jerking around the backseat, "I didn't forget about you, Dusty."

A single laugh bounces her hat, "Idiot."

She shuts off the alarm and gives an exaggerated double-fisted thumbs up paired with double-raised eyebrows, "You good?"

One of the demons gives her a thumbs up, thinking she's talking to it. She can almost hear Dusty's muffled yells, almost, "He's so dramatic."

She rolls her eyes, facing the entrance as Dusty worms between the front seats to the center console for a better view of Custard. As he inches through, he spots her knife on the passenger seat. He's thrown into a goosebumped panic, but her back's turned, her guard's down, too amused by the mansion, she's fucked up and he WILL stab a witch.

Custard knocks, letting herself in, disappearing through the doorway right before Dusty's eyes as it slams, blowing leaves and crunching crickets. He's at a loss, *'What the hell? Where'd she go? Yeah, she went inside, but she just disappeared before it closed. Shit man, what is this hell? Am I dreamin' again?'*

He struggles towards the knife, ribs crushed against everything. He jams through the small space and as his feet tilt towards the roof, his body shifts like a teeter-totter as his head lowers towards the passenger seat. Dusty reaches for the knife across the ropes, a rough burn on his arm hair, self-inflicted pain for a sliver of safety. He manages to hover above the knife and drops, hoping he's aligned. He grabs the tightest he's ever held anything, the blade slicing random fingers as he squeezes blindly with tied wrists. He catches his breath through his nose-sweat as he starts to slide face-first into the leg area of the passenger seat. Dusty rams his skull into the glove compartment, crunching neck bones under body weight. He manages to lock his foot behind the driver's seat, pushing off with his head, correcting himself to the back.

He sits for a moment, exhausted as his nostrils burn for air. His arms are asleep and there's no way to cut the ropes holding the knife so close to his body. He checks the mansion, seeing Custard's still gone, thinking, *'What the fuck do I do now? I can't escape tied up.'*

He sweats, stretching his sore neck, slamming his head into the cushion, pissed. Dusty manages to slide the knife under his belt after a few stabs to the pelvis, hiding the handle under his shirt. He sits breathing heavily in the quiet, wondering when she'll return as the wind wobbles the car. The quiet's broken as Dusty hears a dog bark from the road behind. He strains to see anything, '*Please don't be a fuckin' stray!*'

He sees the dog, but no one else, '*Please!*'

Dusty looks back at the mansion, Custard's still gone, '*Please be on a fuckin' leash!*'

He's ready to lunge through the car and honk the shit out of the steering wheel, '*I can't honk until I know someone's walkin' that dog. Once I do, that bitch is gonna come runnin'.*'

The dog squats in front of some bushes to shit, 'Great, yea take a shit while I die, come on dog, move!'

The dog finishes wiggling its ass, starting a happy, poop-dropped run up the driveway, '*A stray. Fuck! What good's this dog gonna do my ass?!*'

He watches the dog drag a leash past the window, '*It's not a stray, where's the owner?*'

Dusty turns to the road, frantic to see, as someone rounds the corner. A blonde-haired girl in a black V-cut top and baggy white and blue striped pants is chasing the dog, her body littered with bouncing jewelry. Dusty screams for help in a sock-stuffed mouth no one can hear, "Shit. Hey, HEY! HELP ME!"

The girl chases the dog, her cries muffled by the storm, as Dusty shoots through the car, face-slamming the horn. It wails in his ears as the dog runs past the fountain onto the porch, Dusty worming to the back to see, '*Did she hear me?*'

The girl stops at the car door as the gusts blow her large, messy blonde bun atop her head high above dirty makeup. She meets Dusty's eyes, realizing the situation and pulls at the locked door, looking back at the road with dread. Dusty slams into the window, grasping at the door, realizing Custard must have used a curse as they won't budge even while unlocked. The girl's eyes are helpless, "I'm sorry."

The invisible demons banter, "Look at this meat mound. You think Custard will let us eat his brain? I want his brain juice. I hear it squelch with thoughts."

Another demon laughs, "I want to eat this girl. All of her. Make her gone."

The girl's blurred through fogged glass, turning to the road as Dusty now sees what she's looking at, someone coming. She shrieks, running towards Black Manor as the dog barks through the wind. Dusty watches her fight the storm towards the porch realizing the girl wasn't chasing her dog, she was being chased with her dog as he feels sick with terror, '*No no no no no no no, what the fuck?*'

Dusty sees a man in dark pants and a tan police shirt emerging from the darkness up the driveway. He's wearing a gold Roman-style cavalry mask with curly gold hair. The helmet's cut off just below the upper lip and the bottom of his face is exposed, black and blood-burnt skin with jagged teeth. He dangles a chainsaw marching towards the house as Dusty freaks, '*What the fuck!? Shit, no no no, maybe he didn't see me. Fuck, what if he heard the car horn. But, he's chasin' that girl. Fuck it, maybe he'll keep chasin' her. I can't take this shit man, what the fuck is this place?*'

Dusty lies flat across the backseat, holding his breath. His blood freezes with the sound of the chainsaw growing closer and his eyes are wide as he swallows anxiety. The dog barks from the porch as the stutter of the chainsaw moves past the trunk. Dusty watches the moonlight disappear, then return, realizing the man's moving around the car. Dusty can't see, tied up near a man he can't run from. The chainsaw stops next to the window behind his view, a shadow covering Dusty's body. He strains backward, trying to see something he'd rather not, as his body petrifies. He hears the chainsaw behind, stuttering in vibration, close enough to smell the gas. He looks around the car, helpless and spooked beyond belief, wondering, *'Why is he just standin' there? LEAVE! Just fuckin' leave, please! GOD!'*

The man taps the window twice with the blade of the chainsaw as Dusty freaks out with the widest of eyes. He never had to force himself to do anything harder in his life as he slowly sits up, turning towards the man. The rain pelts the sheriff's uniform as the tall man stands with cold purpose, his eyes barely visible under the gold slits of his helmet. He spews words from a charred, black jaw, lightening behind him, "'Ay man, yo' ass here for supper?"

His voice is deep and surprisingly normal despite his scorched appearance. Dusty's afraid to give the wrong answer if a correct one existed, nods his sock-filled head in an uncontrollable vibration. The black mouth smiles, "Guess imma' see you later, white meat."

The man gives Dusty a final, unsettling glance and revs his chainsaw, moving towards the porch. Dusty begins a spazzing struggle, kicking the window hoping to crawl away from this place forever. He hears the girl scream in the distance as chainsaw sounds make their way around the yard in horror too far away to see. The dog's on the porch, barking towards a garden where the man stalks the girl out of sight like a creepy musical. Dusty thought it might be better that way, surprised Custard hadn't come out after he honked, thinking it might be better that way, too. He hears the girl shriek, "FUCK YOURSELF, SHIT BRAINS!"

She's dragged through muddy grass towards the steps, dirt sliding up her back. The dog clenches wet fangs into the cop's meat-gushing leg as he shouts, scaring it to hide somewhere the girl wishes she could. He pulls her up the stairs by her hair as his chainsaw and her head hit each step with a rude thud. He doesn't care. He squeezes the girl's neck red, lifting her just above her feet, effortlessly choked against the wall as he punch-knocks the door. The black door opens as they both become shrouded in clear nothingness, disappearing like the end of night sweats, the girl's shrieks warped to silence.

Everything's quiet, the wind picking up enough to clean the trees of their leaves. The silence is too calm for murder and Dusty's heartbeat throbs with panic. Imagine if he could see the demons. The front door opens, Custard stepping out as if from nothing into existence. Behind her, the cop appears through the doorway, spacetime rippling like an unspillable pool of liquid vision. The cop pushes his chainsaw into her arms, ordering her, "'Ay, hold this, Marshmallow."

Custard points, "He's in there."

The cop laughs, "Naw, really? He ain't in the other taxi? Bitch, there's one car on this whole farm. Yellow fuckin' taxi, stickin' out like yur' white ass in this black house."

Custard's unamused as the cop makes his way towards Dusty, muffling out, "No, no! Shit! Leave me alone you gold-faced fuck!"

Dusty jerks every muscle, trying to break anything for freedom as the cop stands outside the car, ready to pounce. He smashes the back window with an elbow as Custard watches from the porch, "Doom Cop, did you really just ruin the car?"

She stares dominant eyes, straightening her tie like she's managing a meathead in a butcher shop. Doom Cop looks at her with an agitated gold helmet, far down the driveway. At least she thinks it's agitated, she can't tell, as he talks shit she can't hear, "Bitch just met me an' already up my ass."

He yells, "Listen 'Custard', we ain't all got Black Magic, witch, some of us just black an' my ass got one kinda magic, destruction. That's what I got, you feel me?"

Custard stares, dumbfounded, "Yea, and this is what 'I got'!"

Custard holds up car keys as they have a staring contest, one that's almost funny if not for Dusty's glass-covered quivering. The stare-off ends as he throws a hand towards Custard, brushing away her pointless suggestion, "It ain't your ride, why you gettin' all sentimental an shit? Danglin' keys at me like she ain't watch my ass walk all the way up this shit. Coulda' pushed that junk five minutes ago, now let me do my thing."

Doom Cop reaches in, grabbing Dusty's ankles with thick hands. He rips Dusty out as his chin slams against the window frame, biting his tongue. He drops onto the concrete in agony, a blood-soaked sock swelling in his mouth like a well-fed leech. He's dragged across moon-twinkled glass as the gold-faced helmet stares down, Dusty lifted over Doom Cop's shoulder, carried towards the mansion as the road behind shrinks. Doom cop scoffs, "Said I'd get you, didn't I?"

Dusty struggles up the porch through the doorway of invisible liquid. Custard follows behind, nicely carrying Doom Cop's chainsaw, smiling like Dusty's arrived for a pumpkin carving contest, welcoming him, "I'm glad you could make it, Dusty!"

As Dusty's carried through the decaying wood of the doorway, the mansion's interior is magically restored. Dank smelly wood becomes colorfully rich, creepy and clean, closed off from reality as a small Black Bird chirps, "Welcome to Black Manor."

CHAPTER TWO

Black Bird Dinner Party

The warmth of gelatinous nothingness coating the doorway melts the night's chill off Dusty as the door to reality slams against the quietness.

That quietness, broken as he struggles across brilliantly embroidered gold and green carpets. Doom Cop, Custard, and Dusty pass through a thorn-engraved doorway, its black polish reflecting moon-blue from skeleton-framed windows. Gargoyle chandeliers flicker blue flame as Dusty gags muffled cries in a slobber-soaked sock, a beggar in a colorfully creepy castle. He's lugged over Doom Cop's shoulder like a candy sack past a staircase with two carvings of green wolf's mouths, large enough to consume heads. The glow from the moonroof dances with pops of a cozy, demon-horned fireplace as Custard carries a heavy chainsaw through the heavy atmosphere.

Dusty's abductors follow feather-littered air from the fire-lit entrance to a large dining room filled with floating colored candles. Vines of monstrous potted plants sprawl up walls, climbing elegant wood engravings and strangling statues dead. The dead stone faces glow from blue torches, those flames nearly flickering them to life. Four cages sit by a long window spanning the room

overlooking a pool and garden outside. Dusty notices the cages, Custard notices the pool, a lagoon monster floaty, drifting, "Should have brought a bathing suit. Least I've got my birthday suit."

Doom Cop spits, "Ain't nobody wanna see no witch titties up in here."

Custard strolls by, winking at Dusty, draped over Doom Cop's shoulder, "Speak for yourself, Cop."

Custard smacks Dusty's ass past yellow roses sitting on a black-draped dinner table. A skull-shaped radio above the fireplace plays Halloween songs 24/7, besides occasional commercial

interruptions, "Ghostly Gum! You'll be quivering with fright and tingling with delight! Every ghost is stuffed with an eternity of flavor waiting to torture your tastebuds! Get Ghostly Gum anywhere they're sold and for a limited time, each pack of Ghostly Gum comes with a prize murder mystery weapon! Which weapon sent your ghosts to their delicious doom? Find out today!

23

Collect all 666 toys! Ghostly Gum! Just $19.99! Hunger sold separately, batteries not included."

Dusty notices the blonde girl from earlier, her cries muted by a wicked and whimsical barrier surrounding her cage. Her dog chases bugs in the garden behind, ignorant and happy. The rusted steel cages clash against the expensive room, too clean for killing, a nicely set Halloween party in an expensive part of town. You know, the ones that give the fat candy bars. The bird lands at the head of the table, squawking, "Good evening, welcome to Black Manor. I'm Crackle, and I want to be the first to thank you for following through with our request to bring your own victims to dinner. Our two other guests should be arriving shortly, so if you wouldn't mind placing Dusty in the cage next to Kylee, they can be neighbors while you two get acquainted."

Doom Cop unties Dusty, yanks the sticky tape-stuck sock out past his teeth and kicks him into the cage like a dog tricked into a crate while its owners eat treats. Doom Cop grills him, "Don't think about tryin' to peace out, man, ain't time to run. Not yet,"

Doom Cop towers over him as Dusty backs himself into bars like a criminal, realizing Kylee's mouthing words muffled by magic. He inspects the blackish matter pulsating around her cage, swallowing all sound, reaching for the liquid, hoping to pierce through as Kylee mouths, "It burns!"

Dusty pulls back, hands palm up in a "Now what?" manner, huffing as his panic pumps adrenaline and he threatens,

"Hey, listen, bird. You better hope I don't get up out this cage. I'll step on that little neck! And look at this gold-faced freak. How you ever get a job as a cop, huh? Oh, and ain't this some shit, check this out, I get kidnapped by a witch an' find out 'er name's Custard. It's already a fucked up story, throw that name in and I mean, come on!"

Doom Cop stands, dragging his chainsaw across the tablecloth as Dusty scurries to the far end of the tiny cell with shattered confidence. Doom Cop Snarls, "Crackle, you better shut yur' boy up 'fore I wreck his shit!"

Doom Cop kicks the cage, spitting white drool from a black devil's mouth as Crackle flies, landing on Dusty's cage, squawking, "Have a seat, Dexter."

Dusty instigates, "His name's Dexter? What kinda bad-ass, black man wielding a chainsaw wearin' a mask's named Dexter?"

Doom Cop threatens Dusty, "Keep runnin' yur' mouth, gonna find out what I'm about, Meat Bag! Blackest man you ever met and the last you gonna!"

Doom Cop throws himself into his seat, slamming his chainsaw against plates as silverware scatters. Custard holds her laugh at his tantrum, Doom Cop frustrated like a tired employee in a haunted house breakroom. Crackle addresses Dusty, "It seems you have quite the mouth, Dusty, but not to worry, yours will be permanently silenced soon enough. For now, let's take preventive measures to ensure a wonderful evening for everyone."

Crackle opens her beak, spouting voodoo, black magic and unrecognizable words of incantation as the blackish mass

25

around Kylee's cage stretches to Dustys, enveloping all sound. All Dusty can hear is Kylee's breath and it's comforting amongst the madness as she apologizes, "Hey, sorry I couldn't help you earlier. At least we can talk now. Nice hat."

Dusty remembers what talking to a regular person's like as he inspects his hat, "Just a souvenir from New Year's. I'd sure love to 'Blackout' with my 'rack out' right about now."

Kylee almost smiles, first time in days, "Yea, no shit. I'm Kylee."

He nods, "Dusty."

Kylee sits in awkward silence as Dusty looks at the back of heads he'd rather not see turn. She notices his rope-burned wrists, brushing her bangs out her mascara-streaked face. Dusty thinks she's attractive, Kylee knows she is. A New York model dragged through haunted hayride mud, Dusty beeps like the tractor, "What got a girl like you mixed into this shit?"

Kylee questions his choice of words, perky-pissed, "'Girl like me?'"

Dusty scratches his sunburnt neck, ashamed, "A fashion model type, yur' a model, right?"

Kylee looks away, feeling figured out, "Why?"

Dusty skims over her jewelry-draped body, twinkling spooky lights on a spooky night, "Ain't no one in this town got clothes without holes in 'em or that much makeup on girl, come on. Ain't no fancy fashion stores 'round here either."

Kylee's annoyed at his correctness, "I was contacted for a New Year's photo shoot, paid in advance. Money's not worth

26

this shit."

Dusty guesses, "So you show up to the photoshoot an' ol' gold face is there waitin' for ya'?"

Kylee could cry, but she's empty, "He chased me for two days. This cage is a fucking sanctuary."

Dusty relates to her corpse-like posture, tired and without answers as he inspects the cursed aura around their cages, "They can't hear us, can they?"

Kylee, never thinking twice, turns to them, "Can you motherfuckers hear us?"

Her mouth hangs open like it's waiting for Ghostly Gum, Dusty panicking at her reckless blurting as nothing happens. She makes a 'satisfied yet?' face, "They can't hear shit. That bird put this bubble around me cause I kept screaming. Guess they want a nice dinner before killing us, sick fucks. What'd they expect me to do, politely lay down and die?"

Dusty looks at the three, unable to hear a word, their relaxed posture irritating as Kylee blows chapped lips, "What brings a guy like you here?"

Dusty thinks at the floor, "Same as you, money. You know, I'd say a talkin' bird would freak me out, but that don't scratch the surface a shit I seen tonight, where we at anyway?"

Kylee stares out the window, a lifeless mirrored world, "Some alternate reality? I mean, everything's the same, but like, different. The house was shit, we walk through the door and it's fixed?"

Dusty eyeballs monster-shaped garden shrubs, "Ain't got no clue, but we gotta find a way up outta here before this cult does what cults do best. One thing I don't get, how's your dog still out there? If we went through a portal, he'd be gone, right? Everyone else is. I ain't seen a damn car drive by this whole time."

Kylee watches her dog chase crickets in the glow of a moon-washed sidewalk, "Maybe he came in?"

Dusty almost doesn't care, "Maybe. I barely saw shit tryin' to fight my way up out this place. What's its name?"

Kylee notices two empty cages, barely hearing his question, "Dollars. Ya' know we're not gonna be alone tonight. Fuck, I should have stayed in the city! What do we do? We're screwed! Tonight's the night we die, that's it."

She panics as Dusty sweats, "Would ya' give it a rest? 'Ey listen, I got some dogs myself back home. Angie an' Rox. Good pups. 'Cept Angie's always humpin' on Rox's leg, she's a weird girl."

Kylee doesn't hear him. She's spacing out, practicing breathing exercises and calming affirmations that clearly aren't working as she starts yoga-instructor self-help, "This is fine. It's gonna be fine. I'm ok. Alright, think. Just think, Kylee."

Dusty notices the three at the table turn towards the entranceway as the bird leaves towards it. Doom Cop stands, watching Dusty, taunting Jackal's teeth, awaiting lamb's flesh. He regrets everything about tonight as Kylee watches Dusty's eyes flood three feet from his executioner. Custard gets up, standing in front of Dusty's cage, a small witch staring business up at the towering cop, warning him, "He's mine."

Doom Cop lays his hand on his chainsaw, enlightening her, "You think Imma' let you kill him after he talked all that shit, you lost your damn mind. His ass mine now an' ain't shit you gonna do about it. Power pose all you want, you ain't run shit here, so best you sit yur' little witch ass down before you get put down."

Custard clenches her fist hard enough to break fingers, "I brought him, I kill him. You kill him, I kill you."

Doom Cop grits heat down at the fearless white witch, two boiling bodies itching for violence, smiling at the size of her balls, "You one tough son of a bitch, huh witch?"

Custard's gaze is locked, chin up, no fucks as she mentally flexes seriousness, ordering, "Sit. The fuck. Down."

Doom Cop laughs, her lacey white hat below his tall gold mask, "Girl, you 'sit the fuck down', shit. I bet he outruns your pint-sized ass, Marshmellow."

Custard fixes her shirt's cuffs, pulling her pants up as she plops her ass down, "The next time I have to correct you, Doom Cop, you better hope you can outrun my 'pint-sized ass'."

Doom Cop snarls like a pissed hog at a firecracker as Crackle brings in a girl wearing a large metallic, spiked ball helmet. The spike ball has two slits cut wide enough to see from, but too dark to see her face.

She's got tattooed arms with a sleeveless leather vest.

And a slime-green tank on a caramel skin chest.

Her bloody red sneakers squish at the ends of black tights.

And metal-studded booty shorts with bloody splattered fright.

The spiked girl holds a large fireman's ax handle around the throat of a girl in a yellow sundress. The choking girl's blue side braid whips past her neck as she's forced into the room from behind with authority. The spike ball girl's a feral dog thrusting a purebred into submission as her boyish voice echoes out from metal like yelling in a sewer, "This is what you get, dude! You messed with the wrong chick and now you're gonna pay! Hey, what's up, guys? Yo, this place is hella sick. Look at this mansion, dude, straight money! You want her in the cage or...? Hey, where'd that bird go? Oh, hey, yo, Crackle, it cool to just dump her in any cage, dude or...?"

Crackle bird nods, "That would be fine, Peyton, thank you."

Peyton shoves the girl in the cage, "Peyton's dead, dude, it's Wrecker now, 'kay? Grave Wrecker. I'm like an anti-hero or some shit, it's wild! Serves these fuckers right for messin' with me. You're gonna get what's coming to you now, Dakota. 'Best friends forever' yea, my ass! Shoulda never abandoned me, dude. Now you'll pay!"

Dakota isn't crying, she's not even fighting back, her Latin punk friend somewhere lost beneath a spiked helmet and teen-drama turned horror-trauma. Dakota lowers her blue bangs under the cage, accepting everything that's happening as her gold, bell-shaped earrings swing. She sits on her hands, her

30

yellow knee-length dress riding up, revealing black boots, mud-stained from the chase. Dakota adjusts her large circular glasses at the two hostages next to her, analyzing them. Her neck flaunts a dark choker with white font labeled "Calculate". She processes the room and its current situation, calculating her odds of survival. She notices the chainsaw, the fireplace, she counts the number of knives on the table. It took nineteen steps to get from the front door to this room, same as her age, one more than Grave Wrecker.

The dog's playing outside as she checks the weather, the storm's gone. The drastic change suggests something's off. A tornado warning was in effect, now the world's calm. Dakota notices that the gold-masked cop fidgets, the white witch seems too polite, the Black Bird's a liar and Grave Wrecker, well, she knows Grave Wrecker's secret, '*But where is the man I saw in the driveway? The one with the pink hair.*'

She hears the hum of the energy-filled aura around the other cages, '*I can't hear them and if I can't hear them, they can't hear me or the killers. If I can't hear the killers, my survival percentage greatly diminishes. I need to win one of the killers over, but can they be played? Can they be backstabbed when they're the ones holding the knives? Wrecker's out, she hates me. The bird's out, she organized this event. If the pink-haired man shows up, that's a potential 3 out of 5 victims, a sixty percent chance.*'

The pink-haired man arrives. A clean-shaven Japanese man in a lacey black ball gown dress glides in, pink hair flowing three feet down. The black lace dress covers his neck, stopping at his biceps, soft face covered in slashes like the meat cleaver he's holding can make. His limp grip on the blade and feminine mannerisms are elegant, his poofy dress cascading to the floor like black frosting. He brushes soft pink bangs from his blemished, toughened scars, speaking in a polite and airy voice, "Hello, darlings. My name is Hachimitsu, Honey in Japanese. I traveled far to be here tonight. Thank you for having me."

Honey starts a knife-wielding bow, ending in a dress-wielding curtsey. He fancy-scoots to a seat next to Custard, brushing his dress out before sitting. Honey notices Doom Cop and Wrecker, immediately feeling a bit put off by the burnt man and girl with a giant spike ball head, asking Custard, "Are they wearing costumes, like cosplayers?"

Custard jokes, "I think they shop at those edgy punk stores in the mall, Snot Topic? My niece drags me through there. Sometimes if I feel like treating myself, I'll pick up an unsuspecting t-shirt or victim."

Honey laughs, "I love your hat."

Custard's polite, "Thank you, I love your gown! I got this hat from a woman at my father's church. She didn't need it anymore. Her head rolled down a hill into a creek, so..."

Honey touches Custard's arm, laughing like he's sharing secrets in a cemetery. He clasps his hands, throwing his hair to the side, having a lovely time as Crackle chirps, "Thank you all for showing up, I appreciate the efforts you've taken to get here tonight, though I am curious, Honey, did your victim not make it?"

Honey points his pink fingernails to the hallway, "He's just in the entranceway, tied up, love. Can someone help? He's dreadfully heavy."

Crackle looks at all the guests as Grave Wrecker jumps up, "I got it, yo!"

She military salutes her spikeball and squishy-shoe runs her dirty tights across the once clean wood floors to the entrance. Her voice echoes back like a child lost in the woods, "I don't see him. Wait. Oh, wait. Ok, yeah, Got 'em!"

She returns slower than she left, dragging a large garbage bag with girly strong grunts through a ghost-scented hall. The bag leaves a blood streak as she puts her red sneaker up on the bag and leans on her knee, exhausted, "Yeah, I don't think your boy made it, Honey."

She kicks the bag with a plastic fleshy splurt as Honey brushes his pink hair over his ear, fingernails to chest, "Sweety, please don't kick my father."

Wrecker holds her hands up in apology, stepping from the lumpy flesh-filled bag, "Oh shit, sorry dude, that's your dad in there? Damn, that's savage."

Wrecker wipes her bloody sneaker on her chair as Honey explains, "Your request was to bring our own victim. I've made good on that request. Granted, he's hacked up into chunks, we should still respect his remains."

Crackle looks deep in bird thought, "Honey, this is unexpected. However, this twist might inspire our guests and make tonight a bit more competitive. Allow me to explain."

Crackle paces bird-footed taps, "The night after New Year's, tonight, is considered to be the first day of the thirteenth month, a one-day-long month, unrecognized by normal society. We utilize this special day for The Abyssal Harvest. The Harvest is celebrated here at Black Manor, where a feast for you all takes place. After the feast, a show of sportsmanship will commence in which you all partake in a ritualistic hunt of your victims one by one in an attempt to impress me. Once the hunt is completed, the sacrifices will be offered to the dormant, ancient eldritch beast, Blood Taker. After consuming your offerings, Blood Taker will choose one of you to be given regenerative properties. You will then use your healing abilities to continue population control on Earth, working directly with us to help balance the planet's overpopulation while keeping yourself alive with your gift-"

Grave Wrecker interrupts, "Wait, wait, wait, hold on. This shit sounds like the grim reaper, 'killing people to control overgrowth'. Is one of us for real about to become a reaper 'cause that's fucking metal, dude!"

Crackle schools her, "'Grim's real name was Steven Spinbreaker, a servant to us whose time was cut short by greed. That was long ago when flying skeletons could cut men down in the fields of their corn without proof of their existence. Steven tried wiping out an entire village alone, receiving too many injuries later dying here in the void."

Doom Cop tilts an interested mask, "This some crazy shit, man. So what? Just don't go gettin' greedy, else it's lights out, huh?"

Crackle nods her beak, "Correct, Dexter."

Custard crosses her legs powerfully claiming her seat as a throne, "How empowering, to control the population. What's more controlling than watching a man run for his life?"

Honey notices Custard gouging her nails into her thighs in a lust for power, "I'm sure we'd all love the rush of a chase, I doubt any of us have much restraint or we'd be somewhere else tonight."

Grave Wrecker plops her bloody sneakers up on the table, leaning back in her chair, "Only 'restraints' I have are handcuffs under my bed, you know what I'm saying?"

Wrecker jokes, flicking Doom Cop's dangled cop-cuffs as he drools her a death-plastered, stare, "If you wanna get real kid, I ain't decided yet whether or not to kill yo' whack ass. You stole my shit. I was the only one wearin' a mask. Now, you straight up crampin' my style, jackass."

Doom Cop shrugs away Grave Wrecker as she throws up a sideways peace sign, "It's all good in the haunted hood, my dude. Besides, it's a helmet, not a mask."

She leans elbows on her knees, spike ball resting on her arms as Crackle chirps, "Honey, when the time comes, you'll tell the story of how you killed your father. It won't be a live hunt, but this is your circumstance and opportunity."

Honey nods as Crackle shakes her feathers, "Very good, then. All of you, please get acquainted while I prepare dinner."

Crackle flies through a doorway framed with a purple bat as the four awkwardly sit in silence. Honey puts a finger on his lips in wonder, "Doom Cop, what happened to your face?"

Doom Cop's blood boils, "Why, you lookin' for facial reconstruction tips? The fuck happened to your face?"

Honey side glances the garbage bag, feeling foul, "My father's hate."

Doom Cop laughs, "Least your shit ain't burnt to a crisp. Look at me! You think I scare people? I scare my damn self, man. Lookin' like a burnt ass piece a barbecue chicken."

Honey smiles in surprise at his ability to make light of his appearance as Custard touches Honey's arm. "So what happened to your face?"

Honey's friendly towards Custard, "My father's a traditional man with traditional values. Values that don't include sons wearing dresses or loving other men."

Wrecker jokes, "Least you ain't end up in a garbage bag, dude."

Honey's face is wide-eyed and guilt plastered, "This is true, darling. Oh my, I'm a cretin. Let's change the subject, loves. So, Doom Cop, what happened to you?"

Doom Cop shakes his head at the ceiling, already over story time. He reads the blood-stained warning sticker on his chainsaw, the irony putting him in a better mood for the moment, "This guy got a couple cuts on his face an' wanna ask me 'bout my shit? That's fucked up, Honey. Listen, I live in Texas full o' white-ass, cowboy mother fuckers. All of 'em hatin' black folk, born with that shit burnin' in they blood. Bad night at work ended with a bare-assed cop gettin' chainsawed an' my shit gettin' burnt to a crisp. Ding. Storytime done."

Custard aims her eyes at Kylee's cage, "So why choose her as your victim?"

Doom Cop hitchhiker-points over his shoulder like a gravedigger, "She's a rich white girl who ain't never gonna appreciate shit. Her folks bought her every damn thing she want, she don't know what a struggle is. All she care about is looks, fashion, money. Everything I ain't. She's everything I ain't and ain't nobody gonna make me feel bad for takin' the life of a self-entitled kid who ain't never gonna appreciate it. I worked my ass off for my kids and what happened? They ran from my burnt ass. And now this kid gon' run too."

Kylee sits in her cage, a four-star model in a one-star crypt as Honey adjusts his dress, "I care about my looks, does that make me worth killing?"

Doom Cop lights a cigarette, "No, but killin' your pops does."

Doom Cop picks dried blood from his fingernails as Honey blinks with an irritated smile, "My father was going to kill me, I fought to live."

Grave Wrecker waves Doom Cop's smoke away like a moth stuck in fog. "No offense, man, but a dude looking like a cigarette probably shouldn't be smokin' 'em."

Doom Cop can't help but chuckle at Grave Wrecker's

banter, gazing up through dark eye slits with a puff, "So what's your story, Wrecker? You wear that helmet to keep that big ass mouth in check?"

Grave Wrecker knocks on the metal, "You're actually not too far off, yo! That blue hair chick, Dakota, we were cool till some drunk jocks from school showed up and beat my ass. They fed me raw meat, burnt down my trailer. Dakota ran away when shit hit the fan. I started feeling sick after the meat like a parasite was growin' or something, cravin' flesh. Even my mom started looking at me sideways. After the fire, we were living in her car. Well, till we weren't. She was stressed and lashed out an' somethin' in me lashed back. These bloody worm-like shits came up out of my mouth and ripped my mom to shreds, forced me to eat her!
Got this helmet to keep the tentacles at bay. I got the invitation to come here and decided to get revenge on Dakota for abandoning me."

Doom Cop looks from one mask to another, "Well shit girl, what you expect her to do? Keep hangin' out with you hopin' them tentacles ain't weed whack her ass?"

Grave Wrecker defends, "She abandoned me before I ever had an episode, before a single tentacle left me! She's a coward!"

Grave Wrecker crosses her arms like a grounded gargoyle as Custard rides the drama train. "She's a survivor. Good on her for leaving you, she'd probably be dead because of you."

Grave Wrecker grabs her ax glaring at Dakota, "She will be."

Dakota stares at a long-lost friend whose face can no longer be seen as the skull radio chops the end of a song off with another bloody commercial, "Come to Snot Topic! Are your parents boring old farts with no black shirts? Come to Snot Topic! Wanna scare your fam' with radical spikes on all your stuff? Come to Snot Topic! You wanna poke holes in your face and pay to fill 'em up with plastic bats and skeletons? Come to Snot Topic! If it's snot spooky, it's snot, Snot Topic!"

Grave Wrecker's ears perk up with childish wonder, "Dude, I love Snot Topic! Wait, so Custard, what makes you so special, yo? You judge me for bringing an ex-friend here. What's your story? Let us judge you now. Who's the bro in the cage?"

Custard plays along, "'Bro's' Dusty. His ex-wife is part of my witch coven. She arranged for me to dispose of him. Dusty cheated on her and then used his connections to ensure he'd gain full custody of their kids after they divorced. She wants full custody and that means taking Dusty out of the picture. When I received my invitation to this dinner, the members of the Black Kansas Witches Society discussed who would be my victim. This seemed like the perfect opportunity. Dusty's kids go back to his ex-wife and I gain her seat in the house as the next high-ranking witch."

Grave Wrecker puts her ax down, "Damn, I can't even be mad at that. Had enough dick boyfriends to hate dick for life. Good for her, yo. You imagine being married to a witch and not even know? Crap would blow Dusty's mind if he could hear us."

Custard smiles with mischievous eyes. "Trust me, girl, I've been in his mind tonight, there's not much to 'blow'."

Grave Wrecker nods her head yes in excitement at real-life magic, joking, "Good thing I got this helmet on, keep you out my brain, bitch!"

Custard gives a dismissive smile at her ignorance of magic, "As a witch, I have no problem accepting a talking bird and the existence of this cosmic monster, Blood Taker, but I find all of your easy-going attitudes about this a bit surprising. Are you not afraid?"

Grave Wrecker flips her hand unbothered, "Dude, my home burnt down, belly worms ate my mom, now I'm in a nonexistent Halloween mansion with you jerks, what else I got to be afraid of?"

Honey looks at the moon, "Blood Taker sounds like a Yokai. In Japan's culture, unexplained phenomena are sometimes considered to be the work of mischievous, supernatural spirits."

Doom Cop shakes his head, "You make this junk sound like a fairytale, man. Bro called Blood Taker, it probably wanna take blood! It ain't just some 'mischievous' little spirit. Y'all need to realize, we dealin' with some dark shit up in here."

Honey pulls an earlobe, "He's right, darlings, this being a once-in-a-life opportunity, keep in mind the consequences are once-in-a-life also."

Custard gauges her competition with resting bitch face, "This darkest of gifts surely comes with a price, one I'm willing to pay."

Grave Wrecker starts to panic by the fireplace, "Maybe I am afraid, dude. Shit sounds creepy as hell. How will Blood Taker even talk to us? Does it know English? Or are we just gonna hear its thoughts in our brain? Where're we gonna live, this mansion? Maybe I'm not ready for this shit. I'm still figuring out this tentacle crap, coming outta' my face."

Grave Wrecker's doubt shifts Custard's energy to dominance and Dakota's to calculated. Dakota calculates, '*What is added to a sixty percent chance of survival based on a percentage of that percentage, Grave Wrecker, having doubts? How much is doubt worth as a number?*'

Doom Cop crosses his arms, "An' what you gon' do with Dakota, Wrecker? Let her ass rot in a cage while yo' ass skip away? That Girl's yo' problem, ain't no one gonna clean up after you, kid. Crackle ain't gonna let her ass go, she knows about this place!"

Grave Wrecker sits on a white leather couch beside the fireplace as Honey joins her. "May I sit?"

Grave Wrecker pouts in a dark cave of doubt as Honey gently plops next to her, the black floof of his dress bunching up against Grave Wrecker's fire-warmed tights, "Wrecker, darling, no one's forcing you to do this. Everyone here has a choice."

Honey tries to soothe her as Wrecker cries tears no one can see, "I didn't have a choice not to eat my mom, dude. You had a choice not to kill your dad and you did it anyway. You got to leave your troubles behind, not me. I'm consumed with consuming."

41

Wrecker lays a metal head back on a cushy cushion as Honey reaches his hand out, waiting for her to relax. She accepts, "I didn't leave my troubles behind, Wrecker. My father is over there in a bag. I'm dealing with that and trust me, love, it's not easy."

Doom Cop notices Custard smiling with her black-crossed face looking extra cynical, challenging him as he wonders, "What?"

Custard looks over at the horror pow-wow, "This isn't a sleepover, it's a murder mansion. She's already lost this game."

Doom Cop creeps out a strong glare of intrigue. "Good, less competition."

Custard narrows her eyes at his confidence as Honey comforts Wrecker in a house now haunted, "What's your real name, love?"

Grave Wrecker remembers her mom, "Peyton."

Honey strokes her spikes like hair, "Peyton, everyone carries the burden of life's challenges, yours are just heavier."

Peyton leans her spike ball head against Honey's soft pink hair, "Thank you, Honey."

Grave Wrecker exhales as Doom Cop leans his head back in boredom. "You gotta be kiddin' me. Y'all for real tryin' to turn tonight into some intervention shit? You gon' braid each other's hair, too?"

Custard slips a laugh at Doom Cop's frustration as Grave Wrecker turns her spikes to the nightmare of a man, "Hey, aren't black people supposed to be good at braiding hair? Maybe you wanna join us?"

Doom Cop couldn't give a shit, "Yea, an' little snot-nosed, punk ass kids supposed to be good at ignorin' adults. But here you are, hangin' out with a whole mess of 'em, huh? I bet you ain't no different from Kylee's ass. Bet mommy an' daddy got you every little thing you wanted."

Grave Wrecker feels a hunger in her stomach grow with boiling emotions. "'Mommy' lived in a trailer working two jobs just to feed me and I never seen 'Daddy'. I never caught a break my entire life, dude."

Doom Cop forces laughter through cringe, "You ain't lived life enough to be catchin' no breaks, kid. Lifes a bitch and ain't no one gonna throw you no bones, so best you figure it out 'fore it figure shit out for you."

Grave Wrecker rants, "I'm eighteen and live alone, in a car, with a fucking iron ball on my head. Yes, let me 'figure life out'."

Doom Cop laughs at the very thought of it. "So what? You catch on fire? Cause I did. My kids ain't never gonna see they daddy again."

Grave Wrecker flails. "Maybe they'll turn out as cool as me! Seems like daddy being gone works wonders."

Grave Wrecker flips him off as Honey shakes his head no, censoring her gesture with his hands, waving for Doom Cop to disregard her disrespect. "Respect your elders, love."

Doom Cop hears Honey's joke, loaded, ready to fire. He

unloads, "Yeah, you one to talk. This fool carryin' his dad's dead ass around in a damn garbage bag talkin' 'bout 'respect yur' elders.' What a croc o' shit."

Doom Cop reloads. "Every single one o' you a hypocrite and ain't nothin' you say gon' change my mind."

Custard raises a judgmental eyebrow towards him. "And, exactly how am I a hypocrite?"

Doom Cop fires, "You tryin' to reunite some kids with they mom by takin' 'em away from they dad. That ain't sound like a hypocrite? How you even know Dusty cheated on this witch, word o' mouth? She a witch! Only reason you believe her ass is 'cause you a damn witch, too!"

Custard reveals, "I know he cheated on her because I was the one Dusty cheated with. She doesn't know. She doesn't need to know. Dusty doesn't even know, he doesn't remember. Black magic's problematic that way. As far as he's concerned, Dusty met me for the first time tonight. I got him that hat from Snot Topic! The Idiot."

Custard regards Doom Cop's confused face with glee as he looks like he's trying to read invisible ink, "Wait, hold the fuck on. You forced this guy to cheat on his 'witch wife', your friend, with you, without him knowing about it. Then she found out about it, but didn't know it was you? So how the hell she know Dusty cheated?"

He looks like he's struggling in a dissection class as Custard flunks him. "She knew because I showed her what he was doing through a vision as it happened."

Custard looks proud, like she's closing a devilish business deal. Doom Cop looks like Frankenstein learning about Frankenstein for the first time, "What? But, you were the one fuckin' him."

Custard explains, basking in the attention, "Yes, I altered my appearance, I thought it was quite genius."

Doom Cop's lightbulb flickers, "Hold the fuck on, so you for real showed your 'friend' a vision of you havin' sex with her husband. Then she hired yo' fucked up ass to right that wrong by killin' her husband. Meanwhile, you 'gon take her place in the coven junk once she get her kids back. That shit gotta be the most fucked up thing I ever heard in my damn life."

Doom Cop smiles at the devious act, gaining some messed-up form of respect for Custard as she bathes in her own cunning. "Yeah, and that's coming from a guy who chainsawed a naked cop, so, I guess I should feel, eh, something."

Custard sucks her lips in a rare moment of embarrassment as Grave Wrecker forces a laugh, "Witch? Bitch is more like it. You're what's wrong with the world, dude. A happy home broken by a horny hag with too much power."

Custard corrects, "Not enough power. You're too young to know the struggle women endure for positions of superiority in this life. There's no such thing as good luck, you make your luck by seizing opportunities. I'm climbing to the top of my coven and stepping on the necks of the weak to get there. My determination is my greatest tool and eventually, all men will submit to my will or burn in regret."

Custard sits up straighter, taller, emanating position and power as Grave Wrecker shakes her spike ball in disgust. "Yeah, all men, and all your friends. You're betraying your own coven, your own sisters, for power."

Custard looks like a detective in a pumpkin patch. "Aren't you betraying your friend? Dakota sits in a cage, waiting to die because your feelings got hurt. Don't judge me for backstabbing my friends for power when you're willing to kill yours over ego."

Grave Wrecker glances at Dakota's cage for the first time in a while, an old friend, now a hostage. Dakota calculates, 'Grave Wrecker's only friend is Honey. Honey tries to befriend everyone. Doom Cop gets along with no one and Custard thinks she's the only one who matters. Things are heating up and percentage values will change soon based on those fluctuations. But what will be the X factor? What will be the random variable that disrupts the entire equation? What part of this problem is the solution?'

Something moves inside Honey's garbage bag.

CHAPTER THREE

A House Now Haunted

The garbage bag fills with liquid from the inside as everyone watches Honey, lost in horror.

The sack throbs and swells, stretching the plastic to its limit, unseen liquid sloshing around entrails. It begins bursting with blood, spraying like a yard sprinkler of meat juices. The fat bag rolls across the room as drippy chunks squeeze out slime trails of thick ooze and sticky puddles of parts. It barfs flesh with each rotation, splashing guts and jellied insides, out. Doom Cop dashes, pushing floating candles across the room as the bag vomits gooey fingers. "Naw man, that mess can back the fuck up!"

It crawls towards the fireplace, leaking gore stains on the white couch where Honey and Grave Wrecker sit. Honey unconsciously squeezes Grave Wrecker's hand while

Wrecker very consciously leaves Honey's side, charging her spike ball to safety, "Yea, nope! Not today, Satan. Screw that, man! What the hell's in there? Honey, I don't think your dad's fully dead, dude. Hey, Doom Cop, you're officially not the creepiest thing in the room anymore, yo!"

Doom Cop entertains her joke, "Beat out by a Garbage Bag, that's that bullshit."

The faces of the three in cages are priceless, watching the blubber bag glob melted fat past them. Dakota's fascinated, Kylee and Dusty's faces look like haunted train wrecks. The bag stops rolling at Honey's dress, pink-haired and petrified at his bag-o-dad. "Not here, too."

Honey trembles, backing towards the fireplace, his fingernails floating in space as the bag gurgles slabs of limbs and skin. Dusty's like a hunter spotting a ghost deer, "The fuck, look at that bag just movin' on its own."

Kylee watches the thick sack jiggle sludge and death towards Honey as she breaks out into a cold sweat, "Oh my god, I'm gonna be sick."

Kylee plugs her mouth like a clogged slurpee machine about to blow, her makeup now a rabid Raccoon with chunk-filled cheeks as Dusty scoots away, "Well don't go pukin' in my direction girl, shit."

He notices Dakota, "Hey, check this kid out. She ain't looked at us but one time since gettin' here, but she's over here smilin' at that sack a shit skiddin' across the room. Fuck's wrong with 'er?"

Kylee holds her Raccoon-puke mouth, looking like a cute dumpster fire as Dakota sits, smirking under her rounded glasses. Her blue bangs frame her red-hot ears, swelling with delight at the sheer ridiculousness of their situation. The garbage bag is so disgustingly absurd, she can't help but laugh quietly as the killers run.

Dusty watches Dakota laugh, silenced by the evil magic gobbling all sound as he stealthily pulls out the Knife he stole from Custard. He sits on it for easy access, Hunter Man survival mode.

Kylee looks at Dusty with less trust than before, behind oil-spilled, waterfall mascara as Dusty acknowledges her concern, "Just a little security deposit, darlin', don't worry."

She looks away in secret, deciding if she trusts him, 'Remember Kylee, just cause bitches show up to Yoga, doesn't mean they're your friends.'

She shoots a fake ass smile towards Dusty, the gross bag melting her acting away with a gag as Dakota calculates, 'I first need to assess if Dusty's a coward, only then can I decide if him having a knife adjusts my survival rate. He seems like a friend who's scared. Scared friends are greedy to live. Survival's a natural instinct, but natural instincts with knives are risks when push comes to shove. I'd rather not get into a shoving match with someone holding a knife. I doubt Dusty would hurt us, but I doubt even more that he'd save us.'

The garbage bag levitates, dangling intestines as mucus drips across the carpet. It speaks in an exaggerated, rancid and

49

ghostly voice with slimy pops of sizzling threats, "Honeeeeeey, I am the spiiiiiiirit of your father! Whhhhhhy did you killlllll me!?"

The bag bubbles out creepy context. "Now you will be forever haaaaunted! Noooow I shall have my revenge!"

The plastic mass spirals through the air, whipping intestines as Honey leaps onto the carpet, the sack of slime slamming into the fireplace. Bodily grease and brains explode in every direction with a flash of flames as blood boils on hot logs, mixing burnt flesh and smoke into the room. Toes and fingers and ribs congeal into an unrecognizable heap of human mess, slow roasting.

Honey's pale in a thoughtless stare, lying on the floor as his father's remains melt, "What is this curse?" He stands with shaking nerves, turning to the other killers, their expressions reassuring his reality.

Grave Wrecker scratches the back of her spike ball head in anxiousness, "Well shit dude, that was some fucked upness." She bobs her hands on her thighs like a penguin. "Why am I the only one saying stuff? Don't make this awkward, guys."

Doom Cop sits at the table feeling like a dad for the first time in ages, "Someone go pat the man on the back er' somethin'. Shit, I don't know. He just lost his pops for the second time. Ay' Wrecker, give 'im this cigarette."

Doom Cop points a finger at Honey, giving a curt nod. "For ya' pops."

Grave Wrecker finger-pinch hands Honey the cigarette and gives a punch to his shoulder, bro style, "Uh, it'll be alright, dude? Sorry, for your loss an' shit. Here's a cigarette?"

Wrecker immediately removes herself from the awkward situation, walking her bloody red sneakers to the window, pretending to be interested in the garden, wiping cigarette smell on her shorts. Honey lights the cigarette on the fireplace, lays it on the mantle and kneels to pray while it burns as Custard leaves towards the entrance, "I assume this place has a bathroom."

Doom Cop watches her leave and she knows it. "Enjoy the view, Burn Daddy."

He flicks her off, leaning back with a laugh, "Burn Daddy, funny witch, but I think that's Honey's problem now."

Grave Wrecker holds her laugh, trying to be respectful to Honey's toasted bag-a-dad, laughing anyways, "No offense dude, but I can't take the smell of your Dad's burnin ass much longer."

Doom Cop bursts, "HA! You can't jus' be sayin' 'No offense' then spit some offensive ass shit, kid. 'Ey, what's the problem, ain't got no air fresheners up in that helmet?"

Grave Wrecker jokes, "Dude, can you even smell shit with that burnt-ass nose?"

Doom Cop's weirdly proud, "Nope."

Grave Wrecker passes Honey, still kneeling in prayer, jogging to the hallway Crackle left through, framed with a purple Bat, "Whatever dude, I'm gonna find the bird, maybe she'll get rid of this stink."

Wrecker steps through the Bat's mouth.

ZAP!

She's gone.

With an electric pop, she vanishes through a gelatinous swirl of space-time and life matter. Doom Cop stares past Honey as the seemingly nothingness of a doorway is now a spectacle of rupturing reality. They hear a scream outside.

Grave Wrecker falls ten feet above the pool. Her spike ball head pops the Lagoon Monster floaty as she smacks the water, sinking like an Anchor. Her helmet thuds a metallic gong, muffled by water flooding her spike ball. Her head's immovable, like a cannonball on the ocean floor, as her red sneakers thrash in suffocating, slow-motion kicks. She fails to unlock her helmet, cheeks full of stale water and bubbles bulging her nostrils. Honey, with closed eyes and a calm and steady voice, questions Doom Cop, "You going to save her?"

Doom Cop strolls to the window, nonchalantly stuffing his hands in his cop pockets, "Nope."

Honey's eyes open, "The kid's drowning."

Doom Cop speaks over his shoulder, "Ain't my kid."

Honey challenges him, "My father was an asshole too. I'll save her."

Doom Cop's ears ignite his brain with white flames, "You wanna run that shit by me again?"

Honey walks towards the bat doorway, turning back briefly, "Your wife gave birth, she has maternal instincts, but you lack the nurturing quality of compassion. What kind of father watches another father's child drown?"

Doom Cop's body heat suffocates the room as he rolls his sleeves to his razor-flexed elbows, "How 'bout we go ask your pops 'bout his nurturing ass qualities, huh? And to think I gave yur' pink-haired, bitch ass my last cigarette. Don't go judgin' me for havin' no sympathy for someone else's kid. Ain't my problem. That upset you? Wanna bring yo' pretty boy ass on over, get that hug you always wanted?"

Doom Cop walks by, blocking the bat door as Honey's muscles flex through his dress, "The 'hug' from my father was hands on my throat, he was going to kill me."

Doom Cop exhales a plague of hatred, starting his chainsaw, "That makes two of us."

The three in the cages have front-row seats to a burning hot staredown as Doom Cop drills his anger into Honey. "Maybe killin' you a' stop ya' from runnin' that MOUTH!"

Doom Cop lunges towards Honey, chainsaw screeching.

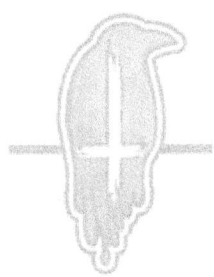

Meanwhile, Custard sits quietly on a cold stone-carved snake mouth toilet in a snake-themed bathroom, witch hat up, business pants down. She closes her eyes, the brain-humming quiet is irksome, but meditative. She hears her mind's energy like ocean-filled ears stuck in a low, water-swallowed rumble. She can't hear herself peeing anymore, she's drowning in quiet on a toilet. She giggles at the silence, quickly regaining her relaxed state. Her heartbeat slows down so still, her blood pumping rattles her bones. She could die peacefully on this toilet and not even care.

Custard's lost in her subconscious, *'I've never peed with my eyes closed. It's too relaxing.'*

She feels each heart throb swell her fingertips with sweet blood, *'My eyelids are locked shut and I like it.'*

The heat from her nostrils could melt her face paint, *'I never wanna talk again, too much effort.'*

Her mind liquifies her physical existence into carelessness, *'Is this what the absence of life feels like?'*

She panics, *'Why do I feel like I'm dying?'*

She's stuck in the black, suffocating and her heart wants to burst, *'It's not me, I can breathe!'*

Her ass is falling asleep, but her mind's alert, *'Someone's dying.'*

She wrenches her eye muscles open, struggling against the black of her brain's heavy, destructive state. She stares wide-eyed at projected images, traveling through the manor in her mind, searching for death. Down the stairs, through the hall, past the candles, over the cages, through the window into the pool.

SPLASH, *'Grave Wrecker. Dammit kid.'*

She bites her fingertip like a spider, smearing a circle of blood on the wall in front of the toilet. Her throat rattles out bizarre spellwork as her fleshy eyes turn a marble black. The bricks inside the circle glow like magma with ear-piercing heat. Rubble and dust explode out onto Custard's lap as a portal in reality drains the backyard pool into the upstairs bathroom. Massive amounts of water smash into Custard as she sits on the toilet, nearly drowning. Grave Wrecker's sucked through the hole, landing in Custard's lap, pants down, knee deep in pool water. Grave Wrecker chokes out the last of the Chlorine as her spikeball head drains onto Custard's bare legs, Custard sporting the most unamused face she's ever worn, "You owe me."

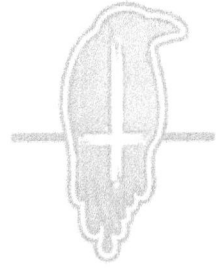

Downstairs, Doom Cop's chainsaw vibrates under the table, gargling gas as he lies next to it, gargling blood. Still, he talks shit, "For a guy in a dress…you hit like a truck, Pink, I'll give ya' that."

Doom Cop crawls towards his chainsaw. "Must…" he coughs up blood, "Must be takin' some hormone vitamins. Got a little testosterone stuffed up that dress, huh? I tell you what, you better kill me, ain't no pink ass pansy gonna lucky punch my ass an' live if I'm still breathin'."

Honey stares into the fireplace like a ghost, "Two burnt fathers in one room, one of them a spirit. Maybe he wants company."

Doom Cop uses his chainsaw as a crutch, "Ready to visit 'em? Maybe he misses you."

Honey remembers his father, "Make sure to ask him

for me."

Doom Cop growls at Honey's threat, clashing with each other as Dakota calculates, '*If the killers end up killing each other, we'll be stuck in these cages and this room will quickly become a graveyard. They're outnumbered three to two now, but for how much more time? Time is an especially dangerous variable in an equation of survival. What value is time worth as a percent when the remaining amount left is unknown? I'm sorry, Dusty.*'

Dakota yells, "Dusty has a knife!"

Doom Cop and Honey pause their choking competition, staring at Dakota, a new voice in a scientific tone.

Dusty doesn't know why they're suddenly looking his way and it instantly shatters him, "What? WHAT!? Why they starin' at me!?"

He shakes as chills in his neck move to his earlobes, his bones aching as Kylee unintentionally throws gasoline on his panic fire, "Maybe, you're the first."

Dusty spazzes, "The first what!?"

Kylee looks down, hoping not to have to say as Dusty realizes, "No! Leave me the fuck alone!"

His eyes dart wildly. 'Shit shit SHIT, what do I do? Do they know about the knife?'

Dusty stares at Dakota's calm and secretly guilty face, then Kylee's finding no answers as Doom Cop pushes Honey off him, ready to investigate. Dusty regrets all the things he said to Doom Cop earlier, "Dammit, no! Go back to killing each other for fuck sake!"

Doom Cop grabs the lock, scorching his hand on the aura around Dusty's cage, "AHH, Mother Fucker! How we get this shit up off these damn cages? Where the fuck's Custard's magic ass at anyhow?"

Grave Wrecker and Custard walk in drenched,
"I'm right here, Crispy Cop, am I under house arrest?"

Honey greets Grave Wrecker, "Glad you're alright, darling."

Grave Wrecker awkwardly fist bumps Honey's chest, who went for the hug, "It was actually a rad fall 'cept for the almost drowning part. Don't walk through the bat door less you wanna eat cement dude, all the pool water's upstairs now."

Doom Cop informs them, "Dusty's got a knife. Dakota ratted on 'em."

Grave Wrecker blurts, "Course she did, she only cares about herself."

Dakota dismissively stares at her old friend in judgment as Dusty slides the knife into Kylee's cage in a nervous panic. The killers turn to the cages, Kylee now holding the knife, caught in the act. Dusty looks at Kylee with guilt-filled cheeks, turning away in shame. Kylee shifts from betrayal to fury as she clenches the knife, stabbing at Dusty through the bars as he panics, "Shit, shit ahh, HEY! Look, girl, I'm sorry, but I ain't tryin' to die up in this place. Someone gotta take one for the team. We all die, what's the damn point?"

Kylee stabs at his feet as he kicks the bars,

"Fuck you! Traitor shit hick! Want them to see me with a knife, huh? Ok, let's give 'em a show, coward! I hope they kill you last so no one sees your ass die, ALONE!"

Dakota watches the two, '*My survival percentage rate has increased, my friend percentage has dropped. We're not friends here and that assumption is a mistake worth your life. Am I a bad guy, a killer now? I've potentially sent someone to an early grave. Do you become a killer to survive one? Maybe the X factor of the survival equation is a variable which represents whether or not you're able to make the hard choices to save yourself.*'

Custard approaches the cages, "The knife's mine. Dusty stole it from the taxi. He's set Kylee up. He's a coward."

Dusty looks at Custard's lips moving. He can't hear her, but he knows her eyes judge his betrayal as Doom Cop rubs his gold-masked temple, "Just get rid of this voodoo ass jelly junk 'round the cages so we can get the damn knife. You'd think I wouldn't burn no more with this charred ass skin, but shit burns somethin' hot for real!"

Custard straightens her witch hat like an instructor pretending to understand the type of spell Crackle used, "Alright, kids, time for the magic show."

She sits down in front of the cages as Dusty panics, "The hell 's this she-devil doin' now?"

Kylee holds the knife out from her chest defensively, "Maybe she knows you're a piece a shit! Coming to have an intervention with your traitor ass."

Custard closes her eyes, breathing out all the air in her lungs as she leans forward with wide eyes, sucking the magic jelly up. She inhales a belly full of liquid air, sparkling red and clear swirls of gelatin energy, popping on her tongue. Her cheeks glow purple, revealing a silhouette of teeth as her neck swells, protruding light down her throat. Custard's eyes space out on the edge of bursting as she quivers with dark energy crawling through her skin. She squeezes the cage bars tight enough to bend steel, fighting the spell's power in her belly. The mass is gone, completely filling her from inside as she grits her teeth with hot black energy seeping from her pores.

Her upside-down cross face paint glistens with glowing sweat beads as she drools mint-flavored magic. Her body lifts itself off the ground with sparkling slobber, dripping at her shoes, dragging just above the ground. The killer's backup as her body twists into upright floating posture. Wrecker takes wet sneaker steps back, bumping the table, "Satan, is that you?"

Honey watches Custard twitch in worry, "The spell's taken over her body."

Custard's hand reaches out for the knife instantly sucked from Kylee's, the sound of an evil church choir chanting a single ominous tone in sync with her pointed fingernails. The blade leaves a trail of gashes on every finger, shooting through the bars into Custard's grasp as Kylee jerks, "AHH, SHIT! ERRAAGH!"

She holds red-smeared fingers, rocking as Dusty watches Kylee thrash in pain he knows he's caused, "I'm, I'm sorry. I'M SORRY, DAMMIT!"

Custard's body spins like a scarecrow, tilting towards the killers, halting with an eerie stillness. Her feet drag, smearing magic dribble into the wood as her face is expressionless, enlightened with loss of control as she speaks in an unnatural voice, "Return me to my caster!"

Custard screams bloody murder, screeching past everyone towards the bat doorway. She easily passes through the portal that Grave Wrecker couldn't, down the hall Crackle had flown earlier as Doom Cop jokes, "Damn man, imagine forgettin' to bring her the child support? Ok for real though, who 'gon check on her possessed ass?"

Grave Wrecker reminds him, "Can't pass through that portal, dude. Also, fuck that mess, yo."

The remaining three sit at the table in silence, three killers guarding three prisoners.

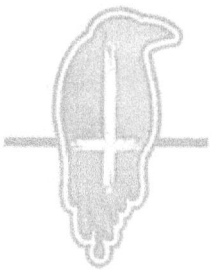

Custard's body rockets down a purple-draped hall of thorns and white roses, her shoes nearly sparking at the speed they drag. Her legs dangle behind, leaving a trail of prismatic slime from her mouth as her knife reflects speedy candle blurs. Her head flops as if she has no neck bone, like a rocket-fueled corpse with a rainbow fountain mouth.

Custard's skull crushes into a thorn-covered door, blasting it off the hinges into a swamp-style kitchen near a bubbling, warm bog. Crackle squawks in surprise, losing feathers in food, flying with a wooden spoon, stirring a goblin-headed pot on a stove. The kitchen smells like pistachios, muggy swamp bugs and now Crackles fear, "Custard? My dear, how did you get past the barrier? Actually, I know, I can hear the dark inside your tummy. Oh my. Why don't we get you back-"

Custard torpedoes towards Crackle, snatching her from above the stove, opening her mouth, baring teeth for taste, "Reunite us!"

Custard's mouth is a massive cave in front of a small Black Bird squawking in pillar-esque fingers, Crackle flailing to flap free with fearful squawks, "Damn this bird body to the hells! Custard don't-"

Crackle's shoved into Custard's mouth and swallowed whole. Flaming rainbow ooze bursts from Custard's mouth and nose as she projects ear-shattering howls of liquid-gurgled roars. The swamp kitchen's river spits hot sizzles of slime and muck around her as she collapses in the dirt, tummy full of magic goop, devouring bird meat.

The feathers burn away and the beak sinks to the bottom of her belly slush. Crackle's guts cook in the whimsical stomach acid and her talons float in liquid light. Inside the belly of the bird, in the belly of a witch, a small gem shimmers. As the bits of bird burst, the gem sinks, landing on the bottom of Custard's stomach. It clamps itself onto her stomach lining and begins drilling its way to her brain. It simultaneously repairs the hole as it burrows through her flesh, stabbing out her forehead. It attaches itself, a shiny treasured gemstone of a third eye and the grave marker of a dead bird.

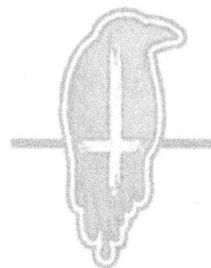

In the dining hall, Grave Wrecker tells Honey about being saved by the portal in the bathroom as Doom Cop stands, "Speakin' of, time for a piss."

Doom Cop walks towards the Bat doorway as Grave Wrecker hitchhiker points to the entrance hall, "Bathrooms that way, dude, towards the front, up the stairs."

Doom Cop laughs, "I ain't walkin' my ass through this damn mansion to take a leak when we got a portal aimed right at the toilet."

Grave Wrecker bounces up, "No way! Ok, wait, wait, hold on!"

Grave Wrecker squishy shoe scatters down the hall, past the green wolf-mouth stairs, up to the snake bathroom. She yells back pumped as shit with an echo, "Ok, go!"

Doom Cop unzips his cop crotch as Honey rolls his eyes. He starts peeing into the portal, the stream going into the bat door as Honey watches out the window, his pee appearing ten feet above the pool. Grave Wrecker watches as the pee from the bottom of the pool falls into the bathroom from the portal, landing in the snake mouth toilet. Grave Wrecker runs downstairs, nearly dying on the stairwell in victory, "You made it! No fuckin' way, dude, that's gotta be some kinda record!"

The three prisoners sit like scorecard judges who've lost their scorecards and will to live. The arua's gone from their cages, but they know not to provoke anyone in the room. Dusty provokes Dakota, "You're a traitor, girl. Funny how you can hate someone you ain't never spoke to, but here I am."

Dakota ignores him as Dusty prods, "Don't worry, either you die before me and I get to watch, sucks for you, or I die first and you feel that guilt of bein' a rat, still sucks for you."

Dakota hears his words, a snake looking to pump venom-fear into her nerves. Grave Wrecker plops down next to Honey as Doom Cop zips his pants, grinning at his accomplishment, taking his aim off the toilet onto Honey, "Honey, when you piss, you sit or stand? I know that dress gotta make it hard at a urinal. What bathroom you use, the girls?"

Honey isn't phased, "I'm surprised you can piss with that flame-roasted dick."

Doom Cop snarls a flame-roasted defense, "My junk's good bro, you ain't just see me portal piss?"

Honey flips his hair, "Oh, was it out? Must have been too far to see."

Doom Cop chuckles, "You a funny dude, man."

He extends his arm towards Honey, offering a handshake.

Honey, on guard with suspicion, offers his hand as Doom

Cop clamps Honey's hand like a vise, pulling him towards the gold mask, "Imma put our little beef on the back burner, but next time that tongue mentions my family or talks junk about me not bein' a good dad, you gonna get real intimate with this chainsaw."

Honey smiles at his threat, the shake ending with some much-needed steam, bursting from golden nostrils as Dakota calculates, 'What does Doom Cop have to gain by befriending Honey? He doesn't want to show it, but he fears Custard. He's a man with no magic that we're aware of and he knows that the enemy of an enemy is a friend. To go from strangling each other to a peace offering is a strange and drastic change of tempo, especially for him. Tonight was about killing victims, but Doom Cop's focus has shifted to survival. It doesn't mean he's one of us, but it does raise questions about where survival rate percentages are. Doom Cop's a wildcard with a chainsaw that's as unpredictable as magic and I'm not sure which is worth fearing more. Is the unpredictable nature of a madman's mind worth analyzing and is he even aware of his own strategies?'

Doom Cop strategizes, "Ay Honey, you and me both know Custard's the one that flew your dad's dead ass into that fireplace."

Honey looks for holes in his plot, "How so?"

Doom Cop flips a hand, "You see anyone else up in here pointin' their hands, makin' shit happen? We ain't careful, these magic folk gonna take our asses out."

Grave Wrecker flops both her hands out in jealousy, "Yo, what about me? These stomach tentacles gotta be at least a little magic. I'm magic!"

Doom Cop chokes on laughs, "You ain't magic, you cursed by magic, dumbass."

Grave Wrecker gives a silent double-thumbs down, leaving the table to snoop through fancy drawers as Honey tests Doom Cop's questionable friendship for bullshit leaks, "You know the last guy to try to kill me ended up in a garbage bag."

Doom Cop nods, "I ain't your family, things go south with us again, ain't gon' be no lapse in judgment and drama-filled dialogue. We just gonna throw hands, and my hands gon' be carryin' a saw."

Honey assures him, "You'll be carrying a saw, I'll be carrying you, dead."

Grave Wrecker nearly dies herself at the corny banter, "You two are so whack with the shit talk, "Oh my god dudes, give it a rest. Doom Cop, what happens when your chainsaw runs out o' gas, yo? Then what, all you got's an ugly ass face? So, then you're just the boogie man or what, dude?"

Doom Cop holds his mask in pain at her question, "Guess we gon' figure it out when it happen, huh? Don't be worryin' 'bout my saw. Junk ain't for you anyhow, it's for that chick's ass."

He points at Kylee, a hopeless, spaced-out mess of a blonde with nothing left to lose. The mess tries her luck. With the magic barrier now gone, she confronts Doom Cop, "Let me kill Dusty."

Doom Cop chokes on air, "The fuck?"

Kylee stares with no regret at Dusty, a traitor now betrayed, "Give me the chainsaw, let me hunt him. He tried to sabotage me with the knife, right? Well, Custard's gone, so I'll kill him for her. Prove to you I ain't a stuck-up snob, show you I got balls."

Dusty shakes his head no at Kylee, turning towards Doom Cop awaiting his dismissal as Doom Cop sentences, "Fuck it, we all bored, let's see how this junk plays out."

Kylee's heart pounds in shock as Dusty now feels betrayal, "NO! Kylee, you gonna kill me? Really, you're ok with bein' a murderer? No, fuck both of you! You think survival's worth the guilt of my life on yur' hands, girl? You makin' a mistake you ain't gon' be able to clean off your conscience. I'm tellin' you, don't do it. You think you kill me, he's gonna let you live? He gon' kill you anyway."

Kylee's a faded ghost, "Probably. Least there'll be one less selfish person in the world."

Dusty blurts, "Are you stupid? Ain't nothin' selfish 'bout not wantin' to die in a cage, bitch. Hop off the internet and join us here in the real world!"

Kylee scolds him, "You don't know anything about me. You're about to find out that the 'real world' is full of young blood waiting to claim the lives of tired people with tired views."

Doom Cop thinks out loud, "I am tired. Shit man, am I old?"

Grave Wrecker interjects, "Duh. Dude, you already got that crinkly-ass grandpa skin too."

Honey thinks about the consequences this could have as Dakota calculates them, *'Custard left the room and now things are spinning out of control. Does that put Custard in the captain's chair? Doom Cop's surly second in command of this ship and no one wants him steering. No one, except Kylee. Does Kylee have what it takes to kill Dusty? I don't understand her logic and what she intends to gain from the act. Maybe she's lost all hope and it's her final thrill. Killing one of us can't amount to anything good in our current situation. Maybe she wants her hands on a chainsaw. Until I see Doom Cop hand it to her, I don't believe he's that reckless.'*

Honey thinks about Crackle, "What about the ritual? Crackle expects you to hunt your victims one by one in competition."

Doom Cop brushes off the issue, "Crackle ain't here, Dusty dies, what's it change for me? And what about you, man? You ain't got no victim. Why you even here?"

Honey stares outside, questioning his purpose,
"Night's young."

Doom Cop rants, "Night's fucked. Ain't nothin' goin' to plan up in here. We all got a letter sayin' come to dinner with three killers. What y'all think was gonna happen? Fuckin' killer intervention? We gon' sit around a table an' work our shit out wit' Kumbaya songs? None o' y'all knew about this Blood Taker shit an' now we sittin' here with our thumbs in our asses, wonderin' what shit's comin. You wanna follow rules, walk out the front door, Honey, cause ain't no rules up in this house. You think I care about what Crackle wants? Bird can kiss my ass. My whole damn life got other people sayin' what's what and I ain't playin' that shit no more. You ain't want folks in charge o' you, take charge of shit yourself. Custard think she in charge, but her ass ain't even here, right? If she know what's good, she gon' show up an' save her boy."

Doom Cop walks over and unlocks Kylee's cage, "Get up."

Kylee lowers her messy blonde bun under bars, wiping bangs out of makeup-splotched aftermath. Her black top, sweat, white pants, blood and dirt. Her hands sting and her jewelry shines like her spirit used to. She looks at Doom Cop, exhausted in the glow of colored candles, demanding, "Open his cage."

Doom Cop engulfs her demand with hot breath, "You gon' get yur' revenge on Dusty. I'm doin' yo' ass a favor, but you know I'm still gon' kill you, right?"

Kylee nods in shaking anxiety as Dusty looks into her defeated eyes with a hanging head of helplessness. Honey's worried as Doom Cop unlocks Dusty's cage, Dusty winking at Kylee.

SMASH! Dusty tackles Doom Cop, shoulder breaking ribs as Grave Wrecker's startled back, "Oh shit, dude!"

Dusty demands, "RUN KYLEE! GO!"

Kylee's goosebumps fuel her terror-charged sprint towards the front of the mansion. Doom Cop reeks of outrage rolling on top of Dusty, squeezing his neck blue with berserking panic, ordering, "GET HER!"

Honey hesitates, taking the situation in as Grave Wrecker charges her spikeball head down the hall, "I'm on it!"

Kylee runs at burning speed, survival instincts pushing past pain and logic as sounds of chaos behind her mute with ringing ears. Her heartbeat's the only sound left as her eyes cry tears she's unaware of. Everything's out of focus as blood-gushing

fingers grab the door handle in shock, turning back one last time. Past Grave Wrecker, Dusty's choked, struggling to see Kylee's fading face as she mouths, "Thank you." Dusty can't respond, wondering why this win feels like a loss as Doom Cop fires orders, "GRAB HER, NOW!"

Grave Wrecker fakes losing her breath, "This helmet, it's too heavy, dude."

Doom Cop Barks, "Then take the fuckin' thing off!"

Grave Wrecker pretends to fumble to unlock her spikeball helmet, buying Kylee time as she rips the door open. Insane amounts of wind rush into the entranceway as Kylee realizes the house is facing down towards earth and the grounds hundreds of feet below. The winds outside spin as pieces of debris and glass violently rotate. Kylee holds the door frame as Honey looks from a distance at the view outside the door, realizing, "It's the tornado."

The inside of the mansion is calm and unbothered as the tornado ravages the exterior of the building, creating two separate worlds. The world outside is a windy hell of flying rubble as Kylee stares out in disbelief, 'What do I do?'

She struggles to hold the doorway as the vortex tears her fingernails across the doorframe, wood-shoved skin.

Grave Wrecker teeters behind her, drunk by winds echoing through the halls as Kylee makes the choice, immediately sucked out.

She's barraged by everything the wind can grab, effortlessly tossed around at deafening speed. The gusts fill her ears and dirt fills her eyes, blindly thrown into things too fast to recognize. She smashes into what's left of the mansion as the building rattles to an explosion of needle-like splinters and airborne fires, spiraling in a low rumble. Kylee can barely hear the air siren wailing in the

distance as cars and trees soar by. Her skull collides with a dumpster, shattering bones as she's stuck in an earth-engulfing vortex of violence. A spinning wall of razor metal and glass shreds everything at an ear-bursting pitch. The outside of the mansion's gone, with its remains thrown everywhere. They're littered across a storm-torn field of pure carnage as Kylee's body rockets, plummeting into the dirt at detrimental speeds. The tornado crawls destruction toward town as police sirens and crickets fade in.

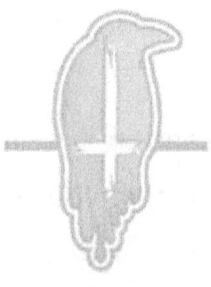

Grave Wrecker carefully holds the doorway of the nonexistent mansion, hundreds of feet above the ground, at the point where the house was destroyed, the portal to the real world suspended in midair. The inside of the mansion is still pristine and quiet, floating in the hidden pocket of another reality. Doom Cop pauses the pummeling of Dusty's face, mesmerized at the front door's view of the earth below. Doom Cop and Honey make their way towards Grave Wrecker in disbelief as Dusty sleeps in a blood puddle. They stare out at the farm nearly six hundred feet to the ground, Doom Cop in awe, "Well, shit."

His head peeks out from nothingness in the sky like the demon under your bed, a mere speck from the ground as Grave Wrecker panics, "If the house is gone, what the fuck are we standin' in? Shit dude, so what? We're trapped here? What the hell kinda mansion explodes in a tornado and the shit's perfectly fine from the inside? Where the hell are we?"

Honey suggests, "Maybe you'd consider this purgatory for our mistakes, love."

Doom Cop orders Grave Wrecker, "Get Dusty back in his cage 'fore he takes off."

Grave Wrecker hops to it, "Word."

Doom Cop stands in front of the door, a staggering drop, "Why'd you hesitate?"

Honey's hair blows in the calm of the aftermath, wind in his dress, "'Not my kid, not my problem,' right?"

Doom Cop realizes, "Oh, okay. I see you flippin' my shit on me."

He looks at Kylee's ant of a body. "Guess we both need a victim now."

Honey looks at him through his mask, dead in the eye, "Guess so."

Doom Cop walks towards the dining hall, blindly ordering, "Close the damn door, you're lettin' all the A.C. out."

Honey rolls his eyes, shutting the world out as he enters the dining room, Doom Cop's agitated and distressed, quietly interrogating himself at the table over losing Kylee.

Grave Wrecker notices Kylee's dog having a field day outside as she leaves through a thin door parallel to the bat door out to the pool's patio. She patrols past the empty pool, starting a jog around the side of the mansion to the front yard, searching for logic on an illogical property. Her tattooed arms flip in a 'What the fuck' motion as she blurts her confusion, "No really, what the fuck, dude?"

She stomps up each step to the porch, ensuring they're real, looking back at the driveway, then the door. She blinks in bafflement as she opens the door to the mansion. She steps into the entranceway, "Okay?"

She turns around to find a six hundred-foot drop back to the ground where Kylee still lays, "OH, SHIT!"

She nearly falls to her death, scurrying away as her soggy sneakers kick the door shut, "Fuckin' fever dream, yo. What the hell? This crap's nuts!"

She scampers back into the dining hall, breathing heavily from her near fall as Doom Cop mocks her, "You doin' laps?"

Grave Wrecker reports, "Dude, I just walked through the front door of the mansion from the outside to find myself lookin' out into a drop from the inside that I couldn't have just been standin' on."

Doom Cop stares at his empty reflection in an empty plate, "You ain't really tellin' us shit we don't already know."

Grave Wrecker's face gets an attitude you can only hear, "Okay, just thought you should know the house is weird."

Doom Cop sighs, "You weird."

Honey clarifies, "Actually, we didn't know that we could walk into the entrance of the house in this reality. We just can't walk out. The Mansion's door seems to be the only portal to reality."

Doom Cop mocks, "So what y'all wanna do, order pizza? What's the point?"

Honey theorizes, "'Point' is, we don't know the boundaries of this realm. What's past the mansion? Can we walk down the road? How far does this reality reach?"

Doom Cop rejects his curiosities, "Ya'll wanna go on a field trip? Bus full o' killers? Bet everything outside this house ain't nothin' but a damn illusion an' Blood Taker's ass just waitin' for your's to get curious. Bottom line, my ass is stayin' put. Ain't nothin' bad happen to me yet an' I ain't 'bout to go lookin' for no problems."

Dusty lifts a bruised face towards Dakota, "You told 'em I had the knife, huh?"

Dakota's silent as Dusty wonders, "Why'd you rat?"

She informs, "Kylee escaped, that's a win for us."

Dusty looks at Kylee's empty cage, "We planned her escape. That's a win for her. We're still fucked."

Dakota calculates odds no one could know as Dusty sits, cramped and too tired for thought, Doom Cop investigating, "Why y'all come here?"

Grave Wrecker paces the table, "Had nothin' left, dude."

Doom Cop points at her, "Exactly, this junk makes sense for you. Even Custard got somethin' to gain here, tryin' to move up in her little witch coven shit. An' me, well, maybe I was hopin' to escape my bad choices, meet some people dealin' with the same shit."

Doom Cop looks at Honey, "But you. Junk don't make sense. Kill your pops, travel across the world, for what? Supper? Naw, it's somethin' else ."

Honey brushes pink bangs across from a curious gold detective, "You're as sharp as your saw, huh?"

Doom Cop laughs, "Maybe my ass 'oughtta join the real cops."

Honey rewards his detective work, "I've killed my father twenty-seven times since he first attacked me. His body continues to rejuvenate and hunt me. His eyes aren't human. His mind doesn't always remember me. Yet, his hatred for my life choices surpasses even death. I'm convinced he's made a deal somehow, unable to allow his soul to rest until I'm dead."

Doom Cop raises an eyebrow no one can see, "So, you figure what? Come here, get answers?"

Honey gazes into the past, "There's an older woman back home who lives in the warehouse of a rundown supermarket. When I first sought answers to my father's strange circumstances, I was directed towards her for guidance. She told me about Black Manor, that she'd been here in the past, but in Japan. Somehow the house moves, I don't know. She had the same name in Japanese, too, Crackle. She had me invited here for a chance to gain the powers we were told are beyond our world's understanding. Her explanation that death must kill death is my only conclusion for ridding myself of this cycle. Do I want to become some otherworldly deathbringer? No. Do I want to continue scarring my conscience with the never-ending murders of my father? No."

Doom Cop looks at the fireplace, "So, them ashes up in that thing gonna come back?"

Honey nods as Doom Cop's lost, "So, when the bag flew 'cross the room and you freaked out, the fuck was that about? You already knew his ass was gon' come back to bite."

Honey looks defeated, "I thought he'd have no power here."

Doom Cop feels deceived, "'Cause you already knew this place wasn't part of our world."

He explains his frustrations, "Well, the Japanese Ghost Granny ain't tell me shit' an I think it's fucked up they gon' lure us here without tellin us facts."

Grave Wrecker jokes, "Dude, you willingly showed up to a dinner party, knowing there'd be three other killers. You can't really be mad that the letter didn't say, 'Oh by the way, the house is haunted, too. Kinda comes with the territory, don't it?"

Doom Cop shakes no, "This shit beyond haunted, you feel me? You feel like we six hundred feet up right now? Cause we are. This place a house o' lies and I don't trust none of it."

Grave Wrecker's curious, "So you willing to work for this Blood Taker dude?"

Doom Cop barely feels his heartbeat in his scorched cheeks anymore, "Fuck I got left? Came here lookin' for answers. This ain't it, then what? Clothes ain't mine, mask ain't mine, this burnt fuckin' face ain't even mine. Family's afraid of me. Killed a man. Kylee's gone. Now some invisible ass beast probably laughin' at my mopey ass. Really, fuck I got left?"

Doom Cop hangs his head in creepy defeat, arms on his knees, as Honey empathizes with him for the first time. Grave Wrecker jumps up and begins human-bulldozing the tablecloth, shoving all dinnerware into a fancy mess. She proudly makes her way to the drawers she'd been snooping through with a bounce, "Check it out."

She lugs a large box over to the table, "I found this earlier, maybe it'll cheer ya' up, dude."

It's a colorfully spooky board game box labeled The House of the Bone Man, with cheesy blood font. Honey holds his hands in a pleased prayer to his smiling lips as Doom Cop stares at Grave Wrecker, already annoyed, "You bein' for real right now?"

Grave Wrecker bounces, pulling out the plastic purple

mansion and little rubber survivors. The dice have symbols of ghosts and skulls, Doom Cop's face is pain and irritation. Wrecker finger-gun points at the fun. "Pew, pew. This shit's metal dude, how can you NOT wanna play this!?"

Doom cop entertains her, inspecting the box, "Says ya' need four players."

Honey looks at the cages as Grave Wrecker exclaims, "Dakota's not playing!"

Honey stares down, smiling with wide eyes, swallowing laughs at Grave Wrecker's immediate, blast off of a blurt while Doom Cop instigates, "What? 'fraid she gon' whoop that ass?"

Grave Wrecker's tattoo scattered arms cross, guarding her penetrable and scattered feelings beneath an impenetrable leather vest, "Dude, why the hell would I play board games with a girl I brought to kill?"

Doom Cop stares at beautifully polished dice just waiting to be fondled, "Kylee out layin' in a field, Honey's dad over there cookin', waitin' for round twenty-eight, Custard's boy got handsy durin' the last field trip. Dakota's the only one left. This gon' help y'all work shit out. She plays."

Honey sucks his lips in anxiety of conflict as Grave Wrecker acts cool, "Whatever, dude. Yo, Dakota, looks like it's recess, bitch."

Doom Cop unlocks Dakota's cage as she approaches a table of killers for family game night, Grave Wreckers insisting, "Handcuff 'er to the chair."

Doom Cop hesitates at any order, still doing as she says, "Ok, she ain't goin nowhere dawg, you good?"

Grave Wrecker switches seats, sitting next to Dakota, "Hope yur' ready to lose the last game you ever play."

Dakota calculates the game's pieces, three rubber survivors, one rubber Bone Man, leaning close enough to see inside Grave Wrecker's spike ball, face to face with a dark old friend. Dakota aims her sights, "Shotgun on The Bone Man."

CHAPTER FOUR

Secrets

Dakota holds the rules for The House of the Bone Man as Doom Cop holds the key to her handcuffed wrist, ordering, "Read 'em."

The three killers are focused on Dakota for the first time since her arrival. No longer hidden amongst the mayhem, she's locked to a chair and their sights. The three impatiently await her reading, like Boy Scouts at a campfire ghost story. Dakota lifts her shackled wrist from the chair, "This really necessary? Where do you think I'm gonna go? Out the door to a six-hundred-foot drop?"

Doom Cop smiles at her suggestion, "Just makin' sure ya' don't end up like our friends."

Dakota thinks about the fall Kylee took, watching a bruised-up Dusty sleep in his cage. She holds the rules card, decorated with lightning strikes and pumpkin-stickered bullet points. She sits up proper, her yellow sundress neat, her black boots stiff. A blue-haired girl who never fit in, now the most normal one at the table. She clears her throat under rounded glasses reflecting rules in a world that breaks them, beginning, "Welcome to The House of The Bone Man. In the game, three survivors attempt to reach the attic of a haunted house while being chased by The Bone Man. The Attic contains a spellbook that when read, protects that survivor from the curse of The Bone Man. The Bone Man wants to reach the spellbook and gain his true power."

Grave Wrecker nods in anxiousness, "Shit's dope!"

Dakota tries to maintain composure, "To start the game, place all survivors at the house's front porch and The Bone Man at the end of the driveway. Take turns rolling dice to move through the Haunted House. Players may only roll to move after they've truthfully answered a question from another player that's been randomly selected by The Liar Snake."

Doom Cop eyeballs the pile of game pieces, "Think we missin' parts, I ain't see no snake."

Dakota's sucked into her reading, "To keep player's truthful, keep your hand in the Liar Snake Bag during your turn."

Grave Wrecker squeezes the blood in her nervous fingers, "That bag?"

Dakota smiles, still reading, "The Liar Snake will only bite you if you've lied during your answer. If it bites you, you'll die. If any of the survivors make it to the attic, that player will be granted one wish by The Liar Snake."

Doom Cop blows air, "Bullshit."

Dakota glances over at his interruption, "If all three survivors make it to the spellbook, the game ends and The Liar Snake will kill the player who's playing The Bone Man. If The Bone Man makes it to the attic before all three survivors have read the

spellbook, that player is granted three wishes by the Liar Snake and the game ends. If any player decides not to finish the game after starting, they will be bitten by The Liar Snake."

Grave Wrecker scoots her chair from the table,

"Dude, there's a fuckin' snake in that bag? Dakota, you're full o' shit."

Honey peeks in the gold bag at a gold-eyed snake, black-scaled and thicker than his wrist, "It's in there."

Grave Wrecker tantrums, "I ain't stickin' my hand in a bag of snakes, dude. Get bent!"

Doom Cop laughs, "It's one snake. Win the game, win a wish? Y'all think this shits for real?"

The Liar Snake nods at Honey, "The snake just confirmed it."

Honey sets the bag between everyone as Doom Cop exclaims, "Maybe this the reason worth bein' here. Win this shit an' change ya' whole life. Feel like this place a mistake? Wish yo' ass back to reality. Feel like you made mistakes? Erase 'em. Shit, I'm in. My kids is waitin' for they dad, an ain't no chance like this comin' again. We all playin'."

Grave Wrecker throws her hands up in exasperation,

"Whatever dude, but Dakota's delusional thinkin' she's gonna be The Bone man. Why should she get three wishes, that's bullshit."

Doom Cop reminds her, "Girl, you just heard them rules, Bone Man got the worst odds for winnin'. We jus' gotta make it to the attic, Dakota don't make it to the attic, that snake gon' kill 'er. Sounds like she fucked herself callin' shotgun before knowin' the rules. Snake ain't gon' mess with us as long as we ain't lyin'."

Grave Wrecker plays along, "Oh yeah, yeah, true, okay yeah, cool. You're screwed, Dakota. No way you're gonna beat us. And if you do, I'll kill you anyways, HA!"

Honey rolls his eyes at Grave Wrecker's ability to flip-flop as Dakota suggests, "Why don't you play first, Peyton?"

Grave Wrecker whips her helmet around in confrontation at Dakota, "Cut the Peyton shit, Dakota. You left 'Peyton' beaten at a burnt-down trailer!"

Doom Cop crosses his arms, "Snake's waitin'."

Grave Wrecker shivers in anticipation, "I change my mind, dude."

Doom Cop lifts his chainsaw onto the table as Wrecker almost pees herself, "ALRIGHT!" She inches her arm towards the bag, hating life, "Ok. Ok. Here we go. Uhh, shit. Shit, shit, SHIT, ALRIGHT, OKAY, I'M DOIN IT, FUCK! ASK ME A QUESTION ALREADY GUYS, GOD!"

Her arm shakes violently as she forces it into the Liar Snake Bag. The snake moves along her hand, cold and hissing torture with each second, as the bag magically ties itself around her wrist. Grave Wrecker now, does pee at least a little, "I- I can't do this shit dude, f- fuck me! Just, PICK! Pick someone, ask a question already, what are you waiting for? Uggggh! Please just, GOD, PICK! I. I can't, I CAN'T! I CAN'T DO THIS SHIT! TAKE MY HAND OUT. TAKE IT OUT! STOP THIS!"

Suddenly, the bag forces Grave Wrecker's hand to point at a random player. She points at Honey, now looking a bit lost, as he doesn't have a question ready. Grave Wrecker unloads, "ASK A QUESTION, DUDE, I'M HAVIN' A FUCKIN' HEART ATTACK BRO, SHIT! THIS! THIS! THIS IS HOW I FUCKING DIE, YO. HONEY, PLEASE, JUST ASK ME! PLE- I JUST, FUCK- I CAN'T I CANT DO THIS SHIT! I'M DONE!"

Honey looks at Dakota, both feeling bad for Grave Wrecker's torment, asking, "Why do you hate Dakota?"

Grave Wrecker screams hysterically, knowing she can't lie, "BECAUSE I LOVED HER, OK?!"

Dakota's ears ring, "You-"

Peyton roars, "THOSE JOCKS TOOK EVERYTHING FROM ME, BUT HER LEAVING WAS THE WORST! I'M ABANDONED, ALRIGHT! I FUCKIN' TOLD THE TRUTH NOW, LET ME GO!"

The Liar Snake Bag loosens its ropes as she rips her arm away in a blood-boiling scream. Everyone's heart is pounding from the violent scene, but not as hard as Dakota's, "You love me?"

Grave Wrecker's nerves tremble hectically as she cries alone in a metal dome, "I said 'loved'."

Dakota stares at a spiked ball, unable to see her pain,

"If you loved me, why would you bring me here?"

Grave Wrecker hides away in a dark cave, echoing an exhausted tone, "My hand's outta the bag, dude, I don't gotta answer shit. Just leave me alone."

Grave Wrecker's cheek's roll tears as a shaking hand rolls dice. She moves her survivor with way less enthusiasm for the game than she started with. For once, Dakota can't calculate, a blushing mess of flustered feelings. Honey feels guilty for his question as Doom Cop acts like an ass, "Well whatta ya' know, the game is fun." He slides the Liar Snake Bag to Honey. "Let's go, y'all. We ain't got all night, we got wishes waitin'."

Honey glides his hand in the bag as it ties, pointing to Doom Cop running a finger across his chainsaw's blade, "Oh snap, I'm up? Ok, let's say you make it to the spell book, what you gon' wish for?"

Honey feels the dangerous sensation of the Liar Snake's rhythmic tongue, "I'll wish to become a woman. I should wish for my father to rest easy. However, it was his choice to torture his own soul pursuing me. I've spent most of life feeling like a woman, it'd be profound to wake up fully transformed. Though I fear the continued killing of my father would trump the happiness of finally feeling complete."

The bag unties as Doom Cop laughs, "This guy get a once-in-a-lifetime wish an' he gon' say 'take my dick'. Junk's funny as hell, man! Snake gonna bite yo' junk off, an' you 'gon say 'Thanks' an' walk out? AH HA HA HA! Man, gimmie that bag!"

Honey rolls his eyes and the dice, moving his survivor as Doom Cop shoves his hand in the bag, threatening, "You bite my ass, flame roasted snake gon' be on the menu."

The bag ties as his hand points to Grave Wrecker, still feeling awkward from her confession, wondering, "You regret killing that sheriff, dude?"

Doom Cop feels like a wanted poster. "I dunno why you all up in my business, girl. Yea, I guess now, not at the time, shit. Life hard enough bein' black in a white ass town. Imagine wakin' up every damn day knowin' people talkin' shit 'bout you 'cause yur' family white. I lived with that junk every day, an' I pushed through 'cause my family was there for me. But the day I went to see 'em and they ran 'cause a argument with a racist fuck led to me lookin' like this shit, makin' my own family run? No, I ain't regret it then. Snake, untie this shit."

The bag unties itself while Doom Cop rolls the dice, throwing the bag towards Dakota as she pets the snake, "Hello, my friend."

The bag tightens as she hides nerves, knowing her calculations may become public as her hand points to Doom Cop, ready to stir the pot, "You love Grave Wrecker?"

Wrecker's throat swells with her heartbeat blocking the air as her fingers shake, relieved her face is hidden as Dakota decides not to calculate, "Yes."

Grave Wrecker's struck with a pit in her stomach as they wait for Dakota to elaborate. The bag unties as she sets it in front of Wrecker, who's having an internal struggle from an assault of thoughts and feelings. Doom Cop blows his burnt lips, "That's it. I spill my guts an' you make me waste my turn with that corny ass 'Yea.'?"

Dakota's tone is chill, "Sorry to disappoint you, cop." Grave Wrecker's relieved at Dakota's lack of elaboration, feeling unimaginable guilt for bringing her here. She watches a candle-lit Dakota from the slits in the dark as she rolls her dice and moves The Bone Man. Grave Wrecker feels way less lonely than before.

Doom Cop points at the bag, "Let's go, girl."

Grave Wrecker's nerves shift from emotional struggle to incapable action, remembering it's her turn as The Liar Snake Bag waits, "I can't do this again, dude, please stop."

Dakota sees Grave Wrecker's hands clenched, ripping at her shorts below the table out of everyone's sight. Dakota takes her hand in secret, Wrecker's eyes in secret shock, hidden in her spikes as her blood pressure spikes more. Grave Wrecker tries to 'calculate,' as Dakota says, but it never really amounts to much. She's gonna try really hard though. *'Dang, she loves me? No way, dude. I was gonna kill her. That's so fucked up, Peyton. Way to be a jerk. Was I for real gonna kill her though? Maybe I was just talkin' mad shit. And the snake didn't bite her, so she's telling the truth! God, I'm gonna have a panic attack if I gotta touch that snake again! I am liking Dakota holding my hand, though. She is too cool for you, you're such a butt. I never had the chance to make my move on Dakota and now I brought her here and she tells me she loves me! This is so wack, you're a horrible person, Peyton. You better start acting way cooler.'*

Dakota whispers, "Don't worry, I'll get us through this."

Grave Wrecker hears only the word 'us', as Doom Cop's patience incinerates, "Y'all done with love letters? Wrecker, get yur' shit in the bag."

Honey opposes his demands, "She'll do it when she's ready."

Doom Cop snorts, "Longer we take to do this shit, more chance we got, somethin' gon' go wrong and fuck our chances of gettin' our wish. I ain't lettin' some kid ruin my chance to start over."

Honey wonders, "That's what you'll do with your wish? Start over?"

Doom Cop flicks him off, "You see my hand in a bag? I ain't answerin' yur' shit for free. Wrecker, get this shit goin'."

Honey sighs as Grave Wrecker squeezes Dakota's hand, hyperventilating as her hand shivers into the bag. It ties itself around her wrist, her eyes tearing up as her muscles tighten with uncontrollable phobia, snake's breath on her skin, "Shit, alright, ok, OK. OK! FFFF- FUCK, PICK SOMEONE! P- PICK OK? JUST, FUCKING PICK SOMEONE TO-. TO ASK ME, P- PLEASE GUYS! JUST HURRY AND-. OH MY GOD, I'M DONE! I SAID I'M DONE! OK? STOP! STOP NOW! STOP, THIS ISN'T A GAME ANYMORE! I JUST- I CAN'T OKAY? PLEASE STOP THIS!"

The bag points at Dakota, who's squeezing her other hand beneath the table, asking without hesitation, "What's your name?"

Grave Wrecker pleads, "PEYTON!"

The bag unties as Peyton claims her hand back, "FUCK THIS SHIT, DUDE!"

She sobs into Dakota's calm body, crying relief, "Th- Thank you…, D- Dakota."

Dakota holds Peyton's trembling body in silence with no need to calculate. She places the dice in Peyton's shakey palm, guiding her hand to roll and move her survivor as Doom Cop jokes, "You keep changin' yur' name, imma start callin' you Ball Bitch."

Honey looks at him in disappointment, "You say you'd like to wish to change things, maybe you should start now. Stop being so cruel to these kids. All you talk about is your kids, but look how you treat these ones."

Doom Cop throws his hands up wildly, "Oh look, other Ball Bitch wanna talk now. It's cause I'm fuckin' starvin', man. How you expect someone to play nice when they ain't eat shit all day? Damn bird left to cook how long ago? Been sittin' here with y'all, killin' time when we 'spose to be killin' her!"

He motions to Dakota, "Crackle don't bring somethin' to eat soon, my ass gonna use my wish for food an' I ain't even gonna be mad."

Honey shakes in dismissal, grabbing The Liar Snake Bag as it ties itself, pointing at Peyton, her spiked head leaning on Dakota's shoulder, asking, "What do you really think about Doom Cop?"

Doom Cop gets up, searching the cabinets for food, "Better cut the shit, Ball Bitch."

Peyton corrects him, "It's Peyton."

He raises hands in mistake, "My bad girl, forgot you a kid, you ain't know shit about you yet."

Peyton wishes her helmet wasn't between her head and Dakota's body as Honey answers, "I think he's the worst one here. Peyton killing her mom wasn't her fault. I killed my father to protect myself. Doom Cop's the only true killer in the room. He chose to kill a man fueled only by his hate."

Doom Cop munches on a bag of stale candy, chuckling with a full mouth. "I'm the worst? Bullshit, y'all heard Custard's story 'bout Dusty, right? This witch lie, cheat, steal, and kill. Now she off in the mansion somewhere creepin' while we sit playin' games. Y'all gonna be mad when she start takin' us out."

Honey wonders, "Why is it you deflect attention off yourself? This isn't about Custard. You're the worst in the room, right now."

Honey tosses his hair as Doom Cop tosses the empty candy bag into Honey's lap. "So, y'all wanna gang up on ol' 'Burn Daddy', huh? Ok, I see you. Don't worry, Custard's freaky ass comes danglin' back up in here, her possessed shit tryin' to eat y'all, I'mma sit back an' watch."

Honey rolls dice and moves his piece, landing on the spell book in the attic, "I... made it to the end?"

He's frozen as Doom Cop mocks, "Good for you. You finally gonna get that pretty princess makeover. Hurry up an' wish so I know I ain't been wastin' my time with this kiddie shit."

Honey watches as the black snake slithers from the bag, waiting as Honey's overwhelmed with choice, Dakota warning, "When you make your wish, use the most descriptive and precise language possible. I suspect The Liar Snake will take every word you say very literally."

This worries Honey, '*How do I accomplish everything I want in a single wish? I want my father's soul to rest. I want to be comfortable in my own skin. I want these kids to be safe. I want to get rid of Doom Cop. I can't wish that this night never took place, that would stop Peyton from ever finding out that Dakota loves her. The kid has nothing else left, I can't take away her only hope for happiness. If I have to kill my father one more time, I'll surely lose myself. I need to trust that Dakota and Peyton will watch over each other and find a way out. How do I give my father back his life and still be happy with myself? I can't just wish that he accepted me. He'd be alive, but I'd still be a man, unable to accept myself.*'

Honey looks at Peyton and Dakota, "Protect each other, alright, loves?"

Dakota stares, fearing survival percentages are about to shift, "Go be happy."

Dakota gives the smile you make to those you're losing as Honey wishes, "I wish I were born a girl."

The snake opens its mouth, blue smoke pouring out as Honey's face morphs from a crying man into a smiling woman.

She disappears.

The fireplace startles everyone as logs fall with the fading body of Honey's father. Doom Cop's blackened jaw hanging open as the snake slithers back inside the bag, "JUNK'S REAL? AIN'T NO WAY IN HELL, MAN!"

Doom Cop paces in excitement. "I can't believe he's gone!"

Dakota corrects, "She."

Doom Cop looks like an idiot, "I see her ass again, maybe 'SHE' can make me believe it."

Dakota explains, "She wouldn't remember you. She didn't wish to turn into a girl, she wished she were born a girl. Her whole life up to this point has played out again as a completely different person."

Peyton sits up, hand on Dakota's thigh, "So rad, dude."

Dakota nods in bafflement, unable to yet calculate the potential of three wishes as Doom Cop grabs the bag, tying it on himself, "Yo, how's this shit real, man. We droppin' like flies up in this bitch. First, Crackle leaves, then Custard, Kylee, now Honey? Guess it's just the three of us, huh? Fuck Dusty's dusty ass. Two kissy girls and the chainsaw man. Least we got our Horror movie title."

He notices Dusty's awake, wondering for how long. "Mornin', Farmer John. Ay, Dakota, you mess this shit up for me, reach the end 'fore I get my wish, yur' little girlfriend gonna wish she never brought yo' ass here."

Dusty thinks, '*I gotta be sleepin' still, are they for real playin' board games? An Dakota's with 'em? I wonder, would she* save me after I called her a rat? She saw me save Kylee, that's gotta be worth somethin'.'

Doom Cop orders the snake, "Pick."

His hand points at Dakota as he smiles, "Speak o' the blue-haired devil."

He holds both hands, snake bag and all, behind a relaxed head, "Sup?"

Dakota adjusts her handcuffed wrist, crossing her legs, "You said you want to use your wish to start over and undo your mistakes so you can see your kids again. You also confessed that you regret killing the sheriff now. If you actually want change like you say, would you still kill again?"

Doom Cop leans towards her, "I'll do what needs to get done, so yeah. I ain't got my wish yet an' I ain't got shit worth livin' for now. If my ass can't do good changin' the past, the fuck reason I got to be good now?"

Dakota reminds, "You confessed they were mistakes."

Doom Cop growls, "So? Just 'cause you realize a mistake don't mean you got willpower 'nuff to not do it again. Ignorant kids. You gonna learn, people weak creatures controlled by they urges. You ain't see people regret junk an' end up doin' the same shit tomorrow? We a race o' animals with overpowered brains, so busy droolin' over our own smart asses, ain't no one take enough time to learn how to control they own animal impulses."

Dakota insists she's helping, "You're not an animal, you're a man who made a mistake and-."

Doom Cop jumps up, throwing his chair, "Fuck off, girl!

You ain't know shit about me."

Peyton's startled as Dakota comforts her with the hand not cuffed to the chair as Doom Cop paces in heat, throwing The Liar Snake Bag on the table, "Gimme them dice!"

He rolls as his player lands one space from the end. "GOD DAMMIT! JUNK'S RIGHT FUCKIN' THERE! HELL NAW, ONE SPACE?! SHIT'S RIGGED!"

He grabs The Liar Snake Bag, squeezes Dakota's wrist purple and shoves it in, tightening the rope enough to rip burns. "Stupid snake shit, PICK!"

Dakota's hand points to Peyton as Dakota apologizes to the snake, "I'm sorry for his disrespect."

She feels the snake's tongue dance on her skin as Doom Cop dances with outrage, "YOU GONNA MAKE FUN O' MY ASS TO A FUCKIN' SNAKE?!"

SMASH! He slams his hardened fist into Dakota's cheekbone, crushing her head between sharp knuckles and Peyton's spike ball head. Dakota's face immediately bruises as she stares unfazed with a blood-flavored mouth, "You feel better?"

Doom Cop turns his back, "Keep runnin' your mouth, devil girl!"

Peyton cries, grasping Dakota's palm, "Don't fucking touch her!"

Doom Cop walks by Dusty's cage, kicking the bars, "Peyton, you a fuckin' moron, huh? YOU BROUGHT HER HERE!

Talkin' bout 'don't touch my chick' when you was gonna kill her ass. Hypocrite ass bitch. Anybody tell me one more thing, thinkin' they in charge, these floors gonna need a mop! Ay, Peyton you better ask Dakota your question, I swear y'all, my chainsaw gettin' thirsty as hell up in this bitch!"

Dakota keeps the bag in her lap and the snake away as Peyton hesitates, "Dakota, why-"

Peyton drops her head in guilt as Dakota reassures her, "It's alright."

Peyton nods to herself, "The night those guys beat me up, burnt down the trailer, basically fucked my life. Why'd you abandon me?"

Dakota feels vulnerable for once, "I'm not good at reacting to things immediately. It sounds like an excuse, but this is who I am. When given the time, I can calculate situations and solve for the best possible outcomes. Making small talk is a nightmare for me. I can't plan out interesting conversational points. Being spontaneous gives me spontaneous anxiety. Regardless of how logically I can think while analyzing something during calculation, when it comes to my ability to react on the fly, my fears overtake the part of my brain that could handle a surprise or emergency with ease. As I ran away that night, my mind couldn't stop the racing calculations of horrible outcomes that could occur long enough to stop my body from seeking out safety. Since that night, I've been able to replay the events in endless calculation, realizing that I was wrong. Rather than drowning in worry over what bad things might have happened, I should have acted in a way that prevented them from becoming a reality. I'm sorry for that shortcoming and the pain I caused you."

Peyton puts her hand on Dakota's wrist near the snake bag, wondering if she's in love, "Ya' know, dude, I waste any more time beefin' with that snake or you, we might lose more time. All beefs are squashed, yo."

Dakota's proud of Peyton as Doom Cop nearly chokes in laughter, "Gag me! Y'all done with Pouty Fest? Roll the damn dice!"

Dakota rolls and The Bone Man lands on a space labeled, "Return to start." Surprised, Dakota swallows her nerves moving The Bone Man back to the front gate of the board as Peyton panics, "THAT'S BULLSHIT! What the fuck dude! What do we do now? He's gonna get his wish on his next turn and I'm way ahead of you, Dakota. There's no way you'll catch up before I make it to the attic and the rules say if we all make it before you, the snake will kill you! Fuck this game, dude!"

Peyton stands up, storming around the table, grabbing her fireman's ax. She marches with purpose towards Doom Cop as he stumbles, grabbing his chainsaw, "Ay, ay, AY! Chill the fuck out, what you doin'? You wanna die 'fore you get yo' wish cause I'll grant that wish, no problem, chick, let's go!"

Peyton continues stomping blood-stained sneakers towards him as he starts his chainsaw, screeching above his head, "C'MON BITCH! BLOOD TAKER'S WAITIN'!"

Doom Cop revs his chainsaw full blast as Peyton turns towards Dakota, smashing the handcuffs with her ax.

SHATTER! "Get up, dude."

Peyton pulls her away, eyes locked on Doom Cops laughter, "FUCKIN' TEASE! Next time you come stompin' towards my- Hey, what the hell?"

Doom Cop's chainsaw runs out of gas. "Oh. Well shit."

He drops it on the table, the engine and his blood still heated, but way less of a threat. He shoves a hand in his cop pocket, motioning the other at the game, pretending he wasn't about to just chainsaw everyone. "So, we gon' finish this shit er' what?"

Dakota whispers calculations into her helmet as Peyton insists, "Yeah, we are."

The two girls sit across from Doom Cop as Peyton puts her hand in The Liar Snake Bag, no fear worth having, struggling to be brave, "Hey snake dude, sorry I was afraid of you before. I mean, I'm still nervous, yo, but look, just don't bite me, man. Cool?"

The snake knows not to move too much, realizing the sensation's new to Peyton, same as her hand on Dakota's. As the snake and Dakota both comfort Peyton, the bag points to Doom Cop, "Oh good, chainsaw man here to ruin things, right? Maybe I ask an easy question, huh? Don't much matter now. I'm 'bout to make it to the end next turn an' y'all ain't gonna see my ass again, just like Honey. That junk's gonna suck, Peyton. Winnin' the game, just the two o' you. Gettin' yur' wish, knowin' you gon' be the reason Dakota's dead. Remember, all three survivors reach the attic, Bone Man dies. An' you can't just back up out the

96

game now that you in it, rules said snake 'i'll bite yo' ass. So my question's simple. What yur' wish gon' be, that's worth ya' girl's life?"

Peyton looks at Dakota, nodding and ready, "Dakota suggested I wish us out of here so we're both safe, but that won't work. Her calculations were wrong."

Peyton sees her spikeball's reflection in Dakota's large glasses. "No matter where we go, she won't be safe from my stomach tentacles. Basically, dude, we need more than one wish. Means The Bone Man's gotta win the game."

Doom Cop spits, "You already passed up the only return to start space there is an' Dakota's ass is all the way back at the start. Even if you roll all ones the rest of the game, she ain't gonna be able to pass you 'fore you reach the end. She's sittin' here waitin' to die. You might wanna start thinkin' of wishes cause she dead. So, wassup, what yur' wish gonna be, worth her life?"

Dakota looks worried as Peyton glares a stare Doom Cop's better off not seeing, "My wish will be to move The Bone Man to the end of the game before your character."

Doom Cop's sudden realization could make him cry, "No. NO!"

He lunges for the dice as The Liar Snake Bag releases from Peyton's hand. Dakota swipes the dice from the table, surprised. "Hey! I reacted spontaneously, without calculation, in an emergency!"

Peyton snatches the dice, "Guess we both got over a fear today, yo."

She rolls them, moves her piece and lands on the attic, the Liar Snake slithering out of the bag as Peyton shouts, "I wish for The Bone Man to make it to the spell book, right now!"

The Bone Man floats along the board making it to the end of the game as Doom Cop grabs Peyton's Ax, slamming it into the mansion, game pieces exploding out, "IF I AIN'T MAKIN' A WISH, AIN'T NOBODY GETTIN SHIT!"

He stands on the table, Ax clenched to kill, smoldering with betrayal as the two girls slowly back away, "YOU TWO-"

Dakota interrupts "I don't usually curse, but do you ever just shut the fuck up?"

Doom Cop's tight teeth squeeze out his own gum's blood, ready for murder, "ENLIGHTENED LIL' BITCH. YOU DIE TONIGHT, DEVIL GIRL!"

Dakota forces Peyton behind her, explaining, "I'm not enlightened, I just use my head. It's what I'm good at. Calculations are fun, you should try it sometime."

Doom Cop crunches game pieces under boots, walking to the edge of the table as the two girls below back themselves against the wall, "WHAT MY ASS GONNA CALCULATE? HOW MANY PIECES TO CHOP YOU INTO? YOU GONNA WASTE A WISH TO KILL ME? DO IT! FUCKIN' DO IT, GIRL! YOU AIN'T GOT THE BALLS!"

Dakota stares at The Liar Snake below Doom Cop, awaiting her three wishes, "You're not worth a wish. If my calculations are correct, don't the rules state 'If any player decides not to finish the game after starting, they will be bitten by The Liar

Snake'? I'm pretty sure smashing the game to pieces constitutes deciding not to finish. Wow, I guess I am enlightened."

Peyton laughs, "Damn dude, you got played, what a Dumb Fuck."

Doom Cop looks down between his legs to find the snake staring up at indeed, a 'Dumb Fuck', "NO, WE CAN STILL FINISH THIS SHIT, LOOK! IT'S NOT-"

CRUNCH! The Liar Snake bites Doom Cop in the dick "AHH, FUCK! GET IT OFF. AHHHHHH!"

He shrieks like a child falling from the table, backward onto a chair, neck first, breaking wood and bones with a meat-bursting crunch. He convulses on the ground rolling in terror as The Liar Snake's fangs and teeth shred his balls to pieces, holey, punctured flesh. He stands, flailing his arms as the snake flails from his nuts. Doom Cop crashes through the large window behind the cages, foaming at the mouth. Slick glass erupts out into a mess of blood and diamond shrapnel as he trips, falling into the empty pool like a lost soul in a pit. His face slams into the concrete, shattering his mask with a brain-blowing smash. His burnt face rolls onto golden mask shards, crinkling metallic sparkles. He faces the sky one last time as the snake continues pumping venom into his junk. He thinks of his family, wondering if his final thought was good enough for redemption as two girls in a mansion pop into his head, "Y'all suck, for real."

He dies as his eyes roll back into his head, his tongue flopping out, boiling in a venom-spewing corpse. He uses his final heartbeat trying to flick them off one last time as Dakota and

Peyton arrive outside, above Doom Cop's cold body, puking purple. The Liar Snake slithers up the pool's ladder as Peyton jokes, "He said the snake was gonna bite Honey's dick off"

Dakota smiles, "Honey was a girl at heart. Guess the snake found the real dick in the room."

Dakota picks the snake up and they bring it to the table as Dusty encourages, "Hey. Ay, lemme' outta here! Ain't no killers left up in this place, right? Grave Wrecker, uh, I mean, Peyton. She's turnin' a new leaf, right? So, open this thing on up an' we can figure a way up out this place, huh?"

Dakota turns her chair to him, "What's your plan? We're six hundred feet up."

Dusty holds a hand up, "I need a plan? Last I checked, you got three wishes. You ain't gon' use one to get us up outta here? It really that hard a concept?"

Dakota explains, "There is an order in which these wishes need to occur. You may not realize it because you haven't calculated the risks. Think about it, I doubt that the Liar Snake will be able to follow us outside this dimension. If I don't make wishing us away from here the last thing I wish for, I'll lose my other two wishes."

Dusty laughs, "Alright, but can ya' 'least open this cage up?"

Dakota informs, "Unfortunately, no."

He yells, "Why the hell not!"

She looks away, "I don't trust you. You'll still be wished away when the time comes, but that doesn't mean I need to endanger our safety now."

Dusty scoffs, "Ain't no safety in this place."

Dakota stares at him, enlightened, "You're right, safety is an illusion, but being in control shifts that illusion more towards my favor. And favor isn't luck, it's an extra percentage added to the universe's variable representing potential outcomes based on choice. Those variables that sway outcomes in your favor have two possible options. Choice and karma. I've gained additional favor percentage from the universe through potential threat mitigation by my 'choice', to keep you in the cage."

Dusty laughs, "All I heard was, 'Imma bitch, screw you Dusty'. Just hurry this shit up, my kids are waitin' for me."

Peyton looks away, "I don't want you to wish for my stomach tentacles to be gone."

Dakota's confused, "What?"

Peyton walks away, "They're the only thing I got left. Only thing that makes me different, dude. I always wanted to be special, now I am. What kinda person uses their one wish to take away the one thing makin' 'em unique? I joked when I got here that I was an anti-hero, maybe it's true. 'Least now I'm a part of this life worth noticing."

Dakota stands showing respect to her, "I always noticed you. It's why I clung to you so much. My parents were practically gypsies, Peyton. Reading palms, selling food from a van. I love them, but don't you think they're the reason I'm so weird?

Whenever they wanted to travel, they left me behind at school. Why do you think I calculate so much? I grew up alone half the time and I spent that alone time in my own head. If it wasn't for you, I'd have always been alone. That doesn't mean you were my only option. You're the only option I wanted. The girl I chose to be around because I liked you. Because I love you. Our relationship never got the chance to bloom because I left the night you needed me. I put our potential in jeopardy. You brought me here and also put our potential in jeopardy. And despite everything the universe threw at us, our relationship grows now more than ever. I need you to know that you're more than those things growing inside you and if we're going to make us work, the first choice we make as a couple is wishing your tentacles gone, protecting what we have."

Peyton's back is turned to Dakota at the fireplace, "You're right, dude."

Peyton faces her, "Bringing you here did put what we had in jeopardy. But, even if we wish ourselves outta here, Crackle knows we were here and there's one person in this house that can magic her ass down the six hundred foot drop back to earth and hunt us."

Dakota realizes, "Custard."

Peyton nods, "Dude, there's no way she won't come after us. She's dead set on impressing Blood Taker to gain regeneration, yo. And there's only two official 'victims' left. You and Dusty."

Dakota looks at a worried Dusty, "We can't leave him here as Custard's sacrifice, the guilt would destroy us."

Dusty sighs in an eye roll, "Gee, thanks."

Dakota plans, "If we want our lives together to thrive, we need to eliminate any potential threat to that happiness. We need to make sure Custard's dead. I can use one of my wishes to ensure she's gone."

Peyton unlocks her helmet, "Don't waste it."

Dakota's neck sweats, "What are you doing?"

Peyton quotes her, "Gaining some 'favor percentage from the universe' with 'threat mitigation'."

Dakota's blood throbs, "Peyton."

Peyton's spike ball helmet drops, with a deep metallic gong. Revealing a long-faced Latina, freckle-speckled, cute and strong.

Her hair's wavy black, blonde streaks, ears unseen.

And double-sided nose rings with her pointed nose between.

Dakota drools, "There's my girl."

Peyton grabs her Ax, hacking the shit out of the purple bat doorway, obliterating the frame as waves of energy pulse, whipping her hair. The rubble rolls by as Peyton grabs a piece, throwing it into the door, watching it pass through, realizing the barrier's gone, ordering, "Wait here."

Dakota, worried and silent, watches Peyton leave towards a witch from which she may not return.

Doom Cop sits dead with the famous "Grim Reaper", Steven Spinebreaker.

CHAPTER FIVE

Parallel Problems

Steven Spinebreaker's who you'd get if you draped a purple sheet over an invisible head and shoved white sunglasses through the eye holes, because that's what he did.

Sure, you can see where his body is, but without the glasses, haters might end up talking shit to the back of his head and that's not cool, say it to his face! Steven was a good friend of Blood Taker and as a favor, his soul was spared when he died at Black Manor. Blood Taker ate only his flesh while Steven's invisible spirit roams free in the afterlife of Nether Black.
He became an upstanding citizen, putting on the purple sheet and running a strip club, of course. Thirteen Sins, as a matter of fact, that's what he'd say. His dancers support their gross kids, making skeezy bucks off sleazy butts. Still not as gross as demon kids, though.

Nether Black's got white lilies growing out from black rocks. And its skies are blue flames where the lightning never stops.

Some people have horns and their crimes and money rule.

Purple Steven runs a strip club, Thirteen Sins, he thinks he's cool.

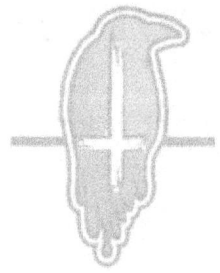

Steven Spinebreaker sits with Doom Cop at the bar in Thirteen Sins, drinking through a mouth hole in his purple sheet head. His voice has a smaller man's tone, carrying the weight of knowing too much while also not giving a crap, "Wow, that stuff will twist the nipples of a crocodile."

Doom Cop scoffs in his glass, "That ain't somethin' people say, but cheers man."

Steven grabs his glass with a purple-draped hand, "Make your own rules, my friend. Drink booze, drink blood, suck blood, it's the afterlife. Time for you to live it up. Well, you're dead, so, dead it up?"

Doom Cop cringes into his whiskey glass reflecting pink lights, "That's worse than the 'crocodile nipple'."

He notices his cop junk still intact, "Least my ass ain't snake neutered here too."

Steven laughs through green smoke, "From your story,

that snake definitely had jungle fever."

Doom Cop wonders, "'Ay man, you naked under that sheet?"

Steven's invisible appendage flops, "Yes, would you like proof?"

Doom Cop builds a wall with his hand, assuring, "I'm good dawg, just glad you invisible."

Steven's white sunglasses reflect colorfully horned bartenders, "It's hard to grab life by the horns or other assets when you can't see your hands."

Doom Cop sips, "Like bein' a baby again, huh? Gotta re-learn basic shit."

Steven's sheet head nods, "I'm curious, are people still spreading rumors that I was a flying skeleton?"

Doom Cop's gold mask strobes lasers to bass-thumping strip techno, "You wasn't?"

Steven shakes his sheet no, "You know, people will believe anything they didn't see with their own eyes so long as they don't have to think hard enough to actually put in effort proving it otherwise."

Doom Cop agrees, "People are sheep, man. Crackle called you a 'flyin' skeleton' too. 'The Grim Reaper'."

Steven fixes his white sunglasses, "I wasn't a skeleton and I couldn't fly, but I was the Grim Reaper. That bird's quite the manipulator."

Doom Cop tries not to stare at girls, "Ain't that the truth, ain't even feed us."

Steven wipes pretzel salt from his purple lap, "Everything in that mansion is very strange. "

Doom Cop catches a glimpse of a leather-strapped ghost girl, cold spikes in hot spots, "Place is straight filled with irony. I joked a dude was gon' get his junk bit off by a snake, end up gettin' my nuts chewed."

Steven jokes, "Was it your birthday?"

Doom Cop exclaims, "Hell naw!"

Steven gulps, "Well... that's just bad karma."

Doom Cop finishes his glass with a slam, "Fuck your 'karma'."

Steven orders another drink, "Would you like something?"

Doom Cop tips a waitress, spooky bikini shoved dollars on wicked chicks flaunting collars, "To see my family again."

Steven slaps the demonic booty of a macho stripper dude, "I actually meant from the bar, but it's good that you have regrets, it means you're healing."

Doom Cop rolls eyes, drowning his lips in liquor, "Don't feel like healin', junk sucks."

Steven's white sunglasses reflect Doom Cop's gold mask, "Endure that pain you feel as a reminder you want change, but put good intentions into the universe. You may be surprised when those changes manifest. Usually, because they come in a form you didn't expect."

Doom Cop blows air, "Sound like someone else I know. This all comin' from a dude famous for slaughterin' folks."

Steven hands him a coffin-shaped business card,

"The 'Grim Reaper's' in the past. I was able to change. You can too."

Doom Cop drinks his troubles away, still too sober for change.

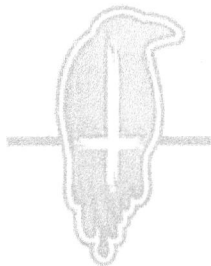

Reality warps from Nether Black through distorted matter, bending time and place, transmitting back to Black Manor, Peyton storming the halls on the hunt.

Her sleeveless tattooed arms flex, patrolling with ax and purpose as she marches through a white rose hall. Her nose rings sway as she stops at the kitchen door, broken from the hinges, she unhinges her spirit, broken free from fear.

Peyton sees Custard sitting on the stove next to a goblin head pot, still hot with smells. She's talking on Dusty's cell phone to his girlfriend, Carol Lin, surrounded by the bubbling of the swamp kitchen. Custard's forehead shines with an opalescent gem and her cheeks have grown black feathers, protruding out toward her ears. Peyton enters, protruding an ax immediately noticing her face feathers, "Sup, Bird Bitch."

Custard holds a 'one-moment' finger up, whisper-yelling, "I'm on the phone!"

She continues her gossip, "So anyways, yea, then Dusty ran through the corn, firing his gun shouting yeehaw or some shit,

I don't know. Then he ran towards the dream taxi, yelling 'Ride 'em, cowboy!' trying to save himself. You really oughta ditch men, girl. Anyways, if you ever feel like becoming a member of the sisterhood, you have my number. Think about it, 'kay? Alright, bye, babe."

Bloop! The phone beeps with a cute tone, Peyton's not so much, "Yo, you ready to kill one bird with no stones?"

Custard squishes her thighs with both hands in a sigh, dangling her short legs off the stove, "Girl, you don't have the blood in you to spill mine. Also, that was corny. What's the problem?"

Peyton's fingers stroke her nose rings, "You're the problem."

Custard strokes her feathered cheeks, "It's soooo hard to care when you look this majestic."

Peyton narrows wannabe-calm eyes, "So what, you kill Crackle?"

Custard chuckles, "You come to kill me for no good reason, but wanna ask me about a bird? Laughable. What's your angle, edge lord? I saved you from drowning, thankless brat. Stop questioning me and start your worship. Praise to Custard, giver of life. You owe me yours, I'm your savior."

Peyton stares through blonde and black bangs, "You're my threat! Don't act like you planned this, that spell took you over dude, you lost control."

Custard drools magic below feathered cheeks, "Honey, you don't know the half of it."

Peyton perks up, "Don't use that name."

Custard drops from the stove, "'Honey?' What, they abandon you too? Just like Dakota? That's right, I saw it all, 'Peyton.' One of Crackle's gifts was telepathic surveillance of this house."

She taps her gemstone forehead with clean white nails, "and a whole lot of magic flavor. Here, have a TASTE!"

She floats, lunging through the swamp kitchen as Peyton clenches her ax, "Too bad it can't see the future, might save you from this splitting HEADACHE!"

She lifts the ax high as Custard torpedoes, "You should be a corpse in a pool, you punk ditz."

Peyton's ax misses, "Wanna join Doom Cop, he's at the bottom of one, waiting!"

Custard presses an orange curse of a star into Peyton's forehead, trapping her in a light-eating blackness. The shadows crawl around her body in a suffocating loom, "Look, your old friend the darkness. Don't know why you took that helmet off, saved us from seeing your busted face."

Peyton swings her ax blindly, hoping to bust Custard's, "Funny you wear white, no dude's ever gonna wait for you at the end of a church aisle."

Custard teleports in circles, "Churches smell and so do men. Why would I want one?"

Peyton swings at Custard's holograms, "Doesn't matter, what man wants to come home every day to a rotten old hag?"

Custard clenches Peyton's neck from the shadows, "I'm twenty-eight, bitch!"

She chokes out gritted words, "Then why you so CRANKY?"

Peyton slams the ax handle up, cracking Custard's jaw as the black dissipates, "Burn to dust, child!"

Custard draws a red circle in the air, palming the center with erupting flames, Peyton sweating, "Only fire that needs smothering is you! Ahh, shit!"

Peyton drops her sizzling ax with black burnt fingers as custard protrudes black nails from her fingertips, rocketing across the swamp, "Too many bitches in my kitchen!"

Custard aims her magic talons at Peyton's eyes, full speed as Peyton's stomach wrenches, coiling meat, "Too many witches in the kitchen!"

Peyton's mouth hangs open as her neck protrudes out with thick tentacles, sliding up her clogged throat. A dozen blood-covered, meaty arms burst out across her tongue, whipping in all directions. They weigh her down, hunched over as she's forced to breathe from her nostrils. Her eyes are fury as saliva spurts out from her mouth's corners, tentacles scraping past her teeth. The arms lift Peyton up, spidering her across the kitchen as Custard retreats, skidding across the dirt, causing magical sparks as she halts near the bog, "Oh, that's attractive."

Custard takes her witch hat off, aims it open-ended toward Peyton and cocks it like a shotgun, unloading a rippled wave of magic burst. Countless bear traps erupt from the hat, circling her in the swamp mud, arming themselves, ready for ankles hidden in weeds, "Sorry for the restraining order. Wanna make up? Come give Mama a hug."

Peyton's tentacles cram down her throat, coiling in her stomach as she lands on mud-splotched sneakers, "I'm eighteen, If you were my mom, you'd have birthed me at ten! Yeah, that makes sense, Haunted ho!"

Peyton's tentacles bulge her throat fast, worming up her neck, nearly breaking her jaw, erupting out past bear traps, grabbing at Custard, "Back off, meat mouth."

Custard pulls green dust from her pocket, blowing sparkled air, lifting bear traps towards Peyton, clamping random tentacles as Peyton bites down in pain. The trap-clamped feelers flail blindly, pummeling Custard's skull. She crawls away as bloody grabbers squeeze her ankle, dragging her across a bear trap. Its mechanism fires, springing shut on Custard's arm.

CRUSH. "AHH, Fuck! Release me, idiot!"

The bear trap opens at her command, hopping away in search of something to chomp in the swamp. Custard wails dark words, dragged across the dirty kitchen floor, cursing Peyton's ax to levitate. It spirals towards the tentacles, thrashing through thick meat, splattering Custard free as Peyton jerks, grunting a tentacle-stuffed mouth, "ERRRRMMM!"

Peyton's eyes are wide, swallowing the damaged feeler as it leaks like a hose, Custard mouthing medical magic on her mangled arm, "Squid-mouthed skank! You'll pay for my pain with yours!"

Custard pukes bright liquid red, splashing the ground as it sloshes around seeking out bear traps, scattering the swamp. The liquid coats the traps, bringing life as they clang their metal teeth with hops toward Peyton. She guzzles dense feelers into bloated cheeks, squeezing past her uvula struggling to her stomach as she struggles for air, "After you're dead, imma' get a tattoo of your hat on my ass cheek."

Custard points in command as her bear traps swarm Peyton, "Why? So every time you take a piss you'll remember how I was on the toilet and saved your ass? Moron!"

Peyton laughs. "I didn't need saving, dude! What kinda witch saves people?"

Custard deflects, "What kinda kid tries to kill their savior?"

Peyton backs away from the traps, "Killing me's pointless, yo. I'm not one of the victims."

Custard stalks forward, "Let's make sure."

Peyton dashes out of the kitchen towards the dining hall as Custard swoops behind, taking control of her traps. She enchants them with flight, soaring them towards Peyton's ankles and wrists, simultaneously clenching her limbs from behind.

CRUNCH! "ARRRAGHH!"

She falls face first as Custard strolls behind, Peyton's wrist and ankles broken. Custard raises her palm as the traps raise Peyton, iron-crushed skin gushing blood into a now-stained carpet. Her limbs are spread apart while her life's spread thin.

Her cool kid sneakers drip from bloody ankle tights.

And her tattooed arms and red wrists hang high with bites.

Peyton's in death-bringing pain that's too much to bear as Custard floats her human piece of art proudly into the dining room, "Heyyy guys. So, bad news, dinner's canceled. But, I brought
entertainment!"

Dakota smolders like the goblin head pot now boiling over, "Release her or die."

Custard smiles, "Have you really even lived if you haven't seen a loved one die?"

Custard squeezes her fist closed as Peyton's stretched further with a squeak, her bangs hanging low with her head. Custard rounds the table towards Dakota, "You have to admit, your girl looks kinda hot, huh? Helplessly splayed, ready for torture."

Dakota stands threatening, "I have three wishes and I will not hesitate to use one as your ticket to oblivion."

RIP! Custard thrashes her hand, bear traps pulling Peyton's flesh, tearing meat from bone, the sound of a helpless squeak haunting Dakota's ears, "DAKO- EEEEEHH!"

Custard stares wide-eyed, "Now you'll have two wishes."

Peyton's leaking limbs thump onto the carpet, squirting to a halt, Dakota locked on a lover's lifeless face. Custard holds Dakota's shoulders from behind, tongue in feathered cheek, her touch like goosebumps, "Don't waste a wish bringing her back. No one wants to see their girlfriend die twice."

The Liar Snake shakes its head in disgust as

Dakota's frozen, calculating wrathful intent, suppressing tears with a daunting thirst for punishment and dead-cold blood. The eyes of a lost love stare lifeless and faded, Dakota stating, "Goodbye, Custard."

Custard serpent's her way in front of Dakota, "And who's leaving?"

Dakota stares at Peyton's ghostly expression, Custard smiling in the corner of her vision, "An innocent girl."

Custard stalks close with a whisper, "She's already in pieces."

Dakota breathes on Custard's lips, "Not her."

Custard's instigates, "Gonna abandon her again?"

Dakota wishes, "I wish to be the most all-powerful, influential witch to ever exist."

The Liar Snake spouts blue smoke as a yellow witch hat appears, floating down to match Dakota's sundress. As the hat fits her head, Dakota feels her veins rumble with black sparks. Goosebumps vibrate her flesh as her vision spasms into clarity. Her breath feels like magic. Her heart feels like vengeance. A deep wind passes her eardrums as her brain grips her spinal cord, pumping favor from the universe.

Two witches stare, ready to kill.

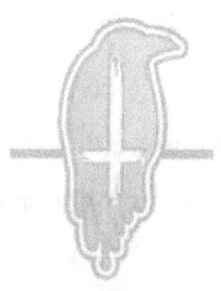

Peyton sits at a bar beside Doom Cop in Nether Black, complaining, "Dude, I can't believe I'm dead. Junk's so wack, yo."

Doom Cop strokes his maskless burnt jaw in a clean purple suit, "Just glad to see a familiar face. Nice one too, can't believe you had that helmet on. You're damn cute ya' know. I ain't hittin' on you. Just bein' nice."

Peyton wonders, "'Ey, that spike ball was rad! Why'd you lose your mask? An' why're you acting so cool? Also, I hate 'cute'."

He orders her a drink, "Time heals. Just go by Dexter now."

Peyton exclaims, "Okay, well Dexter was about to chainsaw us twenty minutes ago, yo."

Dexter laughs through his nose, "It's been twenty-three years."

Peyton's heartbeat drums her throat, "WHAT?"

Dexter raises a glass to Steven Spinbreaker's golden statue outside the strip club, reflecting lightning, "Time's different here. 'Ey listen, I'm sorry 'bout whatever junk went down in the mansion, dawg. Made a lot of mistakes, stuff I can't take back. Was mad at the world for stealin' my family when I'm the one that made them choices, takin' 'em away. Should 'a been mad at my damn self. Was, for a long time, actually. Had a lot of hate. Just ended up hatin' myself. So, how you end up dead?"

Peyton remembers the feeling of being torn apart, "Custard."

Dexter bobs his head, "Witch ain't no joke! I remember you sayin' you was consumed with consumin', cause those tentacles an' shit. That lady's consumed, too. Power hungry. Ain't healthy."

Peyton laughs, "Yeah, clearly works wonders, look at me, dude. Hey, listen, I'm sorry I stole your wish away. I know you missed your family. You were just such a dick back then!"

Dexter fist bumps her, "'S'all good in the haunted hood. Remember sayin' that to me? Man, you were funny. You are funny. 'Ey, that snake tore me a new one, huh?"

He laughs as Peyton's eyes go wide, spitting her drink, "That snake went to town on you, yo! Tore Man Town down!"

Dexter laughs, acknowledging a leaving worker, "Have a good night!"

A demonic chick hoists her purse and jugs, "Later, boss."

Dexter waves like a manager, wondering, "Dakota ever use her three wishes?"

Peyton flips a hand, "No clue, dude. Yo, you think I got a chance at bein' with her again?"

Dexter straightens a golden pin on his purple-suited chest, a sheet-draped ghost wearing sunglasses. He smiles a burnt black face, "Sounds like ya' got three chances. Just hope it ain't in twenty years. Hey, when you know you was into chicks anyhow?"

Peyton wiggles her sneakers, feeling anxious, "Dakota's the only person that's ever been nice to me. Why wouldn't I be attracted to that?"

Dexter lights a cigar, "Make sense, you put it like that."

Peyton's curious, "You've had a lot of time to yourself. What's your biggest regret?"

Dexter thinks back, "Killed a man 'cause he was racist. Pretty sure killin's worse than what I was pissed about."

Peyton cracks open a nut to thumping beats, "Bad vibes bring bad times, dude. People like to think they're entitled to being treated with respect. Harsh truth is, everyone treats people like shit so long as there's no consequence attached. Yeah, there's rare cases of nice people, but most only care about themselves."

Dexter points at her, "Word. You wise beyond yur' years, girl."

Peyton jokes, "Eat your own mom and you'll learn some crap about yourself. How'd you end up with a white family, dude?"

Dexter throat laughs, "You ain't shy, huh? It's all good. I grew up in a white town, nothin' but white folks around. Life gives you lemons, make lemonade for yo' white girlfriend. I don't know, guess you spend time around people 'nough to give 'em a chance, ain't no one you can't fall in love with."

Peyton's Latin brain thinks of 'white girlfriends, "'Ey, you think you'll ever see your girl again?"

Dexter thinks to the side, "She was in her late forties when I left. I been here twenty-three years. My ass even get a second chance, gonna be a grandma waitin' for me. I'm sure she done moved on with her life an' lived it to the fullest by now. Least I had those times with 'er. Losin' yur' family definitely humbles you."

They cheers and drink, thinking of loved ones as Peyton stands, "Where's the crapper?"

Dexter points, "Past the Magic Show room, through the lava hallway. Watch y'ur step an' don't fall in. Lava or toilet."

Peyton remembers, "I'm missin' that mansion's portal toilet already!" She scooches past demons doin' it on the bar to a bridge crossing a lava river flowing through the club. Booty-bouncing music fades as she enters the bathroom, standing in front of a graffitied mirror. Someone wrote Steven Spinebreaker was here in marker. Someone else crossed out Spinebreaker and wrote Dick E-DUR.

Peyton stares into her own reflection, thinking,

'Guess grammar's not a top priority here. What's your priority, Peyton? Dakota. Ok, so how you gonna see her again? I don't know. You gonna end up all crusty and old like Doom Cop, stuck in this hellhole? No. Well, yur' really not makin' me believe otherwise, yur' hiding in a bathroom, bro. I don't have to prove anything to you. I'm yourself, you have to prove it to yourself, so actually, yeah, you do kinda owe me this. By the way, when did you start talking to yourself? When the only girl I ever loved got taken away from me. Actually, you got taken away from her, she's probably fighting Custard in that room. You know, that room where your dead body parts are scattered. Don't talk junk about my body parts. You're body-shaming me. Ok, that was funny, Peyton, but for reals, you need to figure some stuff out. I can't do anything about my crappy situation. I'll throw you a nugget of

knowledge. Dakota believed in you, it's why you think she's super cool. Start believing in yourself and you'll be super cool too. So by 'yourself', you mean you? You already believe in me, Peyton, you're talking to me, right? Ok, but is your name Peyton, too? Well, I suppose that makes sense, but we might get confused on whose turn it is to talk, right? Maybe we should give you a cool nickname. Wait, me a nickname or you? I will be Peyton since I'm her, what should we call you? Well, you used to wear that crazy spike ball, let's call me Spike. Ya know, Spike is a pretty rad name for a girl. Thanks, I thought of it. Ok, see you later, Spike. Goodbye nerd.'*

Peyton winks at her new friend in the mirror, waiting for Spike to wink back as party boy demons laugh just outside, "Hey, you see that girl in the bathroom starin' at herself in the mirror? Bro, like what?"

They smoke, "Yeah, she's been in there like twenty minutes, my guy. She's mad trippin' out. Think she got into the Ghost Worm stash?"

They drink, "For sure, my guy. She's a worm-eater! HAHAHA!"

Spike winks at herself, *'Jackasses keep talking shit, I'm gonna give swimming lessons in the lava pool. I'll watch your skin melt. Goodbye skin. Don't say stuff like that, they're just partying. Yea, but remember when those jocks were 'just partying' an' barbequed your home? Yeah, we don't like party boys. Ok, but these ones can live, Spike. Fine.'*

She puts her eye too close to the mirror, her reflected eye smashed against the real one, "I wonder if I can see you."

Peyton's eye looks at itself, '*Glad to have a new bestie.*'

She high-fives herself as the two party boys are spotted peeking, quickly leaving in laughter as Peyton's cheek rolls a tear, '*Yur' such a girl. Ya know, high-fiving yourself is really just clapping once, right?*'

Peyton flicks the mirror off, kicking a stall door open to piss, "Gimme some privacy, weirdo."

She pulls up her tights as the toilet flushes down the drain, through pipes, past lava, breaking dirt and barriers of intercosmic connection, snapping time back to familiarity, now unfamiliar, Black Manor in ruins.

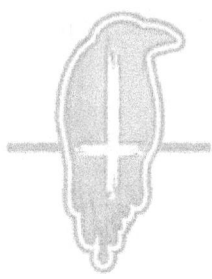

Multicolored clouds drift in every direction, the inside of the mansion a weightless mess of carnage floating in a low-gravity bubble of an energy-gurgling void. Chairs and tables and stair-wells hover, aimlessly gliding around the emptiness to random cracks of energy, pulsing from the sphere of clouds. The Liar Snake flips, Dusty's cage rotates upside down, the entire mansion's an impossible puzzle of devastation. The front door of the mansion is the only thing not spiraling, a secured portal to reality, suspended in swirling chaos. Peyton's limbs flutter by Dakota, a newborn yellow witch, across from a power-hungry Custard. They breathe heavily in a silent stare as the dazzling destruction circling them flows freely with their hostility.

Witch hats tattered, magic minds battered, broken shards of the house drift, slowly scattered.

There is no peace, the world is shattered, the void drinks blood from witch wounds, splattered.

They continue their feud.

Dexter's chainsaw sails between them in slow motion as Custard magically starts the gasless saw, "Doom Cop said it was thirsty!"

The chainsaw spins towards Dakota as she kicks off Dusty's cage, soaring away in a weightless leap. The saw grinds on steel, sparking Dusty's bars as he echoes, "Hey, watch it!"

Dusty grabs at the floating chainsaw only to push it further away as he pleads, "Dakota, unlock my cage! I know you ain't trust me, but trust yur' gut! Do the right thing, I know you lost yur' girl, don't make me lose my kids. Please!"

Dakota glances at the cage as it disassembles its pieces outward, Dusty suspended in space, "Woa, hey, thanks darlin'."

Custard laughs, "Yeah, leave out that door to a six-hundred-foot drop, cowboy. If you're going to sacrifice yourself, at least make it matter!"

Dakota stares, "I doubt Blood Taker cares about you

sacrificing Dusty when you've sacrificed his entire mansion in your greed for power."

Custard's amused, "Let's find out together."

She flies the chainsaw towards Dusty as Dakota mentally pieces the broken cage into a large rectangle, deflecting the screeching saw as Dakota clarifies, "Even if you kill Dusty, Blood Taker won't arrive until all victims are dead. Honey's dad is gone, Kylee's gone and unfortunately for you, I'm not a victim anymore."

Custard brushes her feathered cheeks, "Don't jinx yourself, you can be a victim if you really believe, Dakota! Why are you saving him? What's he done for you?"

Dakota defends him, "He doesn't need reasons for me to respect his right to live."

Custard laughs, "Hop off your girlfriend onto a man, you'll find that ignorant ideal dying with what's left of your self-esteem after a man belittles it. Never thought I'd have to man-splain, men to a witch. What a fucking joke, 'witch', you're a child given too much power."

Dakota suggests, "You're a woman who abuses it."

Custard scoffs, "Better a woman abuses it than give any more to MEN!"

Custard hops onto the stuttering chainsaw, surfing it blade-first towards Dakota who insists, "Maybe you need a girlfriend. You can be the mean one in the relationship, you'd love that."

Dakota spouts voodoo, disassembling the chainsaw as

Custard spins into floating rubble, snarling, "Love's a distraction from the struggle of trying to ascend."

Dakota uses a fizzy blue teleport to Custard, "Love's the reason worth struggling to ascend!"

Peyton's blood swirling head floats behind Custard as she scowls, "Your shallow 'relationship' based on mutual loneliness isn't love. You're with each other because it was convenient."

Dakota smashes black boots into Custard's stomach, a low gravity dropkick to her guts, "Jealous?"

Custard holds herself fetal, "I can calculate, too. Peyton brought you here to kill you. How're you ever gonna forget that, huh? How's your 'odds-defying love' going to survive when you wake up every day knowing the girl you told that you love wanted you dead?"

Dakota rejects her, "People make mistakes. You shouldn't condemn them to misery because they're human."

Kylee's dog floats by in the void as Custard laughs, "There's nothing human about wanting to kill your girlfriend. You're in love with your own slasher. How lonely can someone get?"

Dakota's brain burns, "I'm not in love because I'm lonely. Love just manifests, but you'll never know that."

Custard pinches her white nails into Dakota's throat, rocketing through debris, talking in her ear at full speed, "Lying to yourself's the worst lie you can tell. You already know it's bullshit, but you eat it up anyway!"

Dakota's head smashes through floating parts of the house as she fights the speed to talk, "Forgiving someone for their mistakes isn't lying to yourself, it's empathy, you compassionless wretch!"

Custard's thrown over Dakota's head as she spellcasts a jigsawed coffin, constructed from broken wood, Custard's instigating muffled by the floating box, "You know how good it felt ripping Peyton to pieces?"

Dakota spits on her coffin, "Probably not as good as burning a witch in a box, but I'll take what I can get."

Custard instigates from inside, "Clearly, look at your 'girlfriend'. She's basically leftovers."

Dakota screams as flames burst from her mouth, her blue braid blasts back below a yellow hot hat. The force blows her dress as she stands on the nothingness, floating beside orange scorched wood. She catches her breath and begins spell casting, "Unbreakable Seal."

The Coffin becomes air-tight as the cracks of wood grow closed, shutting out the last of the light, "Forever Flame."

The fires engulfing the coffin will burn for eternity, "Nourishing Nature."

The wood creating the coffin regenerates, never burning away. Dakota sentencing her, "You can heal yourself forever, that's how long you're going to burn."

Custard can't speak, stuck in a continuous loop, chanting a healing spell, keeping herself alive as Dakota whispers, stroking the flames, "Knowing you can't talk makes the silence so much sweeter."

Dakota turns her back on Custard's burning prison, floating towards Dusty, "Hey, I can't risk leaving yet. I don't know if my power works beyond this pocket dimension. I have to save Peyton and you need to be with your family."

She conjures a rope from her palm, magically tying Dusty a harness around his thighs and chest, "This really gonna work, kid?"

Dakota inspects, "If the universe listens, maybe it answers, too. Your kids need you."

Dusty laughs, "Ya' know I ain't really got kids, right?"

She's curious, "You lied?"

He admits, "Puppies."

Dakota smiles, "Still makes you a dad."

She starts casting Mirror Image on the rope, duplicating it over and over until six hundred feet of length wiggles in the void. She summons a gear, magically wrapping the rope around. She casts Clock Work, the floating gear turning a foot every other second, assuring Dusty a slow and safe descent. Dusty's floating in front of the door to reality, turning to her in concern, "Hey, Dakota. Ya' know you ain't like Custard, right?"

The Yellow Witch hovers on standby, "We'll see."

Dusty waves bye, floating towards the door, opening a hole in space. He falls through the doorway, the rope suddenly tight as he rappels down. He hangs, swaying from a seemingly nothingness of a doorway six hundred feet above the ground, his life in the hands of magic, descending from Black Manor to Earth.

Dakota telepathically pieces together wood panels, creating a large makeshift platform suspended near the quiet burn of Custard's Coffin. She enchants the puzzled floor with emulated gravity and spell casts, "Friendly Familiar."

The Liar Snake hovers across the void, landing on the platform as Dakota sits on her hands, her yellow witch hat up across from The Liar Snake, "Two wishes left my slithering friend."

The snake coils up, resting on itself as Dakota calculates, 'There are so many spells in my mind, normal thought has become the hardest thing to comprehend now. A strange challenge I'm not used to. Was this a mistake? I wanted to be able to protect Peyton. What's to stop Custard from killing her again if she escapes? Or someone else. How do I protect her so we can finally be together? Being the strongest witch doesn't protect her, the universe always gets what it wants. What if it wants Peyton? I want Peyton more than the universe. How do I ensure our love will be safe?'

She decides, "I wish that Peyton Sara Sweetjelly can't die."

The Liar Snake spouts blue smoke, Peyton's floating limbs disappearing from the void as she appears in front of Dakota, "Good thing I just got off the toilet, yo."

Dakota runs across the platform to her, "Peyton!"

She's overwhelmed with relief as Peyton's hugged, "You saved me!"

Dakota's comforted, "I couldn't wait any longer."

Peyton hugs her back, wondering, "Yo, where's Dusty?"

Dakota looks at the gear, "Reaching freedom shortly. At a six-hundred-foot drop, a rate of one foot per two seconds puts his descent at twenty minutes."

Peyton notices the destruction-filled void, "Holy crap, what the hell happened? Yo, who's in the coffin? Custard?"

Dakota admits, "Paying her dues. Our fight broke the house and the illusion around it."

Peyton inspects Dakota's hat, "You're a witch."

Dakota raises her eyebrows, "At your service."

Spike talks to Peyton, 'Yo, you were killed by a witch, Peyton! Yeah, a bad witch. Still. Dakota used a wish to bring us back to life, she loves us. Why, what does she love about us? Maybe she loves the idea of being with you. But she became a witch to protect me. No, Peyton, she became a witch to protect herself. Bringing you back was her second wish. Her first priority was herself. I don't know about that, Spike. Now we can be together. You guys are hyping your love up way too much. What if it doesn't work out? Then we kill the witch instead! No, we don't, Spike. We love her. No, you love her, at least that's what you're telling yourself. You loved your mom and you still killed her. That was different, Spike. That was the tentacles. You controlled those tentacles. No, you did. Yes, that's what I said. Don't hurt Dakota, Spike. Then don't let her hurt us, Peyton. You already died once today, dumbass. Stop being mean, dude.'

Dakota repeats herself, "Peyton, are you ok?"

Peyton unfreezes, "I'm with you, right?"

Dakota sits across from her on the floating platform, "What's after death?"

Peyton looks around at the void of colored clouds, "On Earth? No clue. Here? A strip club."

Dakota laughs in concern, "You're joking."

Peyton shakes her head, "Doom Cop's there."

Dakota turns serious, "Did he try to kill you there, too?"

Peyton laughs, "Nah, he's been there twenty-three years. Some time-fuck occurred, I don't know. He's actually cool now. Listen, Dakota, you gotta do me a favor."

Dakota lowers her face to Peyton's. "Name it."

She requests, "You gotta wish for Doom Cop to be with his family."

Dakota's eyebrows lower, "He tried to kill us."

Peyton looks away in shame, "Yeah, I was gonna kill you too and you saved me."

Dakota blinks to the side, "Guess we're not the ideal love story."

Peyton squeezes Dakota's hands, "He's been trapped for years, he's made peace with his mistakes and all he wants is family. And I feel that, ya' know? I wish I could see my mom again, but his family's still on Earth, waiting."

Dakota explains, "You can see her again, we can bring your mom back."

Peyton closes her eyes, "No. She's at peace. She was a good woman, let her rest. I'll see her again one day. Doom Cop's made peace, but he's not at peace. He's learned from his mistakes, but he's still stuck in Nether Black, alone. I have you, he's got no one."

Dakota wonders, "What about your tentacles?"

Peyton's eyes avoid the question, "They're gone. Must a' healed in the afterlife."

Dakota stares through Peyton's stomach at the tentacles, "Oh, good."

Dakota smiles through her lie as Peyton changes the subject, "Yeah dude, so, if there's one thing you taught me about the universe, it's that there's a give and take in place. You've already taken twice, let's give something back."

Dakota wonders, "You're sure Doom Cop's worth this?"

Peyton nods, "I wouldn't lie to you. His name's Dexter Jones."

Dakota's hesitant, judging her lie, "I trust you."

Peyton gives a cute thumbs up as Dakota looks at The Liar Snake, wishing, "I wish that Dexter Jones never killed that sheriff, returning him to his family."

The Liar Snake spouts blue smoke, granting the wish and starts swirling like a firecracker. The snake shrieks, bursting into guts and energy particles, exploding between the two with the third and final wish. Snakey burnt bits float in the void as Dakota questions, "You must really have those tentacles under control."

Peyton looks panicked, "I don't have-"

Dakota interrupts, "Don't lie again."

Peyton's stomach is a pit as Dakota interrogates, "Why?"

She defends, "You can protect yourself, you're a witch now, what do I got?"

Dakota explains, "You have me and I'll protect you."

Peyton questions, "And If I don't have you?"

Dakota brushes off her worry, "You can't die."

Peyton releases Dakota's hands, "Excuse me?"

Dakota's heart punches, "I didn't wish you'd come back. I wished that you couldn't die."

Peyton stands looking down on her, "Are you fucked?"

Dakota looks up at her from the floor, "I can't lose you again, I've already lived that."

Peyton can't comprehend this, "So what, dude? Do I still grow old? What happens when my body dies off, do I float around trapped, watching you and everything I care about die, ending up alone again? Only this time, forever? I wanted to see my mom again, now that's gone! You've fucked me for eternity, Dakota."

Dakota's choice wasn't calculated, "I did it for us."

Peyton turns her back, staring at the void, "It wasn't your choice to make. You're a girl playing a witch, now you're a witch playing one of the gods."

Dakota stands up, "The universe tried to steal you from me twice. How many times would we lose our chance at being together?"

Peyton's goosebumps burn, turning to face Dakota, "I guess one more."

Dakota's cheeks are hot, feeling sick with loss as Spike

interjects, '*Peyton Sara Sweetjelly, The Planet Eater. Stop it, Spike.*'

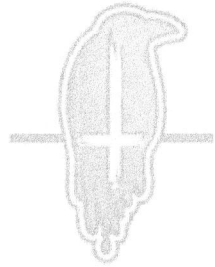

In Nether Black, a log cabin caressed with the slow flow of green lava sits atop a jagged hill buzzing with pests. A peaceful retreat from the hustle and bustle of strip clubs thumping in the distance. Peace ravaged by a classic muscle car, a blue 1970 Dodge Super Bee, white interior matching its hardtop. It rips dirt up a hill steep enough to flip, blue rims holding on for their life. The blue classic jumps the side of the mountain, landing near the cabin, parking with its engine still sizzling. A leather boot steps out, followed by a leather-covered man, a blood-red cape behind his blue wolf's head. His orange eyes are a crazed, wide stare of a beast-headed man who's either drank too much coffee or seen some shit. His hyperactive paranoia has his wolf's head looking like a drug-sniffing pup, patrolling for perps to the cabin porch. His black and white racing suit cracks up the steps as he knocks on a ghost-wreathed door, his man hand scratching his blue wolf head. His spastic eyes suggest he's looking for a fix or flea meds. As the door doesn't immediately open, he impatiently barks, knocking on repeat, "Open, bark, open, open, bark, open the door, dammit. Hello? Bark, Hey!"

The cabin creaks open, an invisible purple-draped man puts on white sunglasses, rudely awakened, "Blood Taker?"

Blood Taker barks, "Get your shit, Steven. We're goin' for a ride!"

CHAPTER SIX

More Than Friends

The blue classic roars like someone doused the blue-rimmed tires with blue hellfire.

Bugs ricochet off a window, one hard acceleration from shattering as the blue wolf floors it, Steven cursing, "Slow your hyperactive roll. I already died once, do you want to kill me again?"

Blood Taker's leather-covered body stretches as he rabidly checks all mirrors, shifting dangerous speeds, the car ripping the edge off rigid cliffs. "Listen, sunshine, no time for grandma speeds. Bark! Get out the road! Damn demon kids."

Steven's purple-cloth hand squeezes the 'Oh-Shit Handle' as some unlucky blur is demolished trying to cross, Steven cursing in neither slang, "Oh Mars, you just hit someone!"

Blood paints the hood, quickly cleared by wind as Steven's breath is cleared from his chest, "Blood Taker! You need to explain exactly what's going on. I haven't seen you in years, can we just slow down a moment?"

Blood Taker's tongue dangles as the engine nearly ruptures, "Two witches tried to destroy each other, ended up destroying Black Manor instead. The place is jacked up, man. Real close to collapsing. That implosion happens, Nether Black's gone too."

Steven's nerves rattle with the car, "I see. You do realize I'm useless to you outside of Nether Black without a body unless you'd enjoy a ghost following you. I suppose I'll be needing some skin."

Blood Taker slams his boot to pedal, hood slamming pumpkin-faced road cones, "We'll stop for skin when we stop for gas. You got a preference?"

Steven suggests, "Something that you would prefer not to eat after we're finished."

Blood Taker barks, "Don't worry, don't plan on eatin' you again, but the three girls that crashed Crackle's house party are lookin' like the Devil's calories."

Steven struggles to read the highway speed limit, "Exactly how is disposing of them going to save Black Manor's dimensional pocket from imploding?"

Blood Taker swerves around a fire-spewing pothole, "That house lives 'cause we feed it souls every year, you know that. But now it's damaged, which means it needs a lot more energy to stabilize the void the house is built in. We don't balance things out, everything in that pocket dimension's fucked, including

Nether Black."

The wheels shred rubber as Steven shreds the seat with invisible fingernails, "I hate to be the buzzkill to your rip-roaring drive fest here, but is there a reason you're trying to blow your car up?"

Blood Taker can barely bark over the engine, "We gotta make it to the transdimensional highway before midnight. Once we're there, time ''ll slow down enough to get us to Black Manor without losing actual time and risking its destruction."

Steven wonders, "And how long is the drive from Nether Black to Black Manor?"

Blood Taker nearly bursts the exhaust pipe, "Give or take a year."

Steven's silent as the thundering engine violently shakes, cutting off cars as Blood Taker admits, "Look, I didn't wanna make the drive alone."

Steven holds onto his sunglasses as the car pulses with adrenaline-spiking power, "If you think I'm going to sit in a car with you for a year just so that you aren't lonely-"

Blood Taker laughs, "I'm fucking with you. Not about the year-long drive, it's gonna take that long. Just about not wanting to drive alone. Truth is, I need you with me. I miss you."

Steven hears birds as Blood Taker skids the car under a crow-infested bridge, explaining, "Look, the yellow witch wished to be the most all-powerful witch to ever live. Her girlfriend's been given immortality."

Steven's heart pumps soul as the throttle pumps gas, "So, how does bringing me along help the situation? Do you 'miss me' now because you need me?"

Blood Taker uses a shortcut off the highway into the suburbs of someone's hanging laundry. "We were best friends. It's the reason I spared your soul in the first place. Crackle wanted your soul and yes, I ate you, but it ultimately saved you. Sorry you didn't see it like that. I had to make it look believable. After I ate your body, I told her that you being The Grim Reaper, your soul was too strong to be fed to the house, that it'd destroy Black Manor, not help it."

Steven braces his invisible legs, "I don't know that I'll be able to solve your problem. However, I'd rather not sit in Nether Black blindly waiting for the end. It's good to have a friend again."

Blood Taker shifts the car like a knife in a witch's back, "Thanks for coming. Told myself if you stayed in that cabin, I'd eat you before the drive."

Steven rattles as they rocket down an alley with too many cats whose faces have too many eyes, "That's not as comforting as you think it is."

Blood Taker laughs, "Didn't mean I'd do it. You never thought of fucked up stuff you're not really gonna do just to get it out of your system?"

Steven leans into a hard turn, holding his breath, "Oh alright, I understand. Like when you think of something bad that you wouldn't actually do because it goes against your morals. Though I suppose if the thought is in your head, it's not completely out of your character. Perhaps a minor fault in your character, blocked by the fear of guilt or being caught."

Blood Taker shakes his wolf jaw, "You're thinking about it too much, man. It's more of an impulse thing. Like, you have a wicked thought and then your pussy conscience says 'No' and cock blocks the fun."

Steven holds tight as the car smokes across a corner store parking lot with the crisp smell of melted rubber, "Give me an example."

Blood Taker jumps a speed bump, sparking cement as they land on a devil squirrel who almost made it back to woods, "Ok, you love your child, but they're also screaming bloody murder about kid crap you don't care about, and a brick-sized hole in their skull sounds like a nice way to start off a weekend filled with you time."

Steven bounces in his seat, "You need a professional's help."

Blood Taker laughs, "See, you're the cock blocking conscience that can't see the comedy in victimless thought."

Steven smirks, "It was 'victimless' until you shared."

Blood Taker mows down a couple of garbage cans, "Now you try it. Just let your mind run wild. What happened to the badass 'Grim Reaper'?"

Steven scoffs, "The only thing grim was the amount of work I did for the farmer housing me in a shit-filled barn. When I answered your call arriving at Crackles, I thought it would help me escape a pointless existence and depression of a medieval peasant's life. You said I'd gain true power, I didn't know that winning her competition, the prize would be to become the 'Grim Reaper'. I didn't know it could get me killed either."

Blood Taker enters a new neighborhood, jumping a curb over someone's lawn, narrowly missing bushes, "Only thing gettin' killed is the mood, man."

Steven thinks back, "We were best friends, why would you lure me to her house?"

Blood Taker admits, "I wanted to be saved, Steven, who else would have listened to a wolf-headed man? You knew me. I killed the other participants that night so you'd win and be given regeneration. I didn't know you'd still have no power against Crackle. I just wanted to be free from her. I'm sorry."

Steven thanks him, "Don't be. You've given me an unrivaled life full of interest and wonder, I forgive you, my friend."

Blood Taker shakes Steven's purple sheet hand, "Thank you, Steven. Ok enough mushy crap, It's your turn to tell me some messed up stuff in your head? Go for it."

Steven thinks, "Ok. What if we drove by a couple having dinner and I yelled out to the girl that she hasn't called me back. The man gets jealous and they get divorced, so their kid gets put into child services after their marriage falls apart. The kid grows up without strong parental figures and becomes a house burglar to support their own kid. One day, he breaks into a home and shoots the family, only to realize that it was his parents from his childhood. He then develops psychological problems due to the trauma, resulting in the abandonment of his kid and he's committed to a psychiatric facility where he rots. He takes pills, turning him into an emotionless waste of space, watching westerns on a television with a busted speaker that's volume is so low, he's gotta make the words up in his psychotic head. One day, his kid comes to visit and the dad doesn't recognize him anymore through the crazy. All the cowboy shows made the dad believe he's a sheriff and his kid looks so similar to his grandfather now, the 'cowboy' believes an outlaw's come back to town ready to finish him off. The chase of his child ends with nurse-issued tranquilizer darts in his head and the kid's head starting its own downward spiral of trauma."

Blood Taker stares at Steven with a dropped wolf's jaw, "You said I need help? You're supposed to make me laugh, man. Now you got me all messed up from that sad ass story."

Steven laughs, "See, this is why these thoughts stay in the vault."

Blood Taker plows through a skeleton's barbeque grill, flames and weiners flying into the windshield, "Five points, see now I don't feel sad. Just like the crazy cowboy."

Steven grits invisible teeth, "There is something I'm actually curious about, if you wouldn't mind letting it out of your vault."

Blood Taker looks over his flexed driving leather, "We got a year on the road, nothin's gonna be left in the 'vault' by the time we get there. Shoot."

Steven looks out to the approaching farmland, "How did you end up working with Crackle to begin with?"

Blood Taker nearly misses a phone poll, "Back when Black Manor was in Europe, you didn't know it, but I made money selling stolen witches' property. A black market buyer wanted proof a spellbook I'd stolen was legit. I was naive, thinking I could reverse a spell after the demonstration. I did a blood sacrifice with a crescent moon instead of a full one. Magic only half worked."

Steven holds the dash as they drive through a grave-covered field, "Alright, so you turned half-wolf, but how did you end up working alongside Crackle?"

Blood Taker crashes through a wooden fence displaying an ad for Thirteen Sins, back to the road. "The spellbook was Crackles and I tried doing other spells to reverse what I'd become. I tried using the spell 'Blood Taker' to extract my own soul out from my wolf-headed body. I ended up erasing the spell 'cause I used it outside Black Manor. Crackle used the spell 'Blood Taker' to feed souls to the house every year. When the time came and the book was gone, she found me with the book missing the spell. I was now Blood Taker, Crackle's only way of extracting souls from the dead. She told me if I ate enough humans, I'd be human again. Truth is, now she needed me to keep Black Manor stabilized, but she only lets me go there once a year to do it. Rest of the time, I'm told to wait here in Nether Black. We're both stronger near each other and I know Crackle fears me. The only reason I help her is to keep that pocket dimension alive. If I didn't, then Nether Black would collapse too, since we're literally the afterlife of Black Manor. Our existence is directly connected to that house, it's like a battery for us."

Steven jumps as a demon deer jumps across the road in front of the car, "So, you opening the portal back to Black Manor's a shot at me cheating death?"

Blood Taker burns gas and tires, "I think so. Well, if you wanna call this 'death'. Seems like we're livin' the life, my friend."

Steven jostles in his seat, holding his glasses stable, "Can you return to Earth if Crackle's dead?"

Blood rolls orange eyes, "Don't want to."

Steven wonders, "Does Crackle know we're coming?"

Blood Taker windshield wipers farm crops off the window, "She should, it's that time of year, but I've lost her voice in my head so I'm takin' things into my own hands while I still got 'em."

Steven bumps into Blood Taker's shoulder as they tip onto two wheels, "Was anyone else but me ever given regenerative properties?"

Blood Taker's wolf ear twitches, "No. You were the only one and it nearly killed Crackle afterwards. She ended up regretting that plan. When Black Manor was built, Crackle didn't know it'd take way more souls than she could harvest every year to sustain the house. It's the reason she held a competition, someone needed to be given power to do more killing than she could manage. You became her answer, Steven, but after you died, Crackle needed souls again. She knew creating another reaper would kill her, so she started throwing dinner parties, luring killers there, knowing they'd do the work for her. But any killer that brings a victim to Black Manor is a fool. There's no reward. Every one of them dies either at each other's hands or by Crackles. Their souls are nothing but fodder for the house."

Steven concludes, "I never knew Crackle was keeping you hostage. Sounds like we'd benefit from offing her."

Blood Taker manages to itch his fur with his non-driving foot as they plummet down a hill. "Problem is, she's way more powerful when I'm near her, we've been connected to each other ever since I read from her spellbook. I'm usually there by now before the 'guests' arrive. I didn't get her message to come there, so she's either dead or those witches blocked her telepathy. We can try to deal with Crackle once Black Manor's stable, but we need to feed those girl's souls to the house. If that dimension crumbles, this reality doesn't exist. I'm getting random visions from her gemstone, it's the only reason I know what's going on. We can exist without Crackle, but not without the manor. Hey, up ahead, there's the transdimensional highway."

Steven jokes, "Good, we can stop at the welcome center. You need to go for a walk."

Blood Taker laughs, "I don't pee like a dog."

Steven jokes, "You smell like one."

Blood Taker barks, "I bite like one, too."

The car drives full speed into a giant wall of green flame, burning through the other side to a black desert. A rest area greets the highway with a sign:

Welcome to the transdimensional highway, take your trash with you.

There's another sign off to the side with the picture of demonic children alone as a minivan drives away.

Blood Taker titters, "Guess people drop their irritating kids here and pretend to forget them."

He takes the offramp, Steven relieved Blood Taker's slowed down to a modest number under one fifty with a sigh, "Oh, there's my regular blood pressure."

Blood Taker rolls crazy orange eyes, "Can it. If your grandpa-driving ass was behind the wheel, we'd never make it. I just saved your life."

Steven corrects, "We're not saved yet. And, considering you've also eaten me, I'd say you owe me and I still need skin."

Blood Taker parks the ride, still smoking from the race. "Ok, a body and a pop and we're even."

Steven mocks him, "Yes, here's your soda, are you no longer mad that I feasted on your flesh, Steven?"

Blood Taker punches his shoulder, "I said we'd be even, I didn't say you wouldn't still be mad. That's your shit to work out. Let's beat feet."

They step out of the sizzling blue classic to a bustling rest stop as Steven feels the engine's heat blow up his purple sheet.

You can die again in Neither Black, the many graves will show.

But if your soul dies more than once, no one knows where they go.

Families take pictures with dead kids and spooky grandpa, too.

Skull-faced cameras take their photos, never cheese they just say 'Boo'.

Stores in membranous bubbles, bloody walls you walk right through.

Workers wearing chained-on aprons, they sell things we call taboo.

Steven yells, "You want anything from the snack store?"

Blood Taker's cape flaps against the sidewalk, "They don't got what I like. Gonna take a leak. Keep an eye out for cool skin."

Steven feels strange searching for a victim, '*Feels like the old days again. Thought these things were behind me. I suppose my needing a body to save the afterlife isn't too much of a crime.*'

Steven yells, "Hey, when we find a body, don't eat their soul to make room for mine, just extract their soul and put mine into their body. No reason to ruin someone's day."

Blood Taker barks, "Grow some ghost balls, man. Besides, I never ate the souls, I extracted 'em. Wouldn't know how to eat one if I wanted to."

Steven sloshes through the blood bubble, un-stained, into the snack store, perusing for a good find, food or otherwise. The store's playing corny elevator music like they're not selling tasers and whips next to Ghostly Gum. The cheesy music clashes with raunchy buy-one-get-one items kids probably shouldn't be touching, but they're already dead, let 'em have some fun. Steven's invisible legs make it seem like his purple sheet's floating down the aisle, laundry riding the air conditioning. He sees a middle-aged demon, wiggling his mustache, digging through a tub of Beast Jerky, '*No creeper 'staches.*'

He hears the grunt of a jacked demon teen, lifting a box of badger food with his mouth hung open, '*Probably compensating, plus he's mouth breathing. That's a no.*'

A short and wingless bat-looking girl bumps into Steven. Her dark, charcoal blue skin the same color as her shoulder-length hair. The blueberry tone clashes with her white, flower-embroidered romper; half sleeves, short shorts. Her voice is dismissively carefree, "Oh, sorry, I didn't see you there. I have trouble with spatial recognition, end up ramming everything in sight."

Steven fixes his sunglasses, their glare fixed on her red eyes between pointed ears, poked out like perches. Her white freckles litter her dark face, stars on blue cosmos. Steven apologizes, "It doesn't help that my limbs are invisible, it's my fault. Ah, you mean proprioception?"

Her head tilts, a ghostly question mark almost visible above her head. "Huh?"

Steven coughs, "The capacity to understand and remember the spatial relations amongst your body and other objects without seeing them."

The lady smiles with gold, metallic teeth, "That sounds right to me now! You're a smarty spirit!"

Steven proposes, "I'm a Steven spirit. Uh, I mean, I'm Steven. You know, being a bodiless spirit like me would probably benefit you greatly, it would surely help with spatial recognition, unconfined to a physical form. Why are you barefoot?"

The lady pats the underside of her feet, bouncing dirty, navy blue toes, "My spatial awareness is super sucky, staying barefoot keeps me grounded at least a little. No pun intended on the 'grounded'!"

Her gold-fanged smile's like a brass knuckle of cuteness and Steven has a crush, "You look like a wingless bat, that's lucky. I'd love to be inside a bat. I mean, my soul. My soul would love to be inside your body. If it were mine, not yours, personally. Not that there's anything wrong with your body. It's actually just what I was looking for. This is going horribly awkward-"

The lady laughs with polished teeth, surprised, "That's pretty forward, but cool. You're weird like me, huh? I am a Bat. Well, I was a Bat."

Steven panics, "No, no, that's not what I meant, my apologies. My thoughts are in disarray as I've never seen a Bat lady before. This may sound strange, maybe even coincidental, but you seem to be the perfect answer to my problem. What's your name?"

The lady gold-chomps a story out, "My pet name, I mean my real name, was Lindsey. I died when I was a Bat. Nether Black changed me, I lost my wings, became a person, well, kind of at least. People started calling me Flimsy, you know, cause I fall a lot and suck at walking. You ever seen a Bat walk? It's more

148

like a crawl. Anywho, I wanted to be a DJ at the Slot Spot, that casino down Kanker Valley. My DJ name was gonna be Rexy. Mostly 'cause dinosaurs are cool. Was hoping people'd call me DJ Rexy Bat. For now, people just call me Flimsy."

Steven blinks invisible eyes, "Alright, Flimsy, this is my situation. My friend, a void-rifting wolfman, needs to put my ghost soul into the physical body of someone here in Nether Black. He wants to perform an exorcism, out in the parking lot, I guess? So that I can have a physical body again and help him correct a catastrophic failure in the dimensional pocket known as Black Manor. Once I have a body, we're taking a year-long road trip through the transdimensional highway to that mansion currently being torn apart by two battling witches. This mansion is the cornerstone to the afterlife you know here as Nether Black. So essentially, by you donating your body to me, for science, by the way, you're taking part in an interdimensional race to save everything that exists."

Flimsy perks up, "Use my body, ghost boy."

Steven's caught off guard, "That sounds way worse than it should. Actually, it's probably better than what's coming. That was way easier than I had imagined it would be, also. Are you sure?"

Flimsy looks like she's star-struck, "This sounds sweet! I'll finally be able to move without worrying about running into stuff all the time."

Steven explains, "You'll still feel things, there's just a lot more leniency as far as spatial laws and physical contact between matter and your spiritual being."

149

Flimsy wonders, "So, where's the dog man? Maybe we should bring him a biscuit."

Steven corrects, "He's a wolf, and, you know what, actually yeah. The dog man's probably out by our car, licking himself. Hey, you want me to buy you something? It's the least I can do, really."

Flimsy scoffs, "Nope. Soon as the exorcism's through, I'm skipping in here, butt ass naked and invisible stocking up, free of charge."

Steven laughs, "You're a peculiar nut that fell off the Spider Tree, aren't you? Please feel free to haunt me anytime. Also, thank you for your help, by the way, it's much appreciated. If you wouldn't mind, let's step outside."

Steven and Flimsy stroll up to a cigar-smoking Blood Taker. Sexy car-leaning, black leather bodysuit, parking lot gleaming, "What's good, Steven? What, you find a volunteer?"

Steven guides her forward, "This is Flimsy."

Flimsy slaps bare feet on hot parking lot, "Don't worry, I don't carry mace. You want some pets, big boy? Nice cape."

Blood Taker flicks the ash of his smoke stick and her fingers off his cape, "She's a she. I mean, she's a girl, and a Bat, bro."

Steven stands beside him, "I know your dog-sized brain can't comprehend my wanting to try something new rather than eating the same bland dog flakes every day. Imagine starting life out again as a Bat. I've lived as a man, as a reaper, as a ghost. It's time for bat boobs, blood, no offense Flimsy. I mean, it will work, right?"

Blood Taker shrugs, "Don't really know. You sure you're cool with this, chick?"

Flimsy holds up rock & roll hand signs, "Take my body, dog."

Blood Taker chuckles a bitten cigar, "Leave it to you Steven, to find someone more fucked up than you."

Steven acknowledges the universe, "The universe listened to my call."

Blood Taker jokes, "Yeah, a bat-girl walking into a convenience store, that's the 'universe'."

Steven warns, "Don't poke fun at the universe, more often than not it will poke back and you will not be prepared."

Blood Taker pops the trunk, rolling out a creepy-symboled picnic blanket, sprawling it across the parking lot, "Ok, girl, lay down."

Flimsy counters, "Okay, big boy, roll over."

Her joke shows the tip of her tongue through her chompers as Blood Taker stares at Steven in silence.

Blood Taker rolls his eyes, "Flimsy, lay."

Flimsy giggles, "Taker, Heel."

Blood Taker looks down at her between serious, squinted eyes and tight wolf teeth, a low growl muffled by neck fur. He barks, "Lay."

Flimsy lies on the blanket, her dark skin sprawled across creepy iconography, as she insists, "Yes, sir. Do me dirty, wolf master."

Blood Taker notices demon families watching, "Oh Mars, don't make this weird, girl. 'Ay, mind your business, Bone Bags!'"

Flimsy explains, "That's just my fam, ignore them."

Steven worries as Blood Taker cautions with his hands, "Shit. Uh, don't worry, guys. She said this was cool."

Flimsy's adopted mummy mom screams, "A WOLFMAN'S GONNA EAT MY BABY! FLIMSY, BLOW YOUR RAPE WHISTLE!"

Blood Taker's orange eyes are wide with worry, Steven panicking as Flimsy yells, "Jeez I hate my family, SHUT THE FUCK UP, MOM! UGH! Wolf, gimmie that hot, furry-"

Blood Taker stops her, "I don't know what you think is gonna happen here, Bat, but it's not kinky wolf sex."

Steven suggests, "Blood, the dad's coming, can you hurry this up?"

Flimsy fake quivers, "Yea, Blood Daddy, no time for foreplay, violate my SOUL!"

Her acting's dramatically cringy as Blood Taker accuses, "Steven, did you drug her or somethin'?"

Steven's appalled, "No! I didn't know she was gonna be some freaky deeky Bat, she was just very willing. I figured it would be easier than mauling some helpless person in the woods. Just perform the exorcism!"

Blood Taker opens his jaws, pouring blood into Flimsy's mouth as it splashes out every direction, Flimsy surely splashing out naughty words we're happier not to hear through her gargling. Blood Taker recites words to the screams of Flimsy's charging family, "Soul inside, out with pride. Leave your cage, you need not hide."

Flimsy's body lies limp as her nearly invisible ghost rises from her corpse. Steven lies next to Flimsy, yelling, "Hurry! Put me inside her! This is starting to sound really gay, by the way. This girl just rubs off on everyone."

Blood Taker recites, "Soul of man, without form. Newfound body, blood still warm."

Steven's spirit enters one of Flimsy's holes, and we don't care to know which one, as Flimsy's ghost cheerleads, "Yea, fill me up, Steven!"

Steven blurts, "Flimsy, shut the fuck up! Oh, jeez, I sound like her. I have a girl's voice!"

Blood Taker throws the picnic blanket back in the trunk with a slam, jumping in the car, "I can't believe those spells worked, I just pulled those rhymes outta my ass! Steven, it's time to move yours, let's go!"

Steven struggles, remembering how to walk in a physical body as he wobbles his girly Bat legs to the car. He barely gets the door closed as Blood Taker rips the road, waving to Flimsy, "Thanks, girl, we owe you! This won't go unrewarded."

Flimsy toga wraps Steven's purple sheet around herself and puts the white sunglasses on her invisible head, "Don't even start with me, Mom, I'm thirty-two! It's my body!"

Her mom snarls, "Then MOVE OUT!"

Flimsy waves invisible limbs to a fading blue classic, "CALL ME!" Blood Taker looks over at Steven's bouncing Bat parts,

153

gyrating with the road rubble, "I'm not callin' you Steven no more."

Steven laughs a girly giggle, "What?"

Blood Taker shakes his head, "Shit's too weird man. You're a chick. You look like a chick, you sound like a chick."

Steven looks down at his Bat Bod, "Just call me Rexy."

Blood Taker looks at him in silence.

"Shut the fuck up, Blood."

Blood Taker judges him, "Yes, ma'am."

They drive off, Bat Babe Body Burglars.

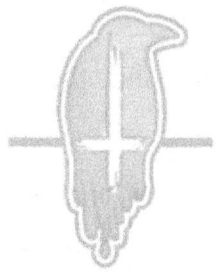

A week's gone by and Rexy finally opens the bathroom door at their hotel as Blood taker day-lays in bed, treasure hunting the TV's ten channels, "Thought you fell asleep in the shower."

Rexy towel wraps shoulder-blue hair, "I had to shampoo and condition my hair. These Bat ears really get in the way, too."

Blood Taker glances at wet and shiny, towel-draped Bat body, "You know, I'd be turned on if I didn't know there was a weasley little ghost nerd in there, right?"

Rexy crosses her sticky, slick thighs, "You know, I'd be turned on if all men weren't dogs, and you're the leader of the pack."

Blood Taker lies, trying not to choke on snacks, "You're

a man!"

Rexy paints her nails at the edge of the bed, "So, if we had sex, would it make you gay? You're a man and I'm a 'man'."

Blood Taker laughs, "No, it'd make you a freak, cause I'm a wolf."

Rexy paints white nails on navy fingers, "So, is your head the only part of you that's a wolf, or do you got some beast balls hanging?"

Blood Taker looks over with the 'What the fuck?' face, "Steven, you're losin' it, bro. I think Flimsy left some hormones in that body. It's been a week and every day, you're sayin' weirder and weirder stuff, man. How am I gonna deal with this for a year?"

Rexy puts her white romper on, "I think, if you expand your mind a little, you'll come around."

Blood Taker puts on his cape, walking to the door, "I'm gonna go expand my stomach with that complimentary breakfast."

Rexy giggles, "There is nothing complimentary about a breakfast when you pay a hundred and thirty dollars for a bed."

Blood Taker laughs, "See, Steven is still in there! First smart thing you've said all mornin'."

Blood steps his leather out into the morning sun as Rexy remembers, "Grab a razor from the front desk on your way back, I need to shave my legs."

Blood Taker walks away without words, 'Grab a razor.'

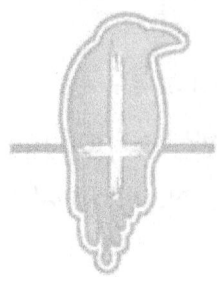

He joins demonic families cluttering up the breakfast bar and their arteries as he sniffs around for the best choice, '*Shave her legs. Ha. Steven, you idiot. Eww, those eggs look like they came out of a bag labeled 'Cooked Eggs'. How hard is it to crack an egg and throw it at fire? What's that? 'Oatmeal'? I bet every person who's eaten that don't even know what the 'meal' part of Oatmeal even is. They just say, 'Oh, it must be food, I didn't have to cook it. It has the word meal in it. It's a meal.' Dumbasses. Yogurt. I'll pass. Does the noise, 'Gurt', even sound appetizing? 'Ah yes, let me put Gurt inside me, now I'm ready for the day. God this food sucks. Least I don't wanna eat a dick for breakfast. I'll pass on those sausages. Mars, Steven's losing his shit for real. Look at this lady, got five kids, how's she even affording this hotel?*'

Blood Taker grabs crispy, overcooked bacon and stalks to the front desk, leaving a crumb trail, "You got razors?"

A pretentious and green gelatinous desk clerk blinks submerged eyes under snobbishly slicked hair on a wiggling, translucent head. "Sir, you'll have to provide proof you've purchased a room. Unfortunately, we can't just hand out supplies for free."

Blood Taker crunches meat, dragging his irritated man hand down his furry forehead, "It's not free. I paid a hundred an' thirty dollars to sleep in the same room as a guy who's slowly turning into a girl last night, ok?"

The protoplasmic face has heard it all, "Is it your birthday?"

Blood Taker scratches his ear, wide orange eyes, "Why, you givin' out razors for birthdays? Ugh, look, it's... It's our honeymoon, alright? She wants to be fancy for our first night... together, and I guess, hair on her legs is the straw that broke the marriage. Can ya' just help me out?"

The slime's unamused, slowly oozing away as Blood Taker finishes his bacon strip, full mouth spitting, "Thanks!"

The gooey man returns with a Princess Pink razor, dead-toned, "Congratulations. Enjoy your birthday."

Blood Taker slowly grabs the razor submerged in the slime, matching the ooze's lackluster attitude. He notices a picture on the wall behind the slime, two people on their wedding day shaking hands in the middle of a hedge maze, white script stating '**Congratulations**'. Blood Taker snaps back to it, taking the razor and walks past a skeleton family sporting sun hats. The parents are way too tired for it to be the start of the day with their kids snarling on tangled leashes.

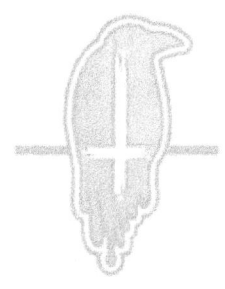

One month passed since Rexy and Blood Taker started their road trip, Rexy asking once more, "What was my name again?"

Blood Taker pours her a handful of quarters as they stroll the arcade, "Your name's Steven Spinebreaker."

Rexy chomps her corndog, "I sound like the jerk. That is a jerk's naming."

Blood Taker laughs, "Yeah, well, you kinda were. Slaughtered farmers while they milked cows."

Rexy's cheeks are stuffed, "I will never do that, you know. So, how old is my age?"

Blood Taker figures, "Least five hundred somethin'."

Rexy's bare feet reflect game lights, "Dang, I am a pretty good-looking one for five hundred, huh, Blood?"

Blood Taker pats her head, "Ya' look alright for your age."

Rexy turns in front of him, walking backward, "You try to act very cool about the feelings. Don't pretend you do not like me in the special ways. Once we, wait, where were we going again? Steven used to remember."

Blood Taker repeats himself all month, "Black Manor, if we don't stop two fighting witches, we and everything else, vanish."

Rexy marches with a spearing Corndog raised, "That's right, we are the special heroes of Nether Black. Well, after the world-saving, maybe we can find a nice place together for being a happy pair."

Blood Taker's reluctant, "I know you're still in there, Steven."

Rexy sucks her lips under red eyes, "I think the friend is gone."

Rexy runs off to play arcade cabinets as Blood Taker sits on a bench, pondering, *'What am I doin' man? Steven was your friend. Not even your friend, let's be real, Steven was your best friend. Then you ate him, let's not forget that tasty tidbit. Now you're flirting with what's essentially a zombified body of a bat-woman possessed by the spirit of your ghost bud, that's slowly remembering how to be Flimsy again? What's wrong with me? There's nothing normal about this situation. Shit, maybe that's what's makin' it so exciting.'*

Rexy yells, "You should stop being the party pooper and come play one!"

She sticks out her blue tongue between gold teeth as Blood Taker grandpa-grunts his leather suit off the bench, "Okay, one game an' we gotta get back on the road."

Rexy smiles scary sharp teeth up to the wolf, "Who is that guy you were driving with again, Blood?"

Blood Taker stands beside her, glowing with game lights, losing the past, "Just a ghost."

He cracks a fanged smile, first in a while, as Rexy laughs to highscore sounds.

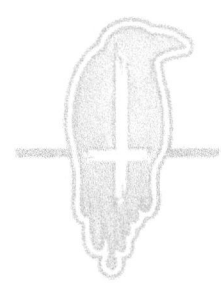

Half a year's gone by as Blood and Rexy slow-roll through dark woods swarmed with Glow Beetles, the blue classic running smooth as Rexy counts bugs, "How much time do you think has been going in that Black Manor?"

Blood thinks, "Don't know the exact conversion. Steven figured something like five minutes per every two months."

Rexy's red eyes reflect blue Glow Beetles, "That is confusing in the brain, we have been driving half a year and only a fifteen minutes has passed for them."

Blood reminds her, "Be thankful. If the transdimensional highway didn't slow down time, we wouldn't be here at all."

Rexy looks wide-eyed, "That is true! Hey, I am sorry that you lost your friend because I exist. I am feeling guilty a lot. I did not know him, but he seemed to be a nice one."

Blood reassures her, "It's all good. He was cool. Didn't really feel like I lost a friend, though, you were here the whole time he faded. Thanks for stickin' it out with me. I know that this whole savin' our world thing wasn't your plan."

Rexy brushes her smoky blue hair over her Bat ear, "Do you believe in lovers?"

Blood looks stoic, "I believe in happiness."

Rexy's gold tooth bites her lip nervously, "I'm needy for something to look forward to if we save everything. I need to realize that you will love me after."

Blood looks at her over his steering arm, "That's a childish thing to say. There's plenty to look forward to even if you're not in love."

Rexy admits, "I am in love feelings."

Blood explains, "You think you love me, but I'm the only person you've spent time with. When Flimsy's soul was taken out and Steven's was put in, it's like he got taken over, like a whole new person emerged. You, Rexy. And you're cool, but you're also too new at life to know love."

Rexy stares, unbothered by his harshness. "Can we promise me, if we save the world, you will be in love feelings with me too?"

Blood smiles at her relentlessness, "Can't promise somethin' I don't know how to do, but I'll promise to make you happy."

Rexy blushes, "There is a big softie behind that leather-strapped wolf."

He laughs, "Bullshit."

Rexy looks at hatching Glow Beetles, "I wonder when is my birthday?"

Blood figures, "Think you got at least three."

She's curious, "Do you also wonder that maybe we should do my first birthday tonight?"

Blood chuckles at her innocence, "Why not?"

Rexy lays her head on his shoulder, "When is your birthday, day?"

He struggles, "Too long ago to remember."

Rexy sits up, looking over, "How about from now on, today is both of our birthday parties and we celebrate those together, every time?"

He can't help but smile, "Sounds perfect. What do you want for your first gift?"

Rexy cheeses, "Say 'I love you too' to me."

Blood laughs, "How 'bout a Corn Dog?"

She playfully slaps his leathered arm, "You are the Corn Dog!"

Blood laughs, "See, you got your gift already!"

Rexy smiles. Custard screams.

CHAPTER SEVEN

The One that got Away

Custard glows in the casket illuminated by a copy of herself repeating healing spells as her real self riots through flames, "Release me!"

Cinders bounce off Dakota, "If I release you, it will be only to burn you once more. You stain the name of your sisterhood with the desecration of their teachings. You killed Peyton to feed your lust for power. You will burn for an eternity by the same magic you abuse."

Custard's words are muffled, "Killing Peyton was, uncalled for. That's my bad, but I promise if you don't free me, we're all dead."

Dakota turns her back to the smell of fire, "Bloodstained lies of a cursed soul."

Custard pounds the wood in front of her, "Listen, Dakota! I swallowed the witch that built Black Manor. That gemstone in my head was Crackle's connection to Blood Taker. He's coming for us, but he doesn't know I'm watching because I haven't contacted him, we have an advantage."

Peyton's intrigued, "You think she's telling-"

Dakota interrupts, "The truth? From The Murder Witch? Yeah, I don't believe so, Peyton. Custard, why would Blood Taker come to kill us?"

Custard sweats, "Nether Black's the afterlife connected to Black Manor. We've destroyed the foundation for that reality. Blood Taker needs this void stable to keep the afterlife alive. That means he has to feed Black Manor souls to repair the damage. Look around! How long do you think this pocket dimension can self-sustain?"

Dakota's round glasses reflect the torched prison, "What's to stop us from walking out that door back to reality?"

Custard insists, "Everything you've become, everything you've wished for. It's all gone if Black Manor ruptures. There's a direct link between your magic and this realm. This place breaks, Doom Cop loses his family, you'll lose your power and Peyton will die... again."

Peyton assures, "She can't kill me again. Maybe we need her."

Custard warns, "There are things worse than death, Peyton. Just because you can't die doesn't mean you can't suffer. Look at me, trapped in this casket, sealed to burn forever, right? Bottom line, void dies, you will too. I'm telling you, let me out so we can correct this."

Dakota shakes no, "Your idea of 'correcting things' last time was pulling Peyton to pieces!"

Custard watches her hologram copy chant spells, an emotionless spawn, "I messed up. Fresh start cupcake, scouts honor."

Peyton stares at her own sneakers, "Let her out."

Dakota can't believe her, "What? You don't-"

Peyton screams, "FREE HER!"

Dakota's startled in an upset frown, "No."

Peyton's stomach tentacles rumble with her emotions, "You both changed my life. She killed me, you cursed me. I'm making my own choices now. You don't get to sentence her to endless torture 'cause you care about me, dude. How am I supposed to deal with that? Knowing someone's cookin' all day cause of me? Yur' not judge, jury, and executioner. That's not the girl I fell in love with. This Yellow Witch is not the girl I fell in love with. Free her."

Dakota stares at Peyton in silence, giving in dead-toned, "Dispel enchantments."

The casket crumbles with dissipating flames as custard's sweltering body instantly cools from the void winds, floating down to the jigsawed platform as her copy firecrackers apart.

Dakota stares silent hatred at Custard as Peyton confronts the roasted witch, "You saved me from drowning, said I owed you. We're even."

Custard dusts off ash, "Agreed."

Dakota addresses Custard, "Well, apparently you made parole, ready for rehab?"

Custard looks out into the electric popping clouds, "Cute. Look, we need to slow down time, now."

Dakota scours her mind's spell library, "I don't have that spell."

Custard rolls her eyes, "Yes. It's not a spell, Dakota. Blood Taker's traveling here by an interdimensional pipeline called the Transdimensional Highway. It allows him to travel from Nether Black without losing time. If we can open a portal and leak the slowing characteristics of that spacetime matter into the void, we should be able to buy enough time to construct a new house to support this dimension. The void should latch onto the house, giving us leeway as far as a "safe" place to confront Blood Taker, but we'll still need to feed the void souls, ensuring its structural integrity is stable again. Blood Taker's soul is surely richer than a human's, it should be able to maintain the void on its own, but slowing down time's our first problem."

Dakota corrects, "No, Custard, you're our first problem. How many souls does the void need?"

Custard blinks, "Do I look like your crystal ball? All this stuff's coming from a dead bird's gem and there's no section on how hungry the void is."

Peyton watches Kylee's dog float through the air, "Yo, how much time we got?"

Custard adjusts her hat, "Right now? Fifteen minutes. They travel two months for every five minutes that pass here. We open

166

the highway, we'll have half a year's time, same as them. That's if we opened it before we started bullshitting."

Dakota calculates, *'That's twelve days lost every minute we waste. There's no way Custard's lying about everything. She's not that cunning to make this all up on the fly. She seems genuine, but genuine people don't kill the ones you love. She might be lying, but I can't lose Peyton again. How do I force myself to trust the woman who so nonchalantly murdered right in front of me? I've already wronged Peyton once because of my fears. She chose to free Custard. I will trust Peyton's choice, I will not trust Custard.'*

Dakota demands, "Impress me."

Custard confronts Dakota, "Unfortunately, as big of a joke it is, you having been gifted power for nothing, your magic's stronger than mine, so, 'impress me'. Can you even sense the afterlife?"

Dakota calms her mind to the void's low rumble, "It's all around us."

Custard twirls her fingers, strolling like an instructor, "Exactly. Death's alllll around us, kept at bay by densely clustered energy forming a barrier. You can't see it, but you can feel it. You can grab it if you're willing."

Dakota grabs the air, "Nothing's happening."

Custard drags her hand down her face, "Yes, it is. You're grabbing it right now, you just don't know you're grabbing it. So, know. Know you're grabbing the barrier. See the energy you pull at. Feel it between your skin and pull it apart."

Dakota pinches at nothing, "I can't feel anything."

Custard eggs her on, "Stop pinching it with little bitch fingers and rip a fucking hole in spacetime!"

Dakota panics, "We're losing too much time, I need to calculate how to do this properly!"

Peyton looks worried as Custard sneers, "We have fifteen minutes before Peyton dies again. Because of you! You wear that choker that says 'Calculate', but your brain couldn't save her the first time. YET, YOU'RE STILL CALCULATING! YOU'LL NEVER BE NORMAL AND MAGIC ONLY MADE IT WORSE! NO SPELL WILL CHANGE HOW FRAGILE YOU ARE AS A PERSON OR HOW MANY TIMES THIS GIRL HAS TO DIE BECAUSE YOU CAN'T SHUT YOUR BRAIN OFF."

Custard strikes a nerve, "GET OUT OF YOUR OWN HEAD AND START LIVING BEFORE YOU'RE DEAD!"

Her words ignite Dakota, white flames erupting from pulsing blue eyes, "WHITE TRASH WITCH, ROT!"

Dakota spasms, thrashing rumbling boiled fingers into the nothingness of the void, nearly mauling Custard, grabbing spacetime and ripping it apart. Custard shields herself, blown back from the ravaged reality in Daokta's palm. The matter of afterlife ripples out from the hole into the void as Custard congratulates her, "Good shit. A little rude, but we take what we can get. By the way, they call me The White Wench, not White Trash Witch. Though it has a nice ring to it. Maybe I'll be the White Trash Witch now. "

Dakota's flaming eyes turn to tears, "Fuck you, Custard."

She floats away in a teeth-smashing sob, sitting alone at the platform's edge as Custard brushes her feathered cheeks, "No time for sad girls, we got a house to build."

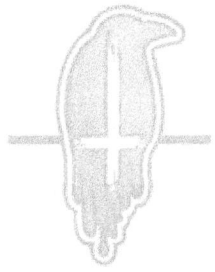

It's been three months since three girls started building a house. Their magic-fueled home supports the dimension that gives that very place permission to exist. A give and take between the void's magical properties and the bones of their safe haven. A surprisingly normal, clean white home attached to the multicolored clouds of gurgling energy and electric snaps drifts calmly across from the old mansion's door to earth. A fresh-cut lawn littered with flowers hugs a wavy sidewalk up to a wrapped porch. A beautiful two-story house with large windows smells like tea as Dakota enters the open kitchen of caramel wood cabinets, a whistling frog kettle sings through the morning. Dakota announces, "Your tea's done."

Custard walks in wearing silk 'jammies' and a silver eyepatch below her white witch hat as she finger combs her feathered cheeks and sleep from her eyes, "You make the best tea."

Dakota smiles behind a yellow-frilled apron matching her hat and dress, "Hard to mess up leaves an' water. Peyton's still asleep?"

Custard sips steam from Dakota's crab-shaped teacup, "Tried not to wake her. Why am I drinking out of your cup?"

Dakota hangs her apron, "Your Magic Meow Meow cup broke, I'm sorry. The emulated gravity's still a little wonky. I can make you a new one if you'd like."

Custard pouts at broken Magic Meow Meow Cat cup shards in the yellow chicken garbage can, "It's alright. We'll get gravity right. Can't have any mishaps when Blood Taker arrives."

Dakota sits at a lace-draped table next to her, asking, "I haven't calculated it. How much time do we have left?"

Custard flirts, "You and me, a lifetime."

Dakota rests her hand on Custard's with an eye roll, "I mean until Blood Taker arrives."

Custard checks the calendar above the chicken can, "Three months. Plenty of time to keep training Peyton."

Dakota fingers tea drips from Custard's cup into the tablecloth, "She's been pushing herself too hard."

Custard reassures her, "She's trying to impress us. She'll make a great witch."

Dakota gets up, kissing Custard's opalescent gemmed forehead, "She's got a great teacher. I'll check on her."

Dakota floats up the stairwell as Custard sips, joking, "Let it sleep! Don't wake the beast." Dakota flies past picture frames of the three making memories, building their home.

Peyton lies drooling across her 'Witch, Please!' T-shirt, her polka dot boxers, pouring sprawled legs as she's manages to

170

take up a three-person bed by herself, "Hey Peyton, you awake?"

Peyton grumbles a face-suffocating pillow as Dakota floats to the bed, sitting beside her, "If you get up, I'll make you breakfast."

Peyton rolls like a log, "Food tastes better in my dreams, dude."

Dakota laughs, "You'd starve for extra sleep?"

Peyton peeks one eye open, "I'd die happy. Yo, who wakes someone up by asking them if they're awake? Just come peek and then leave 'cause yes, I'm sleeping."

Dakota smacks Peyton's thigh, "Are you sleep-talking? Wake up, Pumpkin Cup!"

Dakota hunts for Peyton's scattered laundry and fills a basket, enchanting it to fly to the washing machine downstairs as Peyton's brain struggles to start, "Why don't you just magic the clothes clean?"

Dakota mocks, "Why don't I just magic Bacon into my belly? Some things are just more fun to do."

Peyton closes her eyes, "Like sleep, yo."

Dakota opens the blinds, letting in an artificial sunrise, "Five more minutes and I'm sending Custard up."

Peyton almost snores, "I want a new shirt that says 'Too tired to magic'."

Dakota laughs from the hallway, "Your shirt will be downstairs with your breakfast."

Peyton mumbles in an empty room, "Food's the only reason worth gettin' outta bed. Maybe."

Spike wakes up, *'How long are you gonna let these witches run you? What's your beef with them, Spike? They don't like who you are, it's why they're changing you, turning you into a witch. It's too early for your half-cooked propaganda cookies. You know they love each other more than you, right? It's 'cause they're both tainted by magic. You're wrong, Spike. They both love me and you're jealous. Don't get it twisted, Peyton, I enjoy those two slobberin' magic tongues on us like the next person, but- You're not a person, Spike. You've never felt the touch of a loved one, stop trying to ruin it for me. Let me 'calculate,' as your girlfriend says, your current shit show. First, you love a girl you were gonna kill, now you love a witch who actually killed you? Is that the correct fuckery? Stop judging me, Spike. Look. I'm just tryin' to keep it real with you, Peyton. Someone's gotta keep you in the real world before you lose yourself. You mean before I lose you. You're afraid if someone else is there for me, I won't need you anymore. I'm the OG, Peyton. The only constant in your life. I'm the only one who hasn't hurt you, but keep playin' their game, you'll find out. Go back to sleep, Spike. Peace, nerd.'*

Peyton drags herself downstairs, pulling her 'Witch Please!' shirt off, throwing it into the laundry room, "I'm awake, yo, gimmie my shirt."

Her bare feet slap cold tiled kitchen as Dakota hovers a magically crafted black T-shirt reading, 'Too tired to magic'. She sits by Custard, pulling her new black shirt over her spilling black bralette, sleepy watching Custard sip on spilling black tea, "Good morning, Peyton."

Peyton grouchy stares, too tired for pleasantries as Dakota cooks, "I'm making your favorite."

Peyton slurs with closed eyes, "Food I didn't have to make? Even if I knew magic, I wouldn't cook."

Custard reads a floating newspaper from Nether Black, "Your next shirt can say 'Void's hungriest witch.'"

Peyton chomps Custard's last tea biscuit, joking full-mouthed, "No, that's your shirt."

Custard stares unamused at a sleepy, sneaky Peyton as Dakota insists, "Be nice."

Peyton slurs sleepy words, "She killed me, I get to eat her biscuits for the rest of my life."

Custard jokes, "It's true, witches be crazy."

She takes Peyton's hand, kissing it like a prince, "My apologies, oh master of sleepy world, can you ever forgive me?"

Dakota laughs from the kitchen as Peyton dead stares, "Ask me again tomorrow."

Custard tries to force-feed her tea as Peyton turns her head, "No drinks before food."

Custard nods to Dakota, "Tell that to Coffee Witch."

Dakota defends wielding a baking sheet shield, "How else am I supposed to get you two out of bed?"

Peyton corrects, "I have never willingly asked to be taken out of bed, yo."

Custard agrees, "She's not wrong."

Dakota joins them, presenting a sizzling platter of breakfast goodies, "Happy birthday, Custard."

Custard's feathered cheeks shine with blush below her equally shining silver eyepatch, "You calculated my birthday and you made me pancakes? You're such a dork. You know, it's only been about seven minutes since we started building this house. It's not really my birthday."

Dakota insists, "It's your birthday on earth, so it's your birthday."

Peyton remembers, "There are things I miss. Ya know, back home"

Custard stacks a pancake tower, wondering, "Your life was in shambles, Pumpkin, what's to miss?"

Peyton shares, "I don't know, dude. Just simple stuff, ya know? Music, movies, just people things."

Dakota magically manifests a small orange television behind breakfast, "Here, it should pick up Earth's signals, a little slice of home."

Peyton plays footsies under the table with Dakota, "Thanks, dude! Yo, but it's Custard's birthday, man. Shouldn't she be gettin' gifts?"

Custard admits, "I have two girlfriends and a pile of pancakes, I'm good, Pumpkin, put something on."

She levitates the TV remote to Peyton as she channel surfs, "I can't wait to be able to do magic."

Dakota jokes, "If you've ever seen a lazy person, imagine them with magic and full-blown lazy will be achieved. This will be Peyton."

Peyton smiles, "Less chores means more time to sleep. And more time to go to bed and not sleep."

She exaggerates a kinky wink as she flips channels, Custard nearly choking on a full-mouthed pancake as she spits syrup, "Go back!"

Peyton flips the channel back blurting, "Holy crap, dude, It's Dusty!"

They see Dusty on a Halloween-themed talk show hosted by a cheesy costumed vampire.

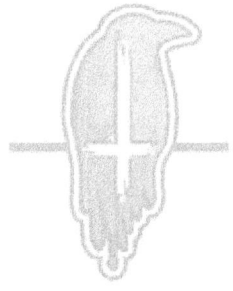

"Welcome to the Late Bite Show! I'm Bitey and it's always a pleasure to have fresh meat. Today's fresh bite is Dusty Dallas, an up-and-coming... ugh... writer, was it?"

Dusty's trucker hat clashes with his sports coat, "We'll ya, if'n ya' wanna call it that. Workin' with a producer who takes my story and turns it to film."

Bitey does a spooky stare at the camera, "Yes, but not just any writer, folks. Dusty's, 'seen the darkness' with his own eyes.

His accounts of, 'real life frights' here in Kansas fuels this passion project!"

Dusty watches studio workers eat, "Well, it ain't so much a 'passion project' as a way to get people involved. See, there's still girls up in that mansion. Well, hole in the sky. Figured if people see it, they might believe it. Send some help."

Bitey mocks him, "Yes, the 'Hooooole in the skyyyyyyyy' Where your friends are, 'HELD CAPTIVE' by the Slasher Club!"

Dusty sighs, "Look, I ain't come here to get made fun of. Every last bit of it's true."

Bitey straightens up, "Yes, yes, how creepy a tale, one the teens will eat alive, I'm sure. So tell the fans, Dusty, when's your movie coming to life?"

Bitey stabs out his fingers as Dusty nearly headbutts an impersonal camera way too close to his face, wondering if anyone's watching, "Well, I ugh... I gotta meetin' with the producer tonight. Want's to show me what he's got so far. Hopin' people see the film and take some sorta' action to save them girls."

Bitey covers his face with his cape, "YES! We'll be waiting for your tale to... rise from its grave, into the homes of all the horror lovers!"

Dusty nods in defeat, "Lookin' forward to makin' it. Thanks for havin' me."

Bitey pushes a button hidden under the desk, strobing red lights as fog fills the studio, "Until NEXT TIME, my lovely boils and ghouls!"

Bitey's chair is pulled back with a rope behind a curtain as a bat on strings swings down like he's transformed. The corny Halloween organ-style music plays to spooky guitar solos as Dusty walks off the set, Bitey yelling, "Hey man, where you goin'? WE CATERED SANDWICHES FOR YOU! What a dick."

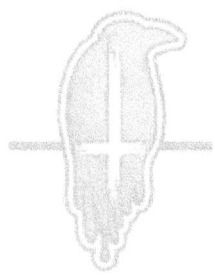

Dusty slams his truck door, ripping down the dirt, "Fuckin' joke, man. Every one of 'em thinks I'm a damn nut job. Serves me right, thinkin' anybody's gonna take this horse shit seriously. Now what? I'm s'pose to just live my merry old life after bein' saved, knowin' Dakota's up there with them freaks?"

He drives in dirt for ten minutes, pulling off the road to a farm where a trailer full of props and actors bakes in the sun near a blood-red barn, "This can't be the right spot."

Kylee rolls up beside his driver's window, her wheelchair mowing down weeds and worms, "Hey, how'd the show go?"

Dusty gets out of his truck, bending down kissing her hello, chair pushing as he talks, " 'Nother joke puttin' us in the crazy hall-o'-fame."

Kylee brushes her blonde hair below her jean dress, "The sports coat looks good on you. Think you'll wear one like that at the wedding?"

Dusty smirks, "Made it this far, we make it down that aisle, I'll wear whatever ya' want, darlin'"

Kylee's chair parks awkwardly in front of the movie's cast as the producer, Chaz Goldstein, smoke breaks towards them. His white pants poke out crocodile shoes, the most expensive piece on the set. His sunburned arm hair and pink Hawaiian shirt reflect in his douchey gold lens sunglasses. His slicked-back hair has shifted from hair gel to sweat and his mustache just started growing back, "Dusty! Karlee!"

Dusty corrects, "It's Kylee."

Chaz absently puffs an antsy cigarette into their faces. "Right, listen, I got some real good shit for ya'. Get your asses in my trailer. You're gonna love it. These fuckers can act!"

Dusty struggles to push Kylee through the grass to a sand-parked trailer as Chaz leaves them behind. Dusty huffing, "Couldn't splurge for a ramp, huh?"

Kylee insists, "It's fine, I'll wait here. Go see what he wants."

Dusty checks, "You sure?"

Kylee smiles in hidden disappointment as Dusty climbs up a dangling metal step into the cramped trailer, Chaz lying on a zebra-hair throw on the couch. He day drinks pointing to a laptop connected to a camcorder beside the sink, burping out, "Play that shit."

Dusty steps over someone's panties, pushing play as the movie starts near a box of thawing Pizza Rolls.

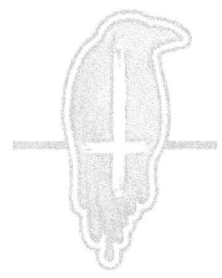

In the movie, a black man wearing a security guard outfit and ghost mask drives a cop car toward a cowboy who's running into the red barn, "We gonna eat you for dinner tonight, Rusty!"

The cop car parks as the ghost-faced man grabs a weed wacker from the back seat, whacking towards the barn, "Hope you are ready to get whacked!"

Dusty pauses the flim and looks at Chaz, "The fuck's this?"

Chaz drinks, insisting it'll get better, "What? This is top-tier shit, man!"

Dusty shakes his head, "I said 'Gold mask', not ghost mask. An' what's with the barn an' weed whacker?"

Chaz assures, "Tool store ain't got no chainsaw under ten bucks and the barn was abandoned, so rent-free! And what difference does it make what the guy's got on his head? A black guy as the villain in a horror flick's fuckin' genius! Just push play."

Dusty sees Kylee waiting out of a dirty mobile window as he suffers through more with a press.

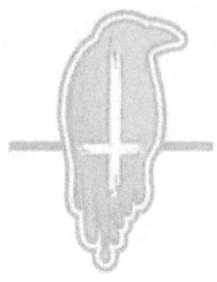

Rusty's actor walks to a large cage beside a picnic table in the middle of the barn, locking himself in. "Hello, my name is Rusty," he says to someone off-camera.

The camera then pans over slightly to a blonde super-model named Carry, who reads lines from a paper on the floor, poorly hidden from the camera, "I'm am Carry, I was talking and the Scarys got mad at me. They put a blanket over this cage so I can not hear them talk anymore."

Rusty holds Carry, "This is a good blanket fort. I will love and save you, Carry girl. Yee-haw!"

Suddenly, Buzzard, a white bikini-wearing girl in a witch hat, walks in, pointing at the ghost cop, "Rusty is mine, Boom Cop!"

Buzzard opens the cage, pushing Carry out, evil slut-strutting her way toward Rusty, "I hope that you are ready for this farm feast. Now I will feast on your flesh."

Buzzard makes out with Rusty as his cowboy hat falls off, nearly horseshoeing his boner as he acts, "Oh no, Buzzard is seducing me again, do not let Buzzard get you Rusty, be a strong man with a strong brain."

Dusty looks up from the movie, wiping his forehead in

disbelief as Chaz panics, "We're, we're gonna cut that out, ok! Just, just watch the rest!"

Dusty forces himself to continue the digital torture.

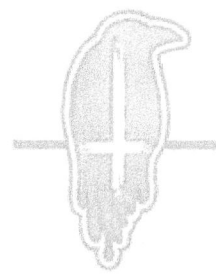

In the movie, someone knocks on the barn door as Buzzard yells, "I wonder who could be knocking the door?"

A girl wearing a blue wig and yellow shirt with a picture of a calculator on it is pushed into the barn by a girl on a skateboard with a band shirt and scuba helmet, "I am Rave Decker, I am here to deck dudes with my skateboard of death! I am mad at you, Delaware. Go into the cage, yo."

Rave Decker tries to pop her skateboard up to her hand, missing several times as Delaware lets herself into the same cage as Rusty and Buzzard, demanding, "Get out of here, witch."

Delaware pushes Buzzard off Rusty, speaking like a scientist, "I am going to calculate how to defeat you. Oh yes, hello. I am Delaware, I am smart and will save us with numbers and logic." Rusty shakes her hand, "Howdy Delaware, I am Rusty. My day has not been a very good one. That witch right there is named Buzzard and she is bad. She made me drink her love juice and now the Scary Club is going to get us. I believe that you will save us, you are a human calculator. Yee-Haw!"

Delaware high-fives Rusty, picking up his cowboy hat, "Oh look, Rusty, a knife was hidden under your hat. The universe is so nice to me. Now we can pick the lock on the cage and be free people."

Rusty knife-taps the cage door with a single clang as Delaware opens the door, Rusty shouting, "Ride 'em, cowboy. I am going to be the new sheriff of this town!"

Suddenly, a man wearing a pink wig, dress and high heels trips through the hay, "I am Sunny. I am a man, but it makes me sad. Someone go get my purse, it's out in my car."

Rave Decker skateboards past Sunny, "Yo, I will get that shit dog, don't even trip."

She fails a kickflip trick as Boom Cop starts his weed whacker, "There be too many people up in this damn house, someone gonna get whacked."

Buzzard walks over to the cage as Rusty hands her the fake knife, "Your weed whacker is no match for my knife, Boom Cop."

Buzzard flails, flopping bikini parts as she pretends a perfectly normal-looking knife is possessing her, shaking as Chaz notices Dusty's shaking head in disapproval, "WE'LL PUT THE EFFECTS IN LATER! JUST WATCH!"

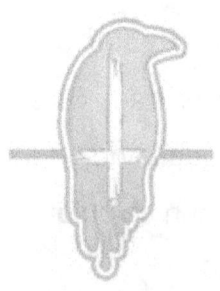

Dusty's lost the will to live as he watches Buzzard dramatize, "Oh lordy, the knife was cursed by the black cat that made us come here. Now I will get you, bad cat. Here kitty kitty, I will stab you!" Buzzard walks off the set, flopping her white bikini through a purple cardboard cut-out door of a cat. Rave Decker skateboards in, crashing into hay bales, "Gnarly crash, dudes. Sunny, here is your purse bag."

Sunny grabs the purse and walks to a fire at the end of the picnic table, "My dad gave me this purse for my birthday. He doesn't like me, though, so I will burn it."

Sunny tosses the purse into the fire, "My cellphone was in there and I did not write down his number, so I will never have to talk to him again. That means that now the curse will be fixed."

Someone turns on a large fan outside the barn door as Rusty headlocks Boom Cop with terrible coordination, "Now is your chance to be a free person again, Carry. Run away to the safe tornado!"

Carry walks towards the fan with zero urgency, trying to act, "For look, it is a bad storm outside. I will risk my life to escape this scary barn. Even though you are much older than me, I love you, Rusty. I hope I will see you after the bad guys lose. I hope that the tornado does not put me in a wheelchair."

Carry walks out of the barn, turning off the fan as Rave Decker brings a Monopoly board game to the picnic table, "Yo gangsters, look it. I have found a sweet game. The rules say it will give us wishes, let us play, dudes."

Everyone sits at the table as Boom Cop pulls a rubber snake from his pocket, holding it to his chest, "Oh no, dog, not the snake of wishes. He has bitten my nipple! This shit whack. With my death, y'all shall have a wish."

Boom Cop runs over to a kiddie pool, falling face first into three inches of water as Delaware looks at Rave Decker, "It is so cool that the snake got him. By my calculations, you are hot, do you want to be lesbians?"

Rave Decker holds out her skateboard, "Only if you kiss my skateboard."

Delaware kisses a lipstick stain on the deck as Rave Decker takes off her helmet, "This helmet is too hot, like your face, lover. I will go and punch Buzzard in her face so we can smooch ours in peace, yo."

Delaware holds a thumbs up as Rave Decker skateboards through the cardboard cat door. She comes right back out with Buzzard holding a knife to her neck, "Haha, I have your girlfriend now, Delaware. If you don't give me a good wish, I am going to do bad things to your wife."

Delaware stands, trying hard to act. "I have calculated that you would do this, Buzzard. But, don't do it though. Calculation completed."

Buzzard pushes Rave Decker onto a mat on the floor, tossing the knife on her, "You see what you get? Now you don't have a girlfriend anymore, for she is dead."

Delaware kneels with a raised fist, "She was going to teach me how to use a skateboard, now I am mad. I wish I was just like

Buzzard with the magic, but a yellow color! I will avenge your sad death, my skateboard queen," Delaware picks up a yellow hat from under the picnic table, "Now I have my power hat and you will regret the bad thing you did."

Buzzard stands in front of the fire, pretending to power up, "Look at how big my flames are. Bring it on, Delaware, you are not even that good of a witch, I bet you will lose and die now."

Rusty puts a referee shirt on, picking up his cowboy hat, "I do not think that this town is going to be big enough for the two of these witches."

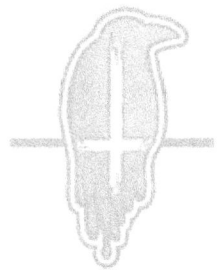

The movie continues playing as Dusty walks out of the trailer, Chaz scurrying behind, "He-, Hey, where ya goin'? You think you're ever gonna make a name for yourself without me!?"

Dusty pushes Kylee's wheelchair through the grass towards his truck as she wonders, "Baby, what happened?"

Dusty's watched by lounging actors as he struggles her wheels through weeds, "Them girls are fucked."

Chaz rants from his trailer doorway, "Hey, I'M CHAZ, FUCKIN' GOLDSTEIN! No movie gets made without me! You'll be back! This is what I was born to do! I'm a visionary!"

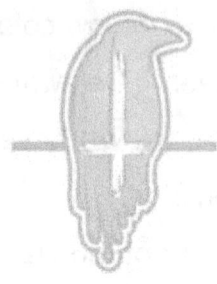

Back at the void, Dakota mutes the orange Visionary brand TV. She places the remote under its legs, crossing hers under her dress, "I can't believe Dusty's going public with all of this."

Peyton braids Dakota's blue hair, laughing, "Dusty's a genius! Get that money, son! Also, I'm watchin' that sweet vampire show every week!"

Dakota floats bad vibes to Custard's good eye, "Dusty thinks we're still in trouble."

Custard attacks pancake tower, "He's not wrong. We need to continue Peyton's practice."

Peyton continues braiding, "Imma' be such a sick witch for real. Ay, who d'you think's gonna play me in the sequel?"

Dakota looks over her shoulder at the hair stylist, "No one as cute."

Custard smiles pancake cheeks as Peyton's grossed out, "Ew dude, you think I'm 'cute'?"

Dakota eats whipped cream with a spoon, "I do."

Blood vows to Rexy, "I do."

CHAPTER EIGHT

Apologies and Prophecies

Blood and Rexy lay on the blue hood of a car, watching 'stars' gleam in blue-flamed sky from afar. Blood jokes, "Great, I'm married to a Corndog."

Rexy playfully smacks his leathered chest, "I said that, 'will you marry me', not do you marry me."

Blood crosses his arms, 'star' gazing, "No time for tradition, might be memories soon. Gotta live fast."

She crosses her ankles below her breezy white romper, "So wait, we say we are married, so it is true?"

Blood chuckles, "What reason we got to live by anyone's rules? If it's true in our eyes, that's all that matters. It's our true."

Rexy thinks, "'Our true' is that, you will not say the 'I love you', but you will marry me. I have found a funny one."

Blood lays his hand in her charcoal blue hair, "You? Ha! Change takes time, but if you're cool, you change for the one you 'love'."

Rexy sticks her blueberry tongue out gold chompers, "I am counting that. You said the 'love'."

He laughs, "Shut up, kid, I'm whipped."

Rexy's red eyes stare up in marvel, "What are the sky twinkles do you think?"

Blood scratches his blue fur ear, "Some say 'stars'. I think they're cameras. People taking pictures, finally achieving their dreams. Everybody spends their life chasin' at least one, right? Maybe those 'twinkles' are the people that finally reached 'em. Takin' a picture to remember in case that dream's ever
taken away."

Rexy smiles, "What is your dream?"

Blood's orange eyes search the cosmos, "Too dangerous to have one right now."

She curls up in his cape like a blanket, "Can I help you find the dream?"

Blood pokes her nose, "Already are."

Rexy cheeses gold shiny chompers, "You are 'whipped' and soft, you are a Whipped Cream."

Blood pushes her off the car, smug, "I ain't that soft. Look at me, pushin' my 'wife'. I'm tough. Divorce me."

Rexy laughs on her ass from the grass, "Push me more, Whipped Wolf. I am liking the bad boy acting."

Blood slides down the hood, helping her up below his cape, "Alright, Corndog, let's go."

Rexy's bat ears perk, "Honeymoon?"

He opens the door for her, "Magic Arms Dealer."

Rexy clicks her seatbelt together, "You are surely knowing what a girl wants, huh?"

Blood twists the car's ignition as his stomach twists more, "As special as we think we are, we're the bad guys in someone else's eyes. If we don't off those witches, we say goodbye, and I'm not good at those. Won't say it to you. Sorry, Love, this is what you married into."

She laughs, "You said the 'love' twice now. I do not need a ring, I can tell that you are loving me."

Blood fist bumps his wife as the blue classic muscles it's way from campground to pavement, shaking the night, Rexy curious, "You know, you are too nice, Blood. I can not see you eating the people."

Blood flicks the headlights on, "You can't see a lot of things I've done. It's in the past for a reason and 'less you start seeing the past or doin' Tarot Cards, that's where it stays."

Rexy's eyes are wondrous, "The Tarot Card reading sounds like the cute power, I will get some when we stop, and learn it. You are the learner, too. You learned how not to let a bad past hurt you. How was that learned?"

Blood switches lanes past a coffin-shaped car, "You let your past fester 'til it eats away at you, you're drainin' your new spirit, worrying about somethin' that hurt your old one. Accept what happened and learn from it, that's what gives the new you strength. You live as long as me, you'll learn."

Rexy bounces over a bony train track, "My hubby is

a smarty man."

He pulls the shifter, "Your 'hubby' has the brain of a Wolf."

Rexy watches as they pass a station wagon of ghosts, "We are kind of like that bolt-neck monster from the hotel TV, huh? That Frankie Slime man."

Blood corrects through laughter, "Frankenstein?"

Rexy remembers, "Oh, yes. Because you are a man with a wolf's head and I am the bat-girl with the spirit of the ghost man inside, right?"

Blood jokes, "Guess someone outta write a book about us, huh?"

She smiles, "I would like that idea. Can we get the Franky Slime cassette player tape when we get the Tarot Cards?"

Blood checks his mirror, "Sounds good."

Rexy rocks in excitement as Blood rocks around cars and thoughts of their uncertain future.

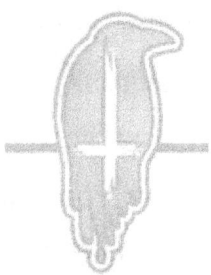

In the void, Custard and Dakota leave a clean white house to a sweat-drenched Peyton, practicing spells in the front yard, Custard encouraging, "You're doing well, Pumpkin Cup."

Peyton grabs their attention, "Yo, check it out."

She grows metal scales, protruding from her skin, covering her arm with repeating metallic clangs as Dakota wonders, "You teach her that?"

Custard shakes her head in surprise as Peyton exclaims, "Mad cool, right? We're gonna be unstoppable, The Three Witches of White Manor!"

Dakota approves the name change, "A suitable name, Peyton, I like it!"

Peyton gives a metallic thumbs up as Custard confirms, "Dakota and I want to go on a date, is that fine?"

Peyton holds up a shiny-scaled peace sign, "Get your love on, yo. I'll make pizza once starvation sets in."

Dakota kisses Peyton's shiny hand as Custard mirrors her on the other, Dakota thanking Peyton for her understanding, "Thanks, I'm proud you're going to cook."

Peyton assures, "I didn't do it yet, don't be that proud."

Dakota wipes sweaty hair from Peyton's forehead, "Ok, let's go."

Dakota waves her hand over Custard's eyes, both of them suddenly submerged in a floating black bubble as Peyton gooey-pokes the magical mass, "So rad."

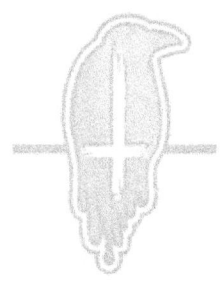

Custard and Dakota sit across each other, in a projected illusion of a restaurant. Elegant white tablecloths lay pristine below candlelit plates. Their wine glasses fill themselves with a whimsical, purple liquid as a breeze blows in from a star-sprinkled balcony. The sounds of chatter all around them from manifested couples, having manifested dinners fill the room with life. A fireplace sizzles below glittered chandeliers, spilling light around low-playing jazz. Gold pillars support a church-painted ceiling as clean white drapes hammock around the evening. Dakota's yellow dress is now a black, sleeveless button-up. The high neck silk, lined with pearl-white buttons. Her skirt is a white pile of flowers and lace, her blue braid with white, cascading flowers. Custard's black business pants and long-sleeved button-up are transformed. Dakota puts her in a peach and floral dress with orange scattered flowers. Her silver eyepatch shines above her black-feathered cheeks. They're both without witch hats, Custard's black hair swaying atop a colorful dress, looking pleas- antly normal for once as she notices her clothing, "I don't do dresses."

Dakota smiles, "You and Peyton both. Just, amuse me tonight."

Custard signals for a ghostly waiter, "I'll be needing another drink."

A second glass appears beside her first one, both filled and waiting as Dakota's curious, "Do you like the restaurant?"

Custard floats her glass towards Dakota, to cheers, "Beautiful ambiance to accompany my beautiful company."

Dakota blushes as a bowtie flaunting ghost floats menus, "Here you are, ladies, everything tonight is on the house."

Custard laughs, "I thought you wanted a date, at least let me pay."

Dakota shakes her head, "You've 'paid' enough."

Custard sets her menu down, "How so?"

Dakota adjusts her glasses in worry, "It's just that, I wanted to say I'm sorry about your eye."

Custard sips glass number one, "I killed Peyton and you're asking for forgiveness over an eye. I never thought you'd forgive me for killing her."

Dakota looks out the balcony, "I never said I did. Peyton needs us, that's reason enough to move forward."

Custard wonders, "How can you be in a relationship with someone you can't forgive?"

Dakota explains, "I care about the person you are now. We share a home and we share Peyton, doesn't mean you didn't make a mistake, just means I don't condemn you for the person you used to be."

Custard laughs, "That burning casket says otherwise."

Dakota holds her hand out, "Heated moment."

Custard takes her hand, unconvinced, "And the eye?"

Dakota thumb-strokes the top of Custard's hand, "My mistake that made us even."

Custard finishes her first glass, "Mistakes got us here. You know, I haven't had a drink in a long time. Haven't not been a witch for a long time either. This is nice, thank you."

Dakota scours the menu, "I've fallen in love with Custard the witch, tell me about the woman. You know you have a peculiar name, right?"

Custard rolls her eyes, "My father was a southern pastor with a love for sweets."

Dakota's surprised, "Suddenly your name's not the issue. Your father worked for a church and ended up with a witch for a daughter?"

Custard starts glass two, "He knew I practiced witchcraft, never judged me. When the church found out he was bringing me there, they started harassing him. Called him a heretic, insisting he'd tainted the church. Took it so far as to even bulldoze the property. He lost his job and I felt so guilty, I left home, joining the coven."

Dakota assures her, "Religious types always seem to throw the first stone."

Custard jokes, "I know witches who are better-mannered."

Dakota wonders, "But, what about you? Why did you get into Witchcraft?"

Custard gemstone shimmers, "No one ever asks how you got a hobby, think they just grow from boredom."

Dakota playfully mocks, "'Yes, I'm so bored, let me become a witch'."

Custard nearly spits in her glass in laughter, "It's true! You grow up in the sticks of Kansas, let's see what you start meddling in. You became a witch out of boredom, too! You'll say it was to kill me, right? You could have just wished me dead. The truth is, you were bored of being normal, you wanted excitement."

Dakota smiles at her deduction, "I can't argue that this hasn't been exciting. Now that I've used magic firsthand, I understand your passion for it, but is it your hatred for men that fuels the things you've done for power?"

Custard hands a waiter her menu, "I watched my father devote his life to a church of men who destroyed that very life he dedicated to them."

Dakota admires Custard's dress, "So, you want revenge on them for what they did to your father?"

Custard's one good eye waters, "My cat."

Dakota gets goosebumps, "They killed your cat?"

Custard's nose shakes with anger, "The priests of the church wanted to hurt me without getting into any real trouble."

Dakota stops her, "Please don't tell me what they did."

Tears drip below Custard's silver eyepatch onto silver cutlery, "I was weak then, but I will never let a man hurt me again." Dakota gets up, kneeling beside Custard's chair, comforting her as a ghostly waiter checks, "Is everything alright, miss?"

Dakota handles everything, "Oh yes, she just hasn't eaten all day. Can you bring us an appetizer, please?"

The ghost scurries off as Custard laughs the end of her tears off, "I haven't cried since I was your age. Last time I did's when I buried Moose."

Dakota wipes Custard's tears, kissing her eyepatch, "Moose is way too cute of a name for a cat."

Custard gets up, wiping her wet, feathered cheeks as she makes her way to the restroom, "I'll be right back."

Dakota nods as a colorful Custard gets lost in the hustle and bustle of dinner service.

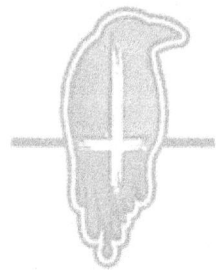

Peyton's lying in the grass, ten feet from their black bubble, "Dang man, I feel like a slug."

She breathes rough from a sweaty and sticky shirt up at the colorful rumble of clouds in the void above their house, echoing cracked electricity, Spike echoing cracked words, '*What a blissfully ignorant airhead you are. Spike, why are you always crappin' on my party? People don't say that, Peyton, they say 'raining on my parade'. Ok, well, you're crapping on my parade, yo. You know, Peyton, you were a lot cooler when you had a spike ball on your head and chased people with an Ax. I never chased 'people', I chased Dakota and I apologized to her. Dakota's a moron, forgiving you for wanting to hack her to bits. She's a double moron, forgiving a Witch for KILLING YOU! We moved on from that, Spike. What the heck? How does somebody move on from bein' killed? You're a limited-edition toaster pastry, huh? Spike, did anyone ever tell you to be nice or can it? HA! You know, they're ten feet from you right now, off having their little love fest while you lay here in the dirt, struggling to change yourself into one of them. I made the choice to become a witch. Peyton, you used to be unique. An*

individual. Now you're shoving yourself into the witch mold. Watch out, everyone, another cookie-cutter witch, headin' for the oven! I need to be able to protect myself, Spike. You wanna die? Yes! I'd rather die as Peyton than witch number three. Well, you don't protect us, I do all the work while you crap on my parade. You know, Peyton, I bet they're having their witchy sex right now. I don't care, Spike. Your insecurities aren't going to affect my feelings about my relationship with them. Don't project your fears onto me, dude. You're either helping or hurting.' Spike storms away, hiding, jealous, and erratic.

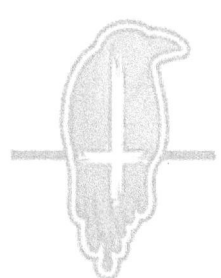

In the black bubble, Custard enters a single-occupant bathroom, closing the door to a busy restaurant, nothing but a door behind her, finding she's entered a vast and windy, storm-brewing field. She sits on a single gold toilet atop a hill, a small basket of toiletries near her ankles. She kicks off her shoes, letting cool grass fill her toes as her dress spills the sides of lemon-scented gold. Custard closes her eyes, a new bathroom ritual, as thunder rumbles beyond the hills, rain too far to see, *'This is the greatest*

bathroom I've ever been in, kudos to Dakota. I'll compliment her on the design, that will be nice.'

Custard's hair blows delicately to the soft sound of grass as her ears fill with wind. She can hardly hear the restaurant, it's faint jazz sounding like a town in the distance. A grasshopper flickers past, Custard's tranquil state unbothered as serene silence enslaves her senses, 'Why is it, I do my best thinking in the bathroom now? Maybe our lives are too busy. Perhaps the bathroom is our one true chance at time for ourselves. I would hope not, that is a sad existence for sure. I hope that crying in front of Dakota didn't change her view of me. That was embarrassing. I guess I shouldn't feel insecure about showing emotion. Moose was a good cat in a cruel world.'

As Custard quiets her mind, a leak springs in her subconscious. A spill from the transdimensional highway's slowed down space-time matter, dripping flashes of daydream-esque reality into her brain. Forehead visions from a dead witch's gem pour into the magic-boiled psyche of Custard's spell-stacked skull. Her dark, feathered cheeks vibrate above her peach floral dress as she seems to be asleep, watching telepathic visions of a Wolf and Bat.

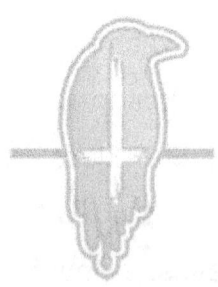

Blood and Rexy stand at the Blue Classic's trunk, parked outside a tent-filled market. Crowded streets glow from the Green Moon Night, this month numbering three, as Rexy opens her first-ever Tarot Cards! She spreads them across the back of the car, announcing, "You now will choose your fate's fortune, destiny's cards tell no lie!"

Blood, a leather-suited beast of a man, towering over the small pointy-eared gypsy of a bat glows from three green moons. He awaits his fate from a trainee, card-fondling vagabond, as Rexy makes magical-like motions over the messy cards. She speaks in a low, wizardly tone, "Dear Blood, fear not the piercing strike of the card's tongue, it tells only what you are too afraid to say to yourself!"

Blood crosses his leather in dismissal, "Yea yea, let's do this, oh mighty Corndog of the desert."

Rexy looks dramatically whimsical, "By the choice of a card, three times picked, the old times, the right now, and the later on, all will be showing the truths."

She wiggles her navy fingers as Blood picks a card with zero thought in his think tank. The card flips, a prismatic deer with three eyes, eating the meat of a lion in blood-splattered snow, reading, "The Gatherer". Rexy tells his fortune, "Ah yes, this is the old past of Blood Taker, the strange beast who eats of the strong, now slain. The snow, his niceness stained from the bad times."

Blood blows air, his cape blows ripples, "Pfft, really? A deer eating, how is that me?"

Rexy stays in character, "He is in a denial already, if only he can learn the embrace to give the truth, then he will not live anymore with a weight of wonder for what will be. Choose your card!"

His face melts from relaxed to spooked like Rexy's become possessed, flipping a card with a reluctant stare. The card flips, a blindfolded black goat wearing a porcelain bell, jumping off a cliff into lava, reading, "The Narrows". Rexy investigates, "Do you not see it with your eyeballs, also? It is your life at the right now, Blood. The sturdy goat, protector of the jingle bell, blind to a danger, ready to gallop the body into the hot flames of a lava to protect his lovely. See, I am the bell necklace."

Blood laughs, "You realize that bell probably melted in the fire along with the goat, right?"

Rexy's gold chompers hang open, unamused at his insolence, still, she presses onward as the fates foretold long ago. "It is time now to see the there, the future seeing, the there that will turn into the now. Make the final choice of your selection, all sales are final, Blood!"

Blood pats her head as she smacks his hand away, never to be manipulated by the non-believers, Blood looking like she's playfully turning clinically insane, "Hey, be nice!"

Rexy laughs, quickly getting back into character, "Seal your fate, husband. It has long been told in the old stories that you can pick a card that is gonna be the one to seal the deal of a lifetimes. No takebacks!"

Blood can't help but chuckle. The card flips, a giant Crab, floating in space, grabbing the red moon, reading, "Space Crab". Rexy looks drunk with power, "We should know this day would come. The water animal, it tumbles in space, so long from its house. It will return to the family only when it finally grabbed its dream. The red moon is your 'sky twinkle', Blood! When you finally grab it, you will be able to go back in the ocean to the home."

He stares dumbfounded, almost impressed at her ability to spout complete bullshit with such confidence. He amuses her, joining her cult, "One day, we the Crabs will grab the moon, only then will we find our way home!"

Rexy smiles, holding the card high like a wand, preaching, "We have got a believer! Praise to the Cards of Time, now prepared, we can make the good choice and be saved from the mistaken path of DEATH! Thank you, Tarot Cards, we accept the blessing of the knowledges."

Blood smirks from behind her as Rexy fumble-cleans her Cards of Mess from Trunk of Car. Blood unlocks the door as she drops cards on her seat, wondering, "So what is a thing that we must get from the Magical Armed Dealer? Are they looking like a magic squid? Seeing them would make me amazed."

Blood takes her hand, walking towards the market, "It's a Magic Arms Dealer. A special vendor selling charmed weapons forged by Spellsmiths. They're lawbreaking Hexmasters that endow metalworks with illegal curses. One of the witches we need to kill can't die. Means we need a workaround, a cheat."

Rexy looks at her bare feet, kicking dirt, "Are you perfectly ready with the witch killing?"

He guides her through the street crowded with tongues and teeth, pests and beasts. "No choice. Black Manor needs souls to exist. No one else knows about the place. Only ones there are the witches. This is our burden if we want to make memories. Are you okay with killing someone to save our memories?"

She's dragged through the bustling market of ghouls and bikes by her leash of an arm, "You have not made me go a wrong direction in life, husband. As a sad feeling it would give after a killing, I should still help how I can to make the cherished times with you."

Blood guides her lower back from behind into a spooky glowing tent, Rexy in awe, "Oh yes, look at all of the wonderful little trinket arts and colored drinkies. I am thinking we should certainly have a good drink together."

They enter the shadowy overstock area of the tent, Blood swiping a drink and tent cloth up. He reveals a small patch of sand surrounded by the backs of market tents, a six-by-six fenced 'backyard', Rexy interested, "This is a most small backyard area."

Blood explains, "This is a hidden place, like a cool secret."

Rexy claps in excitement, "Oh, we are being sneaky crawlers, huh, Blood?"

Blood smiles, walking up to a grill taking up most of the yard, as Rexy sits on a lawn chair, excited. "I am a relaxed Sneaky Crawler and now husband will cook the grilling food for the tummy."

Blood throws a cigar match, lighting the grill as it begins to mechanically lower itself into the sand. It aligns flush with the weeds and locks. Flames erupt from the grill in a pillar as Blood holds his hand out for her, Rexy hesitant, "Will we go in a fire? Is it not a too hot one for burning us?"

Blood assures her, "You only live once."

Rexy has a hard-thinking face, "This is not a truth, Blood. I lived three of the times now. My body had three people in it, so far."

Blood laughs, "Don't go around telling people that, Sneaky Crawler. Let's beat feet."

Rexy lifts her foot, beating it as Blood pulls her through fire, unburned and astonished.

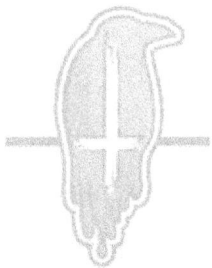

They stand in grey woods, crawling bugs and dead trees.

Thick light choking fog in a silent hot breeze.

A black cabin filled with liquid, in a thorn-tangled grove.

Manifested floating water filling windows, chimney, stove.

Floating water-filled workshop, will not fill your lungs or drown.

Drifting weapons, good and evil, no allegiance to be found.

Use his wares for all your crimes, do not tell from where they came.

Swim on in, pay your fees, make your exit through the flame.

Blood and Rexy snap twigs, stepping from a flame-pulsing grill to frog-pulsing forest. Blood scratches away flies as Rexy tries to eat them, in awe, "Blood, this is a nice and spooky hidden gem. Maybe weird that waters are not spilling from the house. How did you find this one?"

Blood pokes at twigs to disarm traps, "Crackle created everything we know in this reality. Spent a lot of time with her. Shared some secrets with me, probably hid even more."

Rexy's impressed, "Who is the name of the Hexingmaster we are seeing?"

Blood hands Rexy a grub for chomping, "Scribe."

Rexy mashes slimy grub juice in shiny gold chompers, offering, "Do you like a bug to eat with me, too?"

Blood pretends he's not grossed out by the goo-littered smile of his wife, "All you."

Rexy's red eyes lock onto interesting species of flavors, crawling away at speeds sure to end in munching as Blood lifts her. He carries her past traps as she cheers with bug-filled cheeks, "I am liking the no more walking, Blood. Carry me to all the places for now on."

He chuckles, placing her down on the porch. Blood opens the door to the front of the cabin and they look down into the wet space, like peering down into a gutted hangar of an aquarium from the second floor, a large open room below. Elegant tables and chairs sit at the bottom like Roman-style aquarium decorations, as tools and weapons bob along with fish. The inside of the cabin, a white marble landscape of colorful plants and waterproof torches, as Rexy seems puzzled, "We are to go in a water now?"

Blood scoops water from the door, watching it gravitate back to the cabin, "You can't drown as long as you have no desire to hurt Scribe. The water's a living entity that senses your intentions. Keep a calm mind regardless of what Scribe says and never think about harming him."

Rexy nods, pointing to her head, "I will keep the icy cool head and be a friendly friend."

Blood pats her charcoal head as they splash into the rippling door. They swim in water you can hear and breathe in, the oxygen absorbed from all parts of their bodies, as Rexy sees crabs. "Look, Blood, we are closer to the Tarot Crab! Wow, it is a strange thing to talk in the underwater, huh?"

Blood watches her learn to swim, explaining, "Scribe's paranoid someone will return with his weapons, pinning him for murder. And just to be clear, I would NEVER do that!"

The water sloshes, judging his intention as Blood floats, furry head swaying, relieved he hasn't drowned. Blood holds her hand as they descend thirty feet down to the bottom of the living room, Scribe swimming in from the bedroom.

A pink-skinned demon with short black horns stabbing from his forehead sways in a white toga cloth, cascading bubbles over wet muscles. He's a devilishly attractive demon with short black hair, like a pink demonic Cesar. His black eyes flood small yellow pupils, looking like a future seer. His pink earlobes float earrings too dangly for a man, "Smells like a wet dog's ass in here, ya' jackal. What we got, Blood? Thick-thighed bat, that's candy in your hand, Slick. I'll take her. I can pay in cash or ass, got stacks of both."

Blood restrains his temper-raised thoughts, "Rexy's my wife."

Rexy greets Scribe, "Hello, Mr. Scribe, I am loving the home. Truly wet and also wonderful place to be swimming. I am appreciating the compliment of your attraction to my legs, but I am locked down in happily marriage."

Scribe takes a self-appointed throne. "You guys are givin' me whiplash. It's a kind of jacked-up twist in scenarios. Harmless-faced snack bat, humpin' a murder-tarnished mutt. Makes my bones burn somethin' gross."

Rexy shows gold teeth in a defensive grit, "Blood is pleasant with me. Did you know you can also find a love of a lifetime to turn your bad breath into nice words?"

Blood's cape ripples behind in slow-motion waves, "Calm down, Corndog. He tests his guests. We're not here for your head, demon."

Scribe eats blue powder, "Yada yada, pile o' 'chicks' in my room if you guys are hungry for sins of the flesh, just know some got a hint o' man meat. Sheets are clean-ish. You can fuck on the floor, just keep the bubbles in your ass. "

Blood and Rexy swim to chairs at the bottom of the water as Scribe commands crabs to bring drinks. Rexy examines, "I am feeling content with the no sex, thank you for the suggestions. Oh wow, the drinking cups do not spill. Blood, is it a safe one to try?"

Blood nods, clinking cups with her as his wolf tongue guzzles the magically unmixing liquid through the water without fail. Rexy opens gold chompers, figuring out how to drink while underwater as Scribe man-spreads on a soaked throne, "Most guilty dog I know kickin' it with the most peculiar girl I've ever wanted. Real talk, how much for your wife? She bite on command? We can trade. I got high-grade hoes, dealer's choice. Two for one if they're iffy lookin'. Shoot your shit, why's the wolf's neck in my woods?"

Scribe snobby-pinches man nails at a floating bowl of meat as Rexy states, "I am not a property for the buying, sorry this time though. You see, Mr. Demon, we must be killing witches that can not die."

Blood notices a pile of women recovering in Scribe's bed like thirsty fish as he elaborates, "I've lost my connection with Crackle. Black Manor's void is on the verge of collapse and we're killing the witches that did it. One of them can't die, but we need her soul regardless."

Scribe cleans meat from his fingers as bits float to the

ceiling, "Breakin' hearts is easier. Shit show central's what's comin'. Nether Black's tight with the void. It roasts, we're cooked next. I'm brain-smacked, Flea Scratcher. The soul-stealin' dog needs my help!?"

Blood releases his glass as it sinks to the table, "Look, I can't extract the soul of a human who can't die. Can you craft something?"

Scribe swims flexed pink muscles to his tools, "Hire me, they'll be calling you Soul Taker. You ever think about swingin'? 'Cause them wolf fangs gonna wanna bite my sweet pink ass when I'm done."

Blood laughs, "Let's save our world, ya freak."

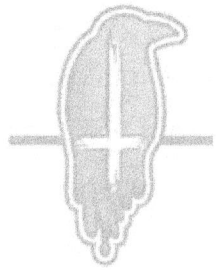

Custard panic-wakes, her butt asleep on the golden toilet as she dresses herself with haste, her vision still tripped. She scampers down the grassy hill to the floating bathroom door into the restaurant, plowing guests to Dakota, "We've got a problem."

Custard explains her vision, both of them deciding to cut their date short and check on Peyton. As the black bubble melts away, Custard and Dakota birth out the bottom. Warm sludge evaporates from slimy skin as the restaurant's music skews out of tune and beautiful ambiance crumbles. The bubble pops a final burst of dream ooze as Peyton lies exhausted in the grass, turning slime green, struggling to speak, "He-... ...Hey guys. How...how was your date?"

They kneel by her, Dakota worried, "Custard, what's wrong with her? Peyton, what happened?"

Peyton coughs out, "I tried, one of the... the harder spells in the book. Junk backfired, yo."

Custard magically lifts Peyton above the lawn, brushing above grass to the living room. Peyton's slime-green head lands on a plump floral couch as Custard urges, "Get a cool rag."

Dakota commands a towel to wrap ice from the freezer, flying it through the house to Peyton's forehead as she jerks, "Ugh, that's cold, dude."

Dakota wonders, "What do you mean by 'harder spells'? What spell did you perform, Peyton?"

Her face strains for thought, "Ani... Animate Death-"

Custard finishes, "Animate Deathborn. It's Demonology evocation. Necromancy. She raised the dead."

Dakota's alarmed, "There's no way she could have used those. Peyton, what happened?"

Peyton slurs, "A pile of bones, screaming underground. Tore out the yard. Had dripping teeth. The darkest. Darkest eyes I've seen. It came at me. I tried a protection spell, but I'm no good at 'em. He bit me."

Custard examines, "Her skin's turning green from the toxins."

Dakota fears, "Do we need an antivenom? Is she going to-"

Custard stops her, "Die? No. She can't die. Even removing the venom is pointless. It should dispel from her with time."

Custard wonders, "And her skin? Will it-"

Peyton interrupts pathetically, "Actually, don't mind it, yo. Looks kinda badass."

Dakota sighs, floating to the kitchen, "I'm making you tea. 'Kinda Badass'."

Peyton sits up, "Oh, ok, with whipped cream though!"

Peyton lays back down pretending to be more sick than she is, hoping to avoid trouble as Custard crosses her arms, "You're not even hurt, you butt."

Peyton closes her eyes, "I'm dying!"

She sticks her dead tongue out with an exaggerated 'bleht', peeking one eye open. She watches Custard join Dakota in the kitchen, speaking in private whisper, "Dakota, we don't use Necromancy for that reason."

Dakota states, "No, we don't use it because we can't."

Custard glances at Peyton, who's now admiring her green hand. "She just started practicing magic and she's already manipulating death. She could become stronger than me."

Dakota reminds, "She could become stronger than both of us. She's a witch who can't die, casting spells we can't do. Custard, I wished to be the most powerful witch to ever exist and I can't even read the language those spells are in. How is she reading them? And how does her mind's spell library even have those books?"

Custard goosebumps rise, "Are you worried?"

Dakota shakes out a heartbeat-rumbled breath, "No, I'm scared."

Spike wakes up, '*Wow, look at this worm. Couch lounging during the day while people wait on her. What do you want, Spike? You know, they're talking junk about you right now, right? They're worried about me, yo. Yeah, Peyton, look at you! They leave you for an hour and your ass is green! You have a green ass, are you happy? We look cool. You look like every default witch that's ever been plastered on a Halloween paper plate! No, we don't. Peyton, you know Dakota and Custard are off having their dates and love, making fun of you behind your back and what do you do?*
Ignorantly accept it all just to be accepted. That's not true, I'm becoming a witch to protect them. No, you're losing control and going to hurt them. They said you're gonna be stronger than them, Peyton. Don't you think once they fear you, they'll do horrible things to protect themselves from you? No Spike, they care about me. Peyton, you're better than them. Stop letting mediocre witches control you. Don't you want to become more powerful than them? No, I want to be their equals. Well, you're not, they're already
plotting against you, that's not what equals do. What happens when their whispers turn into something way more fucked up than gossip? Spike, people whisper because not everything

needs to be known. Do you say everything that's on your mind? Actually Peyton, there is some messed up crap in this head we should probably talk about. No Spike, stay out of my secrets. Oh look, here they come, quick, pretend you're dying again. I bet you like that they overprotect you. Little Baby Peyton, so stupid, she turned herself green. Soon, the universe will know of Peyton, the Planet Eater. No Spike, we're not gonna do that.'

Custard and Dakota bring cookies and tea.

Seasons change on the front yard tree.

Peyton's magical skin starts turning greener.

Rexy sits with a magic-infused vacuum cleaner.

CHAPTER NINE

Making Memories

Rexy smiles gold chompers, tongue-bouncing dangled flap, confused with a pink Vacuum Cleaner perched in her lap. "Blood, for why did the Scribe demon make the Vacuum? Is this really an impressing weapon for the showing?"

Blood drives, joking, "This is all his cooked cranium could conjure."

Scribe, now a pink vacuum cleaner sporting black demon horns from the end of the hose, wiggles his sucking attachments fangs, snapping, "I'm nuzzled against your arm candy's crotch, fur bag. You sure you wanna keep barkin' trash? Maybe, I turn my suck setting from 'Floors & Carpets' to 'Bat Banger'."

Blood shifts, "Scribe, you play nice with my wife or imma' use your face to suck the fur outta these seats."

Rexy pushes random buttons on Scribe. "This is a neato time, having a talking vacuum cleaner friend. I am going to not do a 'Bat Banging' vacuum cleaning for this time, though, thank you. We will be calling you not as Scribe. You are now, Soul Sucker! Do you like the naming?"

Soul Sucker jostles like only a possessed appliance can, "Well, now I'm torn to scorn, you sack of Radishes actually came up with somethin' mediocre, but I'll say it sucks a Pheasant's ass 'cause you two Bed Burners puked it up. So, yes it's cool, but you still suck the big one."

Rexy drums the pink plastic of Soul Sucker, "Actually, you are the 'suck' cleaner, now. That is a hilarious joking, huh, Blood? I wonder Soul Sucker, what was necessary for the reason you put the you into the vacuum?"

Soul Sucker turns his black-hosed brush towards her, "Feel my words, weirdo. Injecting weapons with soul-stealing charms is unstable, okay Bat Breath? When a soul enters everyday crap, the objects ain't strong enough to contain the soul. I make a weapon, it's got some of my magic, but if I am the weapon, it's got all my power, 'nuff to keep it stable, plus it'll look sexy-style with me infused in it. I mean, look at me! Damn, miracle vacuum, extraordinaire!"

Blood glances over, "Only you'd believe your own bullshit that becoming a vacuum cleaner's necessary to save our world."

Soul Sucker taunts, revving his vacuum's motor, blaring the small space with purposeful irritation. Rexy makes up a song about a vacuum cleaner, filling it with a more adorable, yet equal, quality of noise pollution as Blood drives dad-style and spaced.

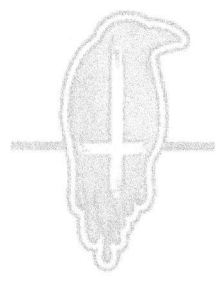

It's been one month since Peyton turned green. Dakota, sharing the morning with her on a void-loomed porch. She jokes into her teacup, "I still can't get used to the green."

Peyton sits at the foot of Dakota's yellow dress, peeling hair removal tape from her slime-green legs, "Yo, you breaking up with me?"

Dakota blows ripples in hot water, "I didn't say it wasn't cute, I said I'm not used to it."

Peyton glances under her black-spiked hat, her wavy hair creeping out as her ick feeling creeps out more, "I'm not cute, dude, this green coulda' killed me if it wasn't for you. Ya' know, I never got to apologize for bein' an ass to you. I mean, well, I could have apologized already, for when I found out I couldn't die an' crap. Caught me off guard, yo. Sorry I was a dick."

Dakota smells diluted honey, "There's no need to worry about it."

Peyton stands, tucking her sleeveless black shirt into her shredded white shorts, "How can I make it up?"

Dakota challenges her, "You could try my tea."

Peyton's ick face is back, "You bein' for real right-"

Dakota blushes in embarrassment, "I'm kidding, I know you hate-"

Peyton grabs Dakota's teacup cup chugging it, her throat struggling almost as much as her face. She swallows, blatantly stating with a tea dripped chin, "I love you."

Peyton's witchy green face dribbles tea slobber as Dakota's silly feelings turn serious. "I know, Peyton. I love you, also. Is everything alright?"

Peyton looks out into the void surrounding their small piece of peace, "Blood Taker's coming for us, dude. No idea what shit's goin' down. Just wanna make sure all my paperwork's in order, ya know? Cross all my T's and whatnot."

Dakota pats her own lap as Peyton sits, green thighs plopped on a dress that smells like pies, "We're not paperwork, we're your family. We're here to protect each other."

Peyton stares off in green-faced doubt, "Why do you guys even like me?"

Dakota's already calculated this, "Peyton, I have never met someone so unapologetically herself as you are. That's not a bad thing. It's something to be admired and we adore you for that. I wish I could wake up every day and say who cares what the world thinks, but I do care. That's me and that's fine, but you don't care. You live in the moment and being with you helps me learn how to be a better version of myself. You give people around you life, you make us better. You're not just a girlfriend to Custard and me, you're a free spirit who brightens our life and makes monotony a little less monotonous simply by being you."

Peyton almost tears up, "Don't make me cry, dude. I'll punch you."

Dakota smiles at the rim of her cup, "See, unapologetic Peyton."

Peyton stands from Dakota's lap, "Yup, that's what they'll call me."

Spike corrects, *'Actually, they'll call you Peyton the Planet Eater.'*

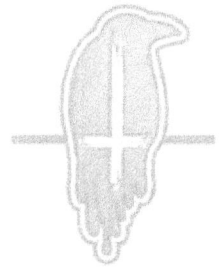

In Nether Black, the Blue Classic sizzles in the middle of a diner through a decimated hole in the wall. A couple demons crawling in a glass pile, nothing worth skipping breakfast over. Spooky families try to eat, staring like they've never seen a car show as Rexy pokes eye holes in pancakes, "I have made the pancake people."

Blood eats bacon like table scraps thrown to a mut, "You're supposed to make a smile with the whipped cream."

Rexy shakes no, "They are not feeling happy. I am gonna eat their face away. I remember calling you the 'whipped cream'. Look, we made the memories, Blood!"

She smiles, licking sprinkles off hot circles, Soul Sucker vacuuming biscuits & gravy, what a waste. "Gut full of gravy with the besties, coolest way to start the day."

Blood watches a vacuum cleaner 'eat', "You're gonna break yourself."

Soul Sucker's hose jiggles thick flavors into a plastic tank, "Silence Half Breed, I'm starvin' somethin' nasty. I'll magic the food gone before it hits any electricals, mind your madness!"

Rexy happy-sips milkshake, "Are you tasting the calories?"

Soul Sucker vacuums crumbs from the table, "NO! Sorry, I'm mad I can't taste. Couldn't eat JACK when I was a sexy demon man, obviously, I was sexy, Peasants. Now that I'm a glorious vacuum man, I'm gonna suck up whatever the depths bring. I don't care if I can't taste it, give me your leftovers!"

Blood tips the Cyclops waitress an insane amount, "Sorry 'bout the hole in the wall, this ought to cover the damages, restaurant and mental."

The waitress whips her apron off, running out through shattered glass, hootin' bloody murder, helicoptering middle fingers at regulars and their kids as Blood picks his fangs, "Well, I tried."

He wraps a leather arm around Rexy, currently trying to eat her weight in sugar, "You happy, Corn Dog?"

Rexy cheeses milky gold chompers from sprinkle stained cheeks, "I am being the most luckiest Bat wife."

Blood chuckles cleaning her face as Soul Sucker cleans plates, "Jupiter's flames, I can't believe, I want what you two Crotch Smashers got."

Rexy points, "This milky shaker was a good one to choose, get that."

Soul Sucker rolls to his seat, "No ya' Batty Ball Breaker. I mean a happy relationship, GOSH! Look at you, Fruit Flies, it's disgusting."

Blood smiles fangs, "I'm sure you'll find the vacuum of your dreams one day."

Soul Sucker panics, "Wait, y'all think I'm gonna be a vacuum forever?! This is putrid particles!"

Blood looks out the window at burnt skies, "Well, how the devils should I know? You put the spell on yourself, jackass! You don't know how to reverse it?"

Soul Sucker looks like a defeated piece of plastic, "Well, no. Not YET! I didn't think that far ahead, ya' Cranberry Snatcher!"

Rexy sucks at the remaining milk-coated cup, "I am sure that once we do a soul stealing, we should find a way for making you a 'sexy man' again."

Soul Sucker vacuums himself, "I bagged so many hottie body demons without a care in the nether world. Now, I take one look at you, Shadow Lickers and realize how much I've missed. On top of that, I transformed my beautiful ass and might never get my shot at it now. This reeks of the curse! No one ever taught me to love. No one teaches a demon emotion. No one yelled, 'Hey Scribe, maybe strike up a conversation after you're done jackhammering that pile of flesh'. I am judged."

Blood Taker fist bumps Scribe's vacuum hose, "You'll find your happiness. You already made the first, most important step."

Soul Sucker apologizes, "Rexy, dammit, I was a Garbage Cactus, my queen. I'm sorry if I ever came off as a Sexy Flexing Bug Jug."

Rexy holds out a high five, "It is a silly remark for saying the sorry for being the true you. I do not find a wrong feeling that you have a sexual energy supply. Just aim for a lover to barrage their brain with the romantic words and they will be awaiting at the love kingdom for a sexorcism."

Soul Sucker wiggly plastic high-fives Rexy's sticky charcoal hand with his face. They tidy their table and hop in the car, reversing through destruction, revving towards the road as families squeal with the tires.

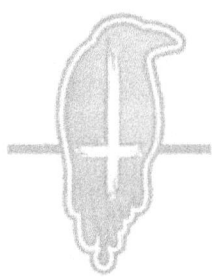

Back at White Manor, Custard and Dakota sit in the TV glowed dark.

Sharing a blanket, eating popcorn, watching a horror movie about a shark.

Peyton drools, sleeping softly on the sofa upside down.

Interjecting funny comments while the fishing families splash and drown.

Custard holds hands under a werewolf-themed blanket as Dakota wonders, "Are you scared?"

Custard makes the 'Really?' face below her movie-shimmered eye patch, "Kota, I've seen worse movies."

Dakota tongues teeth kernels, "I mean that Blood Taker's coming for us. It's this impending doom situation, looming over everyone. I feel like we don't talk about it as much as we should."

Custard asks cautiously, "Are you afraid to die?"

Dakota watches people, faintly gobbled in the ocean, "No, I'm afraid the people I care about will."

Custard lays Dakota in her lap, stroking butter into her hair, "I'm sorry I killed Peyton."

Dakota's eyes shock to the side below glasses, barely watching the movie, speaking from Custard's lap, "We've all done horrible things to each other."

Custard massages Dakota's scalp, secretly rooting for the shark, "I've made you feel the hurt of a loved one, taken away. I told myself I'll never do that to someone again. Truth is, Blood Taker's coming to kill us. Bringing his wife, too. That's all."

Dakota sits up, analyzing Custard's worry. "Are we the bad guys?"

Custard sucks her lips, "Not sure. I don't know how much repair to the void Blood Taker's soul will do. Even if it's enough, what happens to his wife?"

Custard feels sorrow from the future as the background is filled with watery thrashing, Dakota sharing, "I thought becoming a witch would make life easier."

Custard puffs air from her nose, "The ability to do more creates more problems. This is our self-appointed curse to hold."

Dakota sucks her anxiety, "I don't want to be a bad guy."

Custard spaces out as the movie becomes a blur, "Dakota, we're all trying to kill each other just to live another day. There's no good guys in this. Just selfish, scared people."

Dakota thinks calculating is pointless, "I know you don't like to say-"

Custard stops her, "I love you."

Dakota stares like a statue, shaking beneath a blanket as Custard takes her shoulders, "We have enough trouble coming our way, no need to overthink feelings or silly words. Our time to be happy together is now."

Dakota rests her head on Custard's shoulder, falling asleep as Custard roots for the shark in a worried calm.

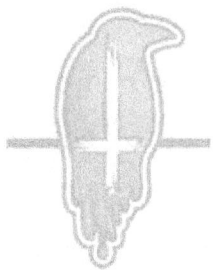

In Nether Black, the Blue Classic vibrates, parked on a green stone road awaiting the gas pedal. Rexy sits behind the wheel, awaiting Blood's permission to slam it as Soul Sucker panics in Blood's lap, "Blood, you fall off your rooster? Ain't no way this Clamp Magnet's ready to drive!"

Blood drinks a Purple Potion Pop, relaxed, "Hush the doubt. She's gonna kill it!"

Soul Sucker's hose anguishes, "She's gonna kill US! Death comes! Do you not see her scolding gleam over the precipice of life's rim?"

Blood fist bumps Rexy as she grins mischievous gold, "This is a dreaming to become true! I will impress my man with the driving! Keep the feets and the hands inside the vehicle as we welcome you to the drive of your destiny. Thank you for having a fly with the Rexy airplane lines."

Blood laughs at Soul Sucker's hysteria, giving the go, "Rip the road, Corn Dog."

Rexy stomps gas with a blueberry foot. The Blue Classic ROARS! It pummels pebbles out like buckshot, the deafening growl of scorching fuel, shrieking brutal screams of skin-rattling force down an empty highway near the Ghastly Graves.
Soul Sucker hyper verbals in terror, "OH MARS! OF ALL THE SLIMEY AARDVARKS THAT'S TRIED TO OFF ME, THIS IS IT!? THIS IS HOW IT ENDS!?"

Blood grabs the frame as they rip through barbed wire, blasting down black rocks past red-horned mountain climbers. Rexy storms the engine past climax, "I am shortening the cut of the drive. This is the secret way! SNEAKY CRAWLERS GOING!"

Blood forgets how to breathe as he questions his choices, "He- Hey Rexy, watch out for those egg sacks. They're baby Titan Slugs."

They mash eggs under death-dealing rubber as Rexy nearly bites the wheel, "We are doing good! Nothing can be stopping these masters of the machine!"

Soul Sucker dies a little, tires digging dirt down the side of the mountain as if falling wasn't fast enough. The mountain rumbles, exploding beside them, Mama Titan Slug ready for revenge. A colossal green and white spiked slug of dirt-coated slime, pussing down the cliffs. It consumes the ground behind them, the burst from its mouth booming the car's exterior. They plow bushes and debris as Rexy stands both feet on the gas, "Not on this day, slug! We are the ones to save the Nether Black! People, keep the buckles connected, we are going for a ride of the nightmares!"

Blood tightens his grip on the vacuum, "Shit! That Titan Slug's ravenous! It's never gonna stop!"

Soul Sucker cries plastic tears, "NEITHER IS YOUR WIFE! CRUEL TIMES INDEED! GIVE MY DARK CASTINGS TO THE RIVER SOULS! I AM SLAIN AGAIN!"

Rexy commands the car go faster as the Titan Slug guzzles a log cabin with thundering obliteration. Wood and rock rupture out in a massive mountain rocking explosion with an ear-destroying screech as the slug flies up in slow motion, Blood Taker staring up out the window, "Clench your asses!"

Soul Sucker watches as a thirty-foot shadow engulfs them, the Titan Slug falling above the car. The drooling snarls grow closer, Rexy pulverizes the exhaust, blasting gravel as they swerve from the landing zone. The slug shockwaves the foundation as it jiggle-slams cliffs. It thrashes down the mountain, obliterating its insides with each roll. Bloody guts rush out the bursting slug, rivering past the car, flooding the mountainside. They rise off the ground, car now a raft, floating in a river of innards. The slug blood river washes them into electrical poles, spinning the car into a guardrail beside a road-wrapped cliff. The guts waterfall over the ledge as the Blue Classic sits in silence to the sound of pouring parts. Blood unclenches his fingers from the door handle, "You guys ever tried Titan Slug meat?"

Rexy's filled with adrenaline, "My body is thrilled with the excitement. Look at the fingers wiggle! I am the captain of a driving seat for now on!"

Soul Sucker's plastic face is frozen, "Bet you Corn Clappers didn't think a vacuum could pee itself."

Blood picks Soul Sucker up, "Did you pee in my car?"

Rexy states matter of factly, "I have also had a peeing of excite. May we do a car washing?"

Blood grins grabbing Soul Sucker, "I know just the vacuum for the job!"

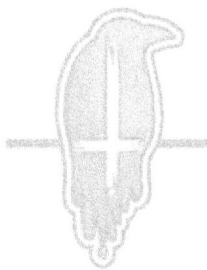

Back at White Manor, Dakota fishes in a creek.

Water mixes with the void, magic fish come up and peek.

Cozy, quiet, fish pole floating, waiting for a hungry bite.

Dakota sits alone in flowers, watching, waiting with delight.

Upstairs, Peyton is measured perfectly. Custard magics her a dress.

A surprise secret for Dakota, she'll be fancy and will impress.

Black-sleeved dress, orange flowers, no skin showing but her face.

Neck-high collar, pearl earrings. Peyton's heart begins to race.

Peyton watches Custard magically sew, "Hey, dude, thanks for helpin' me try to look nice and junk."

Custard focuses intensely on her work, "You're a good person, Peyton. Changing yourself, even for a day, just to make someone else happy is a great show of character. It shows selflessness. Something I've struggled with."

Peyton watches the intimately close stitching below her green nose, "I think you're doin' a rad job, turnin' yourself around, yo. Just gotta learn to forgive yourself. Let the dumb crap go."

Custard smiles, "Says the girl I killed. You know, Peyton, it's your right to kill me when you see fit."

Peyton watches a one-eyed witch swallow her sadness as her hand shakes to apply Peyton's lipstick, "Why would I kill someone I love?"

Custard drops the lipstick, guilty, "Why would you love someone who killed you?"

Peyton picks up the lipstick, taking Custard's hand, drawing a broken heart on the top, "This is a reminder of your heartbreak, yo."

Peyton takes Custard's other hand, drawing a complete heart on top, "And here's a reminder of the love we got for you, despite it. We're all made up of fucked up shit and happy times. But, I don't think anyone has so many bad times in 'em that there's no space left for love."

Custard stares at her hands, "Tattoo over them."

Peyton's green face is stunned, "Yo, you for real?

Custard nods, "I did something to you I can't reverse. Do the same to me. This is the start of my debt to you."

Peyton bounces in excitement, "I promise it's gonna be so sick, dude, I love you for this!"

She switches seats, Peyton magically tattooing as Custard sits in a muted trance, feeling loved as a whimsically buzzing needle stains meaning and memories through her flesh.

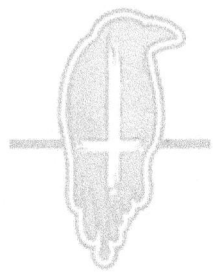

In Nether Black, the Blue Classic sleeps on the shoulder where the road meets red grass. The night's wind pumps the Keeper's South Woods with howls of mint-scented air. The colossal moon, 'Juicy Proud Number Seven', lasers its light through the brush of the fire-gushing trees. Tonight's moon is yellow, a special occasion during the seventh hundred and thirteenth day of the calendar. The Beserk Nectar bugs are plentiful, pulsing their jelly-filled butts at their mates. Their white bodies, no more than an inch, their orange pincers, ten times that. They waddle backward, hoping to run their reproductive organs into a mate, their tiny heads pinned to the ground as they drag their huge pincers in a strut of blind breeding. It's not uncommon for the mates to unknowingly lock genitals with the same sex. After the reproductive act, however, the two bugs continue their sightless search for another mate, neither of them knowing they ever had gay bug sex. Rexy crunches munchy grubs as Blood yells ahead, "Rexy, turn on your flashlight!"

Rexy pounces up ahead, catching bugs for snacking as Soul Sucker's strapped to Blood's back, talking over his shoulder, "Blood, you ever think you'd end up all kissy-faced with a Bug Sucker?"

Blood flashlights through the red grass, a quiet night breeze, "We did a lot of messed up stuff in our time. Never thought I'd find the kind of peace she gives me."

Soul Sucker jostles like a backpack to the crunch of Blood's boots, "She's too innocent for you."

Blood questions over his shoulder, "What you tryin' to say?"

Soul Sucker sways, "Nothing you didn't just say, Crack Dust. You said it yourself, we did a lot of messed-up stuff. She doesn't know about the past."

Blood scratches his ear, "She's not part of my past. She's my future. She's a goal worth reaching. Keeps fools like us on track."

Soul Sucker thinks about the past, "That Bicycle Graveyard Maintenance man would laugh in your face if he saw how pouty you've become, you're like a pillow. What the hell was his name?"

Blood keeps an eye on Rexy, "Double Cross."

Soul Sucker remembers, "Double Cross! Praise Mars, he was cool as shit. I wanted to be him!"

Blood chuckles, "You know he's a Bounty Hunter, right?"

Soul Sucker vacuums bugs away from Blood's face, "Jupiter's flames. So the whole Bicycle Graveyard Maintenance man is just a front!? I've accepted lies! So what? Their store's a fake?"

Blood laughs, "Yup. Just a cover for his real business. Everybody's got their thing. Ya' know, I really hope we see Double Cross again. Gotta deal with fate first though."

Rexy cheeses from a distance, catching her millionth bug as Soul Sucker wonders, "Are you prepared to lose her to fate if it means saving everything?"

Blood Taker checks the yellow moon, "Everything ain't worth nothing if I'm dying alone. Not since I met her. If I gotta live knowing she's gone, death's a welcomed end to a misery I'm not built to endure."

Soul Sucker wiggles, "Now that sounds like something Double Cross'd say! You're so edgy."

Blood watches his wife chomp goo, "You find love, you'll be edgy too when something tries to steal it. Hey, let's promise to see Double Cross again when this is over."

Soul Sucker pendulums, "You think he'll finally give me a date?"

Blood's face is judgmental, "A demonic vacuum has the hots for the Bounty Hunter of the afterlife."

Soul Sucker reminds, "You said, everybody's got a 'thing'!"

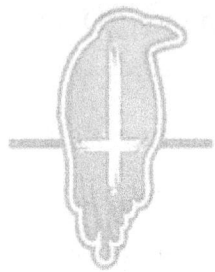

It's night at White Manor, witches digging dirt and stones.

Holding shovels beamed in spotlights, front yard digging dino bones.

Custard learned Dakota's secret, archeology was her dream.

Now they dig bones hidden by Custard, Three Witch Dino Digging Team!

Tables lined with fossils, skulls, tail bones, teeth, claws, and more.

Dakota manages the dig site, Peyton complains that she is sore, "I'm sore."

Dakota manages her clipboard of discovered bones, "You're doing great, my darling. You're a slimy green Archaeologist witch! Probably the first to exist! You're a rare treasure."

Peyton huffs, "Then bury me with the bones, dude."

Custard dusts bones with enchanted bristles, "This is Dakota's special day, no huffing."

Peyton mocks, "Ay, then why isn't she in the hole? And why can't we just magic the bones out of the dirt? An' why can't we eat while the shovels do the work?"

Dakota explains, "The fun is in the digging! With each shovel of dirt, never knowing what contents you'll come across. The process is the thrill."

Peyton scoffs, "Imagine people asking you what you do for a living, 'Oh, yeah, I dig holes.'"

Custard smirks calmly, "I know a Grave Digger who'd love it."

Peyton fake faints at the bottom of the hole, "I am dead."

Dakota floats down to her, wiping her dirty green face, "You are employee of the month!"

Peyton looks up from the dirt, "I'm giving you my two week's notice."

Dakota plays along, "How about I promote you to Museum Curator?"

Peyton suggests, "How about you promote me to Foot Rub Tester?"

Custard dusts bones above the hole, "Jobs already filled."

Peyton hollers from the hole, "You will rub these feet!"

Custard cringes, dusting, "But, they're green!"

Peyton laughs, screams, "Ay, don't be talkin' junk bout my green toes."

Dakota helps Peyton up, "You have the cutest green toes of all the Hole People."

Peyton death stares the word 'cute' and does a mocking, deep announcer voice, "Dakota, mysteriously murdered by WHO?! Could it have been the Green Archeologist? Oh no! Someone's gonna find the Dinosaur bones, but who shall find HER bones, yo? The mystery of the Dead Dino Witch continues!"

Dakota rolls eyes, "Dying surrounded by dino bones and the ones I love would be a gift."

Custard jokes, "Don't tempt her. Pretty sure Peyton'd kill to get out of physical labor."

Peyton admits, "Ya' know, diggin' up the Dino Dead is actually kinda rad. Thanks for forcing me to do cool things, Dakota."

Dakota teases her, "See, there's more to life than skateboards and gang signs."

Custard blurt-laughs at 'gang signs', "Ha!"

Peyton side glances Dakota, holding her laugh, "I have literally never used a skateboard, dude."

Dakota eggs her on, "I know there's a little voice in you that wants to do 'rad tricks'."

Peyton gasps, "Yo, you got that voice too?!"

Dakota reads her clipboard, "No, my little voice wants to color code and label bone piles."

Custard stands at the hole's edge, looking down on them, "Finally, I have you two where I want you."

Custard's hiding something behind her back as Dakota's smile disappears, "Custard, what are you talking about?"

Peyton grabs a shovel, "Yo, I knew she was evil, I had sex with an evil witch, dude. Crap's messed up! Straight evil genius though! Yo, Dakota, how're we gonna handle this? Tag team her ass?"

Custard pulls out a magic camera, snapping their photo, "My two lovelies. More photos for the stairwell. Wow, Peyton, way to look angry with a shovel in the photo. Also, I let you tattoo me and you still don't trust me?!"

Dakota looks at Peyton with a teeth-gritted worry, "You better go make it up to her."

Peyton climbs the dirt like a child, overdramatically wailing, "Custard! Do not leave me, Yo! I LOVE YOU!"

Custard turns with a fake pout, walking from the hole, "Farewell, my Pumpkin Bread."

Dakota floats out from the hole as Peyton remembers, "Oh yeah, magic!"

Peyton flies out of the hole, hugging Custard as Dakota stands next to them both, "Wow, look at all these bones. Let's take a picture together!"

Peyton, Custard, and Dakota stand in front of their bone collection, as the enchanted camera takes many love-filled, silly photos of them and the house that they built together in the background. They do fancy handshakes like they're accepting the key to the city for bone digging. Peyton sticks a bone out her shirt, pretending she's lost her arm. Custard and Dakota attempt to smoosh Peyton's green face with kisses from both cheeks. The camera spits photos, piling the ground with memories of their 'Sky

Twinkles'. A photo of them, smiling. A photo of them, laughing. A photo of them, blocked by a classic blue car.

CHAPTER TEN

Favors from the Universe

The artificial night sky shimmers 'Stars' reflecting off the hood of a blue classic, flexing in the yard's spotlights.

The bone-digging site is a calm ghost town, three witches hiding in their dark home. The closing car doors announce their arrival, hunters with delusion muffled by the illusion of safe walls. Custard and Peyton kneel in a closet as Dakota listens behind the couch in shadow. Blood Taker breaks the quiet, barking, "You know why we're here. Means you know the deaths that are coming aren't personal. You three threaten everything in Nether Black and all I am. I don't expect you to give yourselves up. You got loved ones, means you'll fight. Nothing wrong with it, just know we're good people too. Anyone dies tonight, don't hold a grudge, this is bigger than yourself."

Rexy aims Soul Sucker's nozzle like a gun, "Are you all prepared for the void saving? Whoa, there are so many of the words in my head."

Soul Sucker dangles pink plastics, "Get it together chick, you two Sausage Stompers get me killed, your souls are next for suckin'!"

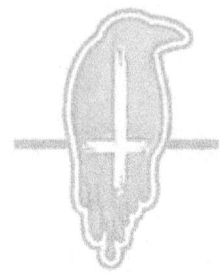

Inside, Dakota cracks the closet, whispering, "Keep each other safe."

Peyton panics, "Yo, what are you doing?"

Dakota faces the yard, "Braving a threat."

Peyton whisper-yells, "No, dude! You'll-"

Custard covers Peyton's mouth, "She's the strongest, Pumpkin. Let her protect us."

Peyton argues, "Why would she go alone? I can't die! Let me go out there, yo! I'll fuck him up!"

Custard warns, "Listen, Pumpkin, they've crafted a weapon specifically to steal your soul. We didn't want to worry you, I'm sorry. We're sorry."

Peyton's worried, "What the hell! Why am I always the problem?"

Dakota kneels close to her, "You're not the problem. You're our reason for fighting. Custard, keep her safe."

Custard stares unspoken words as Dakota creaks the closet closed. The yellow witch cautions towards the porch, swallowing her fears as she nicely closes the front door behind her. She

confronts intruders, "Blood Taker, bringing your wife here, unwelcome, you willfully welcome her to the arms of oblivion."

Blood's cape cracks in void winds, "Brave words from the witch who can die."

Dakota's yellow dress and hat rustle to the chirps of crickets, "I assume, coming here, you're prepared for the potential outcome of death?"

Rexy snarls her gold chompers, "You are not to be killing the husband tonight, Yellow Witch. Your souls are to be band-aids for the repair of the broken void. Prepare for a vacuum to be cleaning the soul. I am also needing a brain cleaning, it is a cluttering mess up there."

Dakota's glasses reflect spotlights, "Have your calculations answered that killing each other is the only solution?"

Blood eyeballs his wife, "Oblivion don't pause long enough to 'calculate' how to correct its path without the loss of life. You built your home in a crumbling void. Void needs souls. I've been watching you through Crackle's gemstone. Wishing your girlfriend can't die won't stop you from losing her if you're dead."

Dakota warns, "I will fight."

Blood orders, "Go say goodbye to your reasons worth fighting, I'll wait."

Dakota's neck sizzles black energy of spell-boiled veins, rumbling blood-pulsed streams of sorcery-fueled particles. Blood Taker explains, "They deserve to know your love was genuine."

Dakota shrieks, "THEY'LL CONTINUE TO!"

Blood Taker barks, startling Rexy, "Ok, Dakota, let's kill each other!"

Dakota prepares her posture for whatever awaits, feeling the heat of fear and power hardening her earlobes. She listens for threats, suspicious of illusions as her brain ignites her eyes with cold intent, arming her hot mind with grim spells to break flesh. Anger squirms her skin with thorned goosebumps, clenching fists hard enough to stab bones through fingerprints. Blood Taker sprints forward, a man running like a wolf as Dakota cocks her shotgun of an elbow, grasping empty matter, ready to conjure. Blood Taker jumps, cape covering fake moon and stars, the ones the witches crafted last week. Those memories distract Dakota as her throat swells. Hesitation takes over as she leaves reality to scour for a spell.

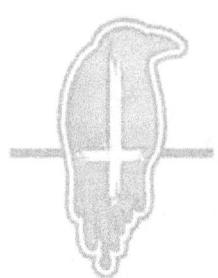

WARP! Reality sucks inward, imploding a vacuum-tightened pop of sparks in her thoughts. Dakota's in her mind's library, calmly perusing for spells in a pile of candlelit books in her brain. She yawns as Blood Taker moves slowly to the tick of a distant clock. Rain fills a yellow lake outside the window, a fireplace popping with the smell of toasted pine. A thunderstorm cracks lightning beyond the lake, a reminder of the danger she's in as she sips a teacup as usual. She opens a book, every page blank, "Strange, this is the first blank book I've found."

The pile of books has grown to a mess across her mind's library, Dakota scouring pages, every spellbook empty, "Why can't I calculate this? Why is this happening? I don't have any spells, so now what? I'm stuck here? My real self sits, waiting to be mauled by Blood Taker in slow motion? I can't calculate how slow time moves when I'm here, but it's still moving. Being here is a temporary solution. Temporary's going to get me murdered. I can't hide. I have to warn them. I have to run."

The library melts away in a deep vibration of sound waves, sizzling light popping with high-pitched sparks as matter manifests from congealed visions, the world's speed normalizing. She hears the snap of electricity loading her senses into position as life plays out again. She remembers, *'Blood's dropping down on me!'*

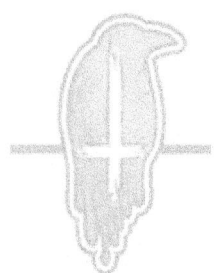

CRUSH! Dakota's smashed into a wooden crater blown into the porch. Her limbs jolt out around Blood's leather-tightened arm, a man's fist powered by a wolf's intensity. She coughs out, "Wha... What did you do?"

Blood's leather creaks back from the strike, smoking hot, "I punched you in the stomach, Dakota."

Dakota's head dangles dizzy, "To my. Ma... My, magic?"

Blood looks down on Dakota like a snapping turtle on her back, "Shouldn't you ask yourself why I came here? Think about it, why would I throw myself at three witches without a plan? You think 'cause you see yourself as the hero, that means you're awarded uncontested survival?"

Dakota's lips taste like iron, "Whe-, Where are my spells?"

Blood calls Rexy over as she frolics her white romper to the porch, charcoal fingers waving into the hole, "Hello, The Yellow Witch."

Blood asks, "Rexy, who owned you when you were a bat?"

Rexy thinks back to Flimsy's memory bank, "Ok, I will say it to you again. The lady was having the name of Sleeze Cheeks."

Blood paces, leading his cape. "And, who was she?"

Rexy remembers another life, "The job of a witch."

Blood insists, "Right, and why did she kill you?"

Rexy frowns in thought at her own death, "She killed Flimsy, because I couldn't stop the word spell erasing. Now, I am having a jumbled brain of spell-words again. Please don't kill me more times."

Blood stares, a beast above a fool, "Rexy's a sponge for human witch magic. Enough of a threat that Sleeze Cheeks killed her. You've feared the wrong person this entire time and your death as a powerless human will be Steven Spinebreaker's final act and the void will be saved because of him."

Dakota's lost in pain, "Custard told me... She can... see you so. You're... connected to a witch."

Blood scoffs, "I was made from witch's spells, I don't use them. Think of your Sky Twinkles one last time, Dakota, the universe commends your effort, but awaits its reward of your failure."

Dakota glances to the side, suddenly, RUNNING! Down the porch, dodging Blood's grasp as she slides under the wooden railing, darting through grass past the side of the house, screaming, "Our magic's gone! RUN!"

Custard and Peyton hear the muffled cry, staring at each other in uneasy silence at the bottom of the closet as Blood barks, "Rexy, find the green one. Soul, don't let anything bad happen to her."

Soul Sucker bounces on Rexy's back, "Remember Blood, we got plans after this ya' Fur Yacker. Double Cross is waitin' for us! Don't get dead!"

Rexy strolls into the house like a vacuum-equipped ghost hunter, "Don't get dead! I will not let the husband down. Blood, I am loving you."

Blood's already gone, his cape snapping around the corner, panting towards Dakota.

Rexy closes the front door, sneaking through the quiet, creaking small wooden steps, clicking her flashlight, "Please don't make this a hard one, my friends. Your lives are the saviors of the everything. Come out with the hands up."

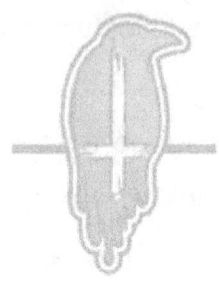

Outside, Dakota runs alone behind their home, past a shed, slogging through a mud-mixed creek into woods splattered with moonlight and tension. The rumble of void-sparked night sky hums low as Dakota's breath shakes in unsettling panic. Her eyes peer wide, exposing her exposed state of anxiety, forced to listen to her own hunt. Her body swims with blood flavored for a wolf's teeth, the breeze through branches playing her last ear's luxury.

Blood Taker stalks with a crazed intent to spill a soul from her skin. A leather-stretched beast at the mercy of a man's stretching mind, steering his nose towards prey. He feels his strength being shared. Crackle's gemstone is near, twisting his mind further, "You think hiding's the last thing you wanna do with your time? I'm chosen by fate to give life, witch. Everyone, everything touching the corners of this reality are awaiting an unknown destruction of their dreams, but I will give them their lives. YOU destroyed this void. YOU threaten everyone's Sky Twinkles. YOU threaten my world." Blood taker twitches out sporadic words, a heretic's spasms of blind action, his gums quivering with drool.

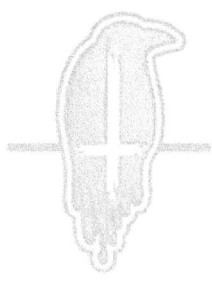

In the house, Peyton watches Custard grow a deep, dark haunting of terror in her soul, hardening electric emotions in her core. A connection with Blood Taker screeches through spacetime, shackling them at the mind through her gemstone. Her brain's a molten sizzle of black hate, infernal mechanisms unlocking secrets of bewitched thoughts and teachings, the strength Crackle knew.

Rexy aims Soul Sucker at the closet door, "I am hearing you, sneaky hiders! This is not a personal attack, you will fix the world! We're happy to be working with you. Goodbye, the friends."

Soul Sucker revs, "Alright you Worm Sacks, you broke this world, PAY UP!"

Rexy struggles to hold Soul Sucker as a wailing storm of a motor roars, sucking at the closet door, shredding wood to dust as Rexy commands, "Suck 'em up good. This is the one for our Sky Twinkles! Your bloods are the fresh paints of the new home!"

Splintered shards needle past as the door shatters away revealing Custard, dark, evil, fucking pissed. Crackle's gemstone blocks Rexy from erasing Custard's spell library. She stands unbothered, blocking the intruders as Peyton cowers below, pleading, "LEAVE US ALONE!"

Hearing Peyton's cries, Custard's corpse froze posture floods with ice-stabbed goosebumps as her vision burns. Rexy aims Soul Sucker at Custard, "You are a nightmare to be washed out!"

Soul Sucker's engine continues a barrage of bone-crushing winds, sucking with deafening speeds. "AHAHAHHA, Praise Mars, the sun shall rise again!"

Custard's body permeates with the hate gifted to those in need of help. Blackening skin rips from bone as it rejuvenates with each sucked flake. Peyton covers her face, crying in her lap below the one she loves, "PLEASE DON'T DO THIS!"

Custard smiles death-flamed eyes at Rexy as she's yet to move from the doorway. Custard is a statue enduring infinite pain with the most pleased chuckle, her mind on autopilot speaking in a dead twisted tone, "You fucking pawn. Step foot in my house. Taint this floor with tears. You will cry. You will beg."

Rexy's fear starts a downward spiral as she takes a shaky step back, dropping Soul Sucker as she pleads, "I am being sorry The White Witch. Give the forgiving to me, please."

Custard floats towards Rexy in a slow ominous presence, Soul Sucker's power halting. The black skin coating Custard's body falls off, her silver eyepatch surely hiding a second stare of murder as Soul Sucker rolls away, "Blood, HELP U-"

SMASH! Custard stomps, obliterating the vacuum into another dimension as a deep booming shockwave shakes their home. Pink plastic and flame erupt around the living room as a wooden crater shards out from her foot. Rexy watches a friend disappear for the first time, "MR. SOUL SUCKER!"

Rexy's hands float in front of her gaping mouth as Custard stares a hate for the ages. Her gemstone pulses deep-toned light waves in sync with her heartbeat as Rexy trips back in tears. Custard sentencing, "The spray of your guts will clean your mistakes, beg your gods for blessings, judgment beckons your life to me."

Peyton watches through soaked eyelashes, "CUSTARD, STOP!"

Custard's body turns to the closet, wretching words through a possessed and blind rage, "WHO THE FUCK IS CUSTARD?" Her eyes drip black flames, ancient power poured from her feeble human shell.

Peyton's side glance is a bone-chilling realization, Custard's lost in diseased magic. Custard holds a palm up, summoning every knife from the kitchen as they loom over Rexy, screaming, "BLOOD!"

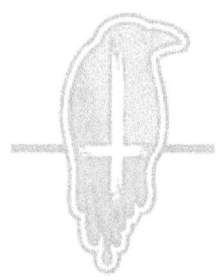

Behind the house, Blood Taker pulls a pitchfork from his neck with a spurt, gritting his fangs as he chases Dakota from the shed into the creek, "You are a pestilence to our future, Dakota."

Dakota huffs in a blood-stained yellow dress reflected in ankle-deep mud, "I am the cure to your future's pestilence."

Blood stomps through muck on all fours, tackling her against wet rocks as he bites at her. His weight is a gravestone on her chest as she loses all air. Dakota grabs Blood's neck with both hands, nearly wrenching her elbows broken as Blood grins fangs, "Go ahead, hag, struggle against your oppressor, impress the universe with your will to live, choke out this darkness and prosper."

Blood drools on her mud-stained cheeks as she growls like an animal herself, hoping to break his neck to pebbles.

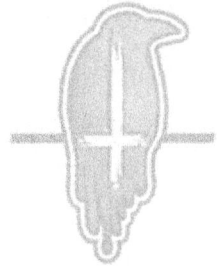

Inside, Custard stands near a couch that's caught fire, illuminating too many floating knives as Rexy lies frozen. Custard sentences, "Guilty." She flicks her finger, Rexy closing her eyes in anticipation as Custard's wrist is grabbed from behind.

Peyton holds Custard's heart-tattooed hand as all the knives clang the carpet, "Custard, you don't have to do this! Rexy doesn't have to die."

Custard laughs, turning with troubled expressions. She sucks smiling lips looking around the room, her tortured giggle bouncing her flame-dripped eyes as she puts her hands in prayer, staring at her own fingertips, "This is a clean house. Trash goes outside."

CRACK! Custard backhands Peyton's jaw, exploding her through the window as she ragdolls to a stop on the driveway, her body ripping across rocks sprinkled with glass. Peyton lies in a dust cloud in front of The Blue Classic, feeling her pain start to form. She listens to thrashing in the creek out back and fire toasting furniture inside, chaos playing hectic melodies to the calm hum of void clouds. Peyton closes her eyes, '*Spike. Yes, Peyton? You were a good friend. I am not your friend, Peyton. That's messed up, yo, I'm laying here in a driveway, dying. You're not dying, stop being dramatic. I am your potential. I have potential? I am every slur aimed your way. I hate name-calling. I am every bully who's stained your conscience. I hate that others messed up my head. I am the fierce, undying nature of a violated psyche who's seen enough. I'm so tired. I am the breaking point of a pure soul, soaked in the stink of hate. Why can't people be nice? I am the lashings, torn skin of innocent people. Be nice or get wrecked. I am the abused emotions of a weaker person. I am not weak. I am terror, brought to the guilty for their crimes. Mess them up. I am the dormant tenacity, stagnant and buried, waiting to rise. Save my family. I do hereby state that Peyton Sara Sweetjelly has been wronged by the universe. Impart her with necessary evil. Avert your gaze from her tonight and judge not her actions as they are justice. Show your mercy to her as she punishes those who have done wrong. Grant her favor from the universe.*'

Spike takes control of Peyton's body, levitating up from the driveway, ascending high above their house. She opens her green lips, a shrill scream ripping the airways between her and their home as the foundation under their house is rocked. Custard loses her footing as Rexy lies on the floor, confused, "First, the white one can still do her magics. Now the green one does the magic? I am here, I should make it gone!"

Spike talks floating high above the house, "I'm not using magic. I'm summoning the ones who created it." She sees Dakota lying far behind the house, struggling under Blood. Dakota's confused, 'Peyton? How is she doing this?'

Spike commands the ground open as their house cracks in half, a boiled-white devil's mouth bubbling from death-soaked hells, swallowing their home as pieces raft in ghost-pale magma rising from the throat of the abyss.

Custard shouts with Crackle's voice from floating rubble, "Blasphemer! This White Wench steals my power and you condemn me? Bring your devils, child." Rexy hides in broken parts of floating house as black bone skeletons crawl out from liquid-white fire.

Spike commands, "Remove her gemstone, a stolen trinket and oddity not gifted to humans." Custard's smug, dodging the grasp of black bones as The White Witch dances on white flame, "From what hells did you rise, kid?"

Spike lowers down into the chaos, as snarling coughs of tortured bones outnumber Custard tremendously. Hundreds of boiling-hot black skeletons grab every corner of her body, pulling her to the brink. Custard is sprawled, ready for ripping as Spike approaches, "Remember ripping me apart?"

Crackle laughs through Custard's voice, "I didn't kill you."

Spike stares, "No, you killed us both."

Masses of skeletons stare at Spike, awaiting her order to ravage. Custard spitting, "Come join me in death, again."

Spike states, "I already died once. You think I'm afraid, you're wrong. You think I'm gonna, you're dead wrong." Spike grabs Custard's jaw with both hands, wrenching it wide, "First we take your lying tongue."

Peyton argues out loud, "SPIKE, STOP! No, she hurt us, Peyton!"

She pounds her own face, skeletons watching mindlessly as she yells at herself, "Weak ass Baby Peyton, watch as others do your dirty work. You're hungry, eat the planet!"

Spike orders the skeletons, "Do it!"

The black bones begin tearing Custard apart, her limbs dropping into the boiling depths. Custard dies calling out, "Pumpkin, I'm sor-"

The White Witch forever gone as Peyton begs, "NOOOOOOOO!"

Custard's clean white clothes burn in clean white fire, her blood instantly burned black, a crying witch claimed by the depths. The hot white lake scorches her existence to ash, a blurry Peyton watching, trapped in her own mind's prison.

Spike taunts, *'Trash Baby Peyton, never good enough to save anyone. I will prove my worth, Spike. I don't believe you. TO MYSELF, NOT TO YOU, SPIKE! So confident once the tears let up, somehow you always end up crying first, though, huh? Ready* to eat the planet yet? SHUT UP! Cry all you want, you're the ruiner of worlds. Planet eating Peyton, the saddest girl in the universe. She ate all that existed and still doubted herself. I have no more doubts. Oh, really, Peyton? Yes, Spike. So, you're ready to take care of yourself? Yes. Uh-huh. And why the sudden change? My family needs me. That's it? Why else, Spike? Seems like a lot. I'll be ok, Spike. You sure? Yes. Alright, say it. I will. I'm waiting, Baby Peyton.'

She watches everything she loves burn around her once more, but for the last time.

Peyton proves, "I believe in myself. I believe in you, too, Peyton. Thank you, Spike."

The predicted outcome spasms, grinding between itself and other universal paths, as Peyton's choice has consequences that impact other Peytons. Her timetable has been spilled on, a mess of fractured sequences and contradictory points in her Karma Blueprint from the start of her cosmic creation to the now fragmented split ends of her destiny. Peyton Sara Sweetjelly has changed fate's fortune.

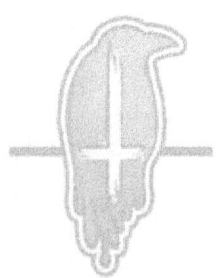

She lies in the driveway of their home again, unbroken, her white jean shorts dirty, sleeveless black shirt still tucked, now ripped. She stands, grabbing her black spiked witch hat, crowning her green stare. Custard readies knives to end Rexy in a perfect white home as Peyton's voice booms, "CRACKLE!"

Custard's body turns towards the driveway from inside their home, yelling, "What is it, trash?"

Peyton runs up the porch, blowing the door in with a quivering stare of madness, "This is my first true home!"

Crackle insists with Custard's voice, "Infested homes require extermination."

Peyton shows grinding teeth, glistening with tears, as she threatens through her closed bite, "Don't get blood in my house."

Crackle assures her, "This is my house, and blood will be spilt."

Peyton's green nose crushes with anger as her mouth bursts tentacles with a stomach-turning roar, lifting herself with meat-bloated cheeks. She spiders towards Custard as dozens of knives fly, stabbing red gashes in green flesh, endless gushing from the spidered pincushion of a witch. Peyton, unable to die, continues rejuvenating endless blood, flooding the entire room red. The floors are smeared, the walls drip thick and the ceiling's speckled. Custard begins cloning knives, shooting an endless barrage of blades into Peyton from every direction. Her body jerks with each stab, sucking in feelers as knives keep her body upright like floating push pins. The splattered room reflects off Peyton, a diamond shrapnel star, spraying above a red river. She leaks in silence, still staring through knives at Custard. Her fury helps her body reject the knives, pushing them out as she walks bare green toes in her own liquid flood. Custard's mesmerized by the sight, frozen in fear and wonder. She watches Peyton run towards her, *'I've never seen such a red room. Look how beautiful she is. The contrast of green on red it's hypnotic. This is a gorgeous way to die. Take it in. Make this moment a memory. She's so close. To witness such persistence is surely a grand and final spectacle to be remembered. I wish I were remembered. I wish I were her.'*

Peyton's knife-covered body slams Custard against the wall, breaking her trance-like gaze. She chokes her neck with a vice's squeeze, "Do you know what hundreds of knives feels like, dude?"

Custard smiles down at her, "A pleasure given only to the weak."

Peyton's green face is masked in total red, reflecting in blades of all directions like a haunted mirror maze. Her blood-bathed body sprays as she tightens her choke, "I was never weak."

Custard stares blue-faced, barely squeezing out, "You can't kill me."

Peyton sentences, "I can erase you." She clenches Custard's gemstone, finger-prying it from her forehead, ripping as she howls a bloodthirsty screech, strings of leeching arms wiggling out as it detaches. Custard's feathers fall from her cheeks as she lies in Peyton's arms, lethargic. Her mind releases the pressure of Crackle's dark energy, pouring madness out her pours. She gains control over her body again as warm evil drips from her body's cold cavities, "P…. Pumpkin, Bread."

Custard nearly passes out as Peyton's worry reflects in steel, "Custard! I'm sorry I hurt you! Please don't leave me again, I need you! I need you so mu-"

SKREEEE! The gemstone shrieks, jumping from Peyton's hand, protruding veins like legs, crawling towards Rexy. It climbs her thigh as she freaks, "No! Get off, Sneaky Crawler! I am having the sorry feelings. Please be a friendly friend!"

The gemstone gouges Rexy's skull, her navy cheeks growing feathers as she stands, hunched over gold chompers drooling death-scented slime. She howls, snarling illness like a feral beast, "If you can't be dead, Peyton, I will force you to the watching of all the ones who can be dying!" Rexy growls a gold-razored bite, running on all fours like a hellspawn, lunging towards Custard.

Peyton, in slow motion, expresses sympathy. "I'm sorry."

She rips a knife from the dozens in her own body with a pained cry, slamming the blade through Rexy's now fractured gemstone and skull. Custard's frozen as Peyton holds Rexy in a hug, hand on a knife driven through her brain. Rexy dies unpossessed with a smile of confusion, wheezing, "Husband?" Her head bursts with energy as Peyton bursts into tears, gem shards sinking in the blood-flooded floor as Rexy's brains paint a room that's already red. The souls of every victim Crackle consumed drift from her hold, sucked from the gem fragments to the void as the skyline stabilizes. The cracks in reality mend themselves as the world goes quiet, the artificial night's stars are replaced with real ones.

Peyton falls to the ground, knives branching in every direction as Custard panics, "Pumpkin!"

Peyton coughs out a joke, "I'm a... ...Pumpkin, carving now, yo."

Peyton's head droops, Custard disapproving of her humor as she begins extracting knives. Peyton cries at the sight of Rexy's headless body and her first kill, Custard assuring, "She rests."

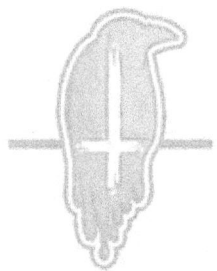

Far behind the house, Blood Taker mounts Dakota, pounding flesh to face in secluded woods echoed with the slamming of her skull. He notices the sky's holes closing up, electric void pops replaced with the calming sound of nothing, the way nature is supposed to be. Blood freezes his lifted fist with exhausted breath, thinking, stopping. He gets up, leaving Dakota in the dirt to sit on a log, lighting a cigar. Dakota's bruised face struggles to sit up, a torn yellow dress and cracked glasses frame her knotted blue side braid as she wonders through pain, "Why... why'd you stop?"

Blood can't look at her, "You can't 'calculate' it?"

She struggles to think in a beaten stupor, "The void... it. It repaired itself."

Blood points his cigar toward her home, "No, it

repaired 'cause Crackle died, I felt it."

Dakota's scared, "Custard?"

Blood smokes, "Maybe."

She thinks of Custard, "So you just... stop wanting to kill us?"

He peers off, "Never 'wanted' to kill you, just took on the burden."

Dakota feels strange conversing with someone who'd beaten her a minute earlier as she coughs questions, "So, now what?"

Blood puts his cigar out on a tree, extending a hand to her as she's helped up. Dakota stares at Blood, struggling to find trust as he hangs his head in worry, "Try to heal."

Dakota's lost, "I don't have my-"

He insists, "Just try."

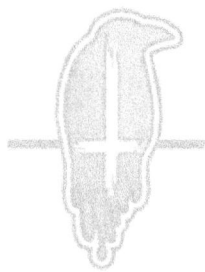

Dakota manifests her mind's library to search for a healing spell as she's immediately terrified by the sight of a table filled with tools she didn't place there, "Is this a trick of Blood Taker? Who's here? This is my mind!"

She's startled by the rummaging of clutter from a supply closet as a hatless Dakota comes out carrying dissection tools. Dakota watches as Dakota sits at a lab table in the middle of the

255

library and begins the autopsy of a snake. Dakota approaches the research area with a trembling walk, watching herself work in silence. Her eyes are wide with unnerving fear she's never felt. The hatless Dakota hands Dakota gloves, "Can you assist me, please?"

Dakota reluctantly takes them, blindly stretching the rubber gloves on, never taking her eyes off Dakota, as she addresses herself, "Asking who you are is a silly question. I'll ask what you're doing?"

The hatless Dakota explains, "I cashed in my favor from the universe for this snake, but he's a liar. He says he can grant any wish, but he keeps bursting after only one. I really need him to have the ability to grant more than one wish. I think every person deserves at least one sky twinkle, don't you? My issue is I need more time to perfect it."

Dakota converses with herself, "How can I help?"

The hatless Dakota rolls out blueprints, "My friend Spike and I created this design for our own game. She called it The House of the Bone Man. Spike guarantees if we create it, she'll make sure Peyton discovers it, but I need more time to under-stand this snake. If you could start building the game board, it would really help free up my time and allow me to solve my calculations for this snake."

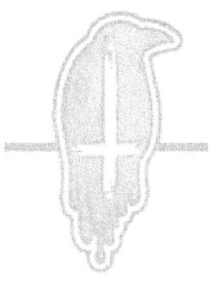

Weeks pass as no time passes, the Dakota's game passing its final test. She holds the game box as she rips a hole in their mind, producing a portal so Dakota can enter through her mind's gate into Black Manor. Crackle opens the front door for Doom Cop, carrying Kylee as Dakota plants the game in a cabinet, Dakota whispering for her to hurry back. She pulls Dakota back into her mind as they stare into their own eyes, undeniably calculated.

She wonders, "So now what?"

The Hatless Dakota clues her in, "You're the most all-powerful witch to ever exist, you can calculate your own answers now."

Dakota hugs herself thank you, as she hears Blood Taker's voice again like deja vu, he requests, "Just try."

Dakota nods to herself, grabs a healing spell and congeals back to reality with a wave bye to Dakota.

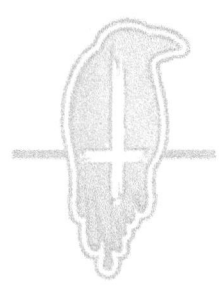

She begins healing her wounds, bruises fading and bones snapping back as Blood Taker's gut feeling twists his stomach with loss, he begins a low-hung sob of sorrow for Rexy. Dakota realizes his realization that with the return of her magic, Rexy was gone. The man with the wolf's head, just a man alone with the curse of loss, he hurts like men do. Dakota steps back, the sound of his anguish too much to listen to, as she's never heard such cries of regret. He crumbles into a pile of loneliness, bawling in the middle of the woods as she cries from the very sound of his pain. Blood pulls at his own scalp, his forehead flat on the dirt as he's sick to his stomach, punching the dirt.

Dakota hugs herself, starting a slow walk back to Blood, kneeling in front of him. She wipes her own tears, putting her forehead on his as he weeps in shame. She hugs him as his limbs dangle, he feels no worth of such kindness, Dakota never lets go. Blood cries with a swollen throat, "What mistake have I made?"

She speaks, pressed against his forehead, "It is no mistake to want to live."

Blood trembles with burning wet eyes, barking, "SHE WAS LIVING!!!!"

Dakota's startled, feeling her skin crawl, grabbing his cheek fur as she searches for hope in his tear-drowned eyes, "You will see her again."

He stares hopelessly, "I will see her now!"

Her stomach turns with worry, "Then I will share that pain with you."

She stands in a serious, tear-run frown, holding her shaky hand out, a slow lift to his feet. Blood wipes his leather across his eyes, holding her hand, requesting, "No magic, please. Let's walk. I've spent the last year in a car. Let's just...walk."

Blood and Dakota start a long, handheld walk through the night woods home.

She smiles sadly through splotched vision, "How the hell do I feel safe with you right now?"

Blood feels a goosebumped guilt, "You're the strongest witch to ever exist, Dakota. What could dare scare you?"

She admits, "Losing you."

Blood stops walking, looking at her, baffled, "What? I just tried to kill you and for what? The greed of existing?"

Dakota takes both his hands, "You've given me purpose. For half a year, I've calculated how to stop you. How to protect Custard and Peyton."

She begins tearing up, "Somehow we won, and it's the saddest feeling I could never imagine. No calculation led to the grief I feel right now. We won and... it's worse than I could have ever known."

Blood frowns in thought, "Because you already know what I'm gonna do."

She shakes her head no, "I need you. We can be friends."

Blood looks away in shame, "I've taken everything from Rexy, she needs to hear words I was too scared to say." Blood takes her hand, leading her, "I'm sorry I hurt you."

Dakota walks with him once more, "Wounds heal, but how will you?"

Blood looks hopeful, "Well, I have a great friend now, things are looking up for me already."

She scoffs in a dismissive shake, "Says a man about to take his own life."

He looks at her in silent head shaking, "I can't be the one to do it."

Dakota stares in fear as their home approaches, looking at him in anger, "I'm not killing you."

Blood smiles, tearing up, "She has to know how I feel, I can't take my own life, Dakota, I won't go where she is."

Dakota cries into his arm as they approach a white house, "No."

Blood fails to hold his tears as they enter the house together, "You've shown me unconditional forgiveness. You're my second-best friend now, Dakota. Bring me to my first."

Peyton sits, being healed at the kitchen table next to a massive pile of knives as she jumps up, still gushing, "IT'S BLOOD! Uhh, DAKOTA! Are you ok?"

Peyton freezes as Custard silently takes in the situation, Dakota walking Blood over to Rexy's headless body. Blood stoically picks Rexy up, carefully carrying her as Dakota gently opens the front door for him. Peyton looks at Custard in guilt as Dakota grabs a shovel from the bone pile table and begins digging a grave in front of the blue classic. Blood holds Rexy, his back turned to the house as Peyton and Custard watch from the porch, Dakota shoveling with great respect. Blood places Rexys body into the ground, asking for the shovel as he makes the resting place as nice as he can. He gets on his knees, patting the cold dirt mound just right, reminding him of patting Rexy's head. Blood stands next to Dakota as she takes his hand, the two girls leave the porch to join them in silence. Peyton cries guilt-drenched tears of regret as Custard comforts her from behind. Dakota holds Peyton's hand, connecting them all in a seamless heartbeat of four lives

synchronizing as one for a moment in time.

Life pauses as the four observe the loss of one, time passes as it does.

Sky Twinkles

Dusty lifted Kylee from her wheelchair in a white dress, carrying her past three fancy witches in a family-filled church, Kylee's dog chasing Dusty's puppies out front.

Honey had a laugh-filled lunch with her dad.

Dexter played with his children at a friendly neighborhood cookout.

Peyton and Dakota brought Custard to Moose's grave site, leaving cat treats.

Soul Sucker, Blood, and Rexy started a house call exorcism service, traveling through the second afterlife, Nether White in The Blue Classic. Occasionally, they bring souls to Peyton Sara Sweetjelly, Custard Ransack, and Dakota Melonie, a family of three witches.

"I love you, Rexy."

ATTENTION!

END OF THE BOOK SPOILERS ARE BEFORE THIS PAGE!

Just a little bonus info, before I knew I'd write a book, I married my editor! Tuesday 2/22/2022! (Can you find our wedding photo in the story? She "edited" it in! What a "Sneaky Crawler"!)

Thank you Brandi!

About the Author

Hey! I'm Matthew King, a 90's kid born in good ol' 1985! And on the 2nd of December, in MICHIGAN! So, probably in a snow storm. I spent most of my life practicing art and game design, only recently realizing that my love for character development goes hand in hand with writing. My hope is that my passion for world building and character creation translates to a memorable experience in my writing. I married a cool lady who's smarter than I am and great at editing my messy, art-brain story into something much tidier for you to enjoy, thanks Brandi! I want to thank you all for taking time out of your busy lives and allowing me the privilege to transport you somewhere else for a moment. It's been great working on this and I hope you enjoy it as much as I have!

www.ingramcontent.com/pod-product-compliance
Lightning Source LLC
Chambersburg PA
CBHW071550110726
47908CB00007B/2053